The Calton Papers

The Calton Papers

Norman Russell

ROBERT HALE · LONDON

ISBN 978-0-7090-8954-4

Robert Hale Limited
Clerkenwell House
Clerkenwell Green
London EC1R 0HT

www.halebooks.com

2 4 6 8 10 9 7 5 3 1

Typeset in 11/15pt Sabon
Printed in Great Britain by the MPG Books Group,
Bodmin and King's Lynn

Contents

Prologue

An Unimportant Auction

30 May 1894

Philip Garamond sipped his brandy and through the distorting bulbous glass, looked fondly at his two friends who were sitting with him in the smoking-room of the New Clarendon Club, which was to be found in a quiet street leading off Pall Mall.

'But what's your special interest in the Calton Papers, Garamond?' Old Penworthy, as usual, couldn't mind his own business. 'After all, you're a botanist, and a Fellow of the Linnean Society. And aren't you always telling us that your ambition is to buy that botanical garden that your friend Da Silva runs in Madeira? Why this sudden interest in the desiderata of the late Sir George Calton?'

Garamond put down his glass, and looked at the questioner. What a blunt fellow the old physicist had become! When taken to task for being so forthright in his questions, he always said that it was one of the few perks of old age.

'Well, Penworthy,' said Garamond, 'I am claiming the privilege of a so-called gifted amateur, and attempting to widen my horizons. Geology has always interested me, but I've no room at Abbot's Langley for great lumps of stone. It's all I can do to confine my collection of rare plants to the present array of

7

glasshouses. Living in Madeira is nothing more than a pipe dream, so I intend to make a bid for the Calton Papers this afternoon. It will be something to read by candlelight on gloomy English winter evenings!'

'You won't understand one half of them,' Penworthy grumbled. 'Calton's style was always impenetrable. Why not buy a primer on the subject and read that?'

Garamond laughed, and his genuine good humour was so self-evident that everybody laughed with him, including old Penworthy.

'Forgive me for being so ignorant of these matters,' said another of the company, a young man in his early thirties who seemed to defer to the others. 'What exactly *are* the Calton Papers?'

'The Calton Papers, Somers,' said Garamond, 'is an assemblage of letters, unpublished essays and research notes left over from the effects of Sir George Calton after the major part of his library was dispersed earlier this year. He died in March, at the venerable age of eighty-two, and bequeathed his renowned collection of mineral specimens to the Royal Geological Society, and the rest of his property to his married daughter, Mrs Catherine Dashkoff.'

'And these papers—'

'Yes, well I'm coming to those, young man. Don't be so impatient! Mrs Dashkoff assembled this collection of papers, and wishes them to be auctioned at Sotheby's this afternoon. Among the papers are Calton's unpublished account of Charles Darwin's journey to the South Seas in the *Beagle*, and a geological survey of the whole of England, which he completed in 1880. It was supposed to be published, but never was. And that, Somers, is the Calton Papers.'

'And are you seriously intending to bid for them, Garamond?' asked Somers. 'They sound very valuable and interesting to me. I expect they'll fetch a high price.'

'Well, by Sotheby's standards it will be an unimportant auction,' Garamond replied, 'but I'd like to have that collection, gentlemen. I actually knew the man, you see. I visited him several times in his declining years, and listened to long reminiscences of his youth. I've brought a hundred and fifty pounds with me, which is as far as I'm prepared to go. I've no intention of bankrupting myself to acquire it!'

'Will you come and visit *me* in my dotage?' asked Penworthy.

'I already do,' Garamond replied, and the old physicist smiled in spite of himself.

'So be it,' said Penworthy. 'We'll come with you this afternoon to afford you moral support. It you succeed in securing the Calton Papers, you can buy us all a dinner here tonight, as an act of thanksgiving. If you're unsuccessful – well, you can buy us dinner anyway, and we'll help you to drown your sorrows.'

His companions laughed. Really, thought Philip Garamond, this little visit to London was proving to be very congenial.

'How are things down at Langley Court?' asked Penworthy. 'Is everyone keeping well?'

'As well as can be expected,' Garamond replied. 'Sir Nicholas is largely confined to the house with heart disease, but he's essentially robust, you know, and they say a creaking gate lasts longest. His sister Letitia looks after him well. He's – what? – sixty-four. There's plenty of life in Nicholas yet.'

'And the sons?'

'Well, Arthur continues to be as absorbed by abstruse genealogy as I am by botany. He goes his own quiet way, as he always has. Lance – well, I expect you know he left the army? He's in want of gainful employment at the moment, but I'm sure he'll find his feet very soon.'

Would those words warn the inquisitive old man not to ask too much about Lance?

'The big news from Langley Court,' he continued, 'is about Sir Nicholas's daughter, Margaret. You know that she was engaged last August? Well, she's to marry later this year, at the end of September.'

'And who's the lucky man?' asked young Somers. 'You wouldn't tell us when we saw you here at Christmas.'

'Well, actually,' Garamond replied, 'he's a man called Jeremy Beecham, who lives nearby, at Horton Grange.' He watched as his audience shifted uneasily. Old Penworthy merely grunted. Somers looked as though he was struck by lightning.

'Isn't that the glasshouse man, the man who built that huge conservatory for Sir Isaac Cohen?' said Penworthy.

'The very same. But see, it's after twelve. If you intend to accompany me to that auction, gentlemen, you'd better do so now.'

The auction room of Messrs Sotheby, in Wellington Street, Strand, was occupied by a score of interested bidders when Lot 14, Miscellaneous Papers of the late Sir George Calton, FRGS, was placed on the auctioneer's desk.

'Gentlemen,' said the auctioneer, 'in that handsome mahogany case reposes a fascinating collection of letters and papers – autograph manuscripts produced by the late Sir George Calton at various epochs of his life. The catalogue will have given you fuller details of the contents. An important and unique collection. Will someone open the bidding above the reserve of fifty pounds?'

'Sixty.'

'Thank you, sir. I am offered sixty. Any advance on sixty pounds? A unique collection of papers – the Calton Papers.'

'Eighty,' said Philip Garamond.

'Eighty. Do I hear ninety pounds? Ninety? Thank you.'

The bidding went on. One or two of those present seemed to get the bit between their teeth, determined not to let the Calton papers get away too easily. It reached £150, and Garamond made a good-humoured movement of resignation. Two strangers began to bid against each other, bringing the price to £300.

'Three hundred pounds,' cried the auctioneer. 'Do I hear three-fifty? Three fifty pounds? No? Very well. The Calton Papers will go to the gentleman in the brown suit unless I hear an advance. Any advance? Going, going—'

'Five hundred pounds.'

A murmur ran through the room, and heads were turned to see who it was who had ventured such a vast sum. The two strangers both threw up their hands in despair.

'I say, Garamond,' whispered young Somers, 'you were well out of that business!'

'You're right,' said Garamond. 'I think I'll abandon any attempt to broaden my mind in future. It could prove too costly!'

'The Calton Papers, ladies and gentlemen,' said the auctioneer, 'are sold to Major Kirtle Pomeroy for five hundred pounds.'

Old Penworthy levered himself out of his chair, and walked across the room to where a small, lithe man with a ginger beard was busy writing out a cheque for the auctioneer.

'Major Kirtle Pomeroy?' asked the old physicist. 'Congratulations on acquiring old Calton's bits and pieces. What ever possessed you to pay that huge sum of money for a wooden box full of paper?'

'Well, you see, sir,' said the man with the ginger beard, smiling rather unpleasantly, 'I am simply acting for Major Kirtle Pomeroy. I am his agent, so to speak, and empowered to do business on his behalf. I don't think I have had the pleasure of meeting you before.'

'Emeritus Professor Penworthy. I don't think I've heard of your Major Kirtle Pomeroy. Is he a noted collector? Where does he live?'

'Well, as to that, Professor,' said the bearded man, 'I don't suppose Major Pomeroy has heard of *you*. Major Pomeroy is a man who minds his own business. As to where he lives, I believe he has a house in Cornwall. I am simply his factor. I know little about him. Let me wish you good day.'

'I say, Penworthy,' said Philip Garamond, chuckling, 'that fellow gave you as good as he got. Serve you right, too, You're always nosing into other people's affairs. But never mind, tonight

I shall treat you all to dinner as promised, and you can help me recover from my disappointment.'

'What will you do now?' asked Somers. 'I gather you came up to London just to bid for those papers.'

'Well, I was, perhaps, foolish to do so, but I shall return to Warwickshire on the fourth of June with no bones broken, and no money squandered. I intend to waste no more time, my friends, thinking about the ultimate fate of the Calton Papers.'

Barney Cottle, commission agent and loan consultant, looked up from his desk as his two associates came into the small, dusty office. Fine fellows, both of them, and ugly enough to put the fear of God into any unfortunate client who might be thinking of reneging on his debts.

'Good morning, lads,' said Barney Cottle. 'How are you both? How's your grazed knuckles, Sean?'

'They're almost healed, now, thank you, Mr Cottle. I wish you wouldn't send me after such bony individuals, though. I could have broken my fingers.'

'Well, never mind that, now. I'll see you don't lose by it. And how are you, Sammy? You're looking very smart in that red and white check suit. I'm glad you could come. Our client won't have seen a black man before, I expect, especially one who's such an adept as you are with a cut-throat razor.'

'Are you expecting this cove to give us trouble?' asked the man called Sean. 'Is that why you summoned Sammy and me up here today?'

'He may be quite straight, Sean,' said Mr Cottle, 'but there are things about him that make me feel a little anxious. That's why, when I hand over the stuff to him, I want you two here as a reminder that a bargain's a bargain. But hark! This will be the patter of his patent leather shoes on the stairs. Pull out a chair, Sammy, and get ready to open the door when he knocks. "Open locks, whoever knocks. Enter Macbeth".'

'Patent leather! You're a caution, you are, guvnor.' Sean laughed, and looked fondly at his master. What a genial old cove he looked! Well, he *was* genial in his own wicked way – a bit like that Mr Pickwick, except that Pickwick was a nice man all through, whereas Mr Cottle was a wicked old devil.

There came a knock on the door, which was opened by Sammy, and the expected client walked into the room.

'Why, if it isn't Major Kirtle Pomeroy!' cried Barney Cottle, half rising from his chair. 'It's nice to see you up in London once again. Sit down, sir. Let me introduce my two colleagues, Mr Sean Molloy, who, as you can see, was once a noted boxer – hence the flattened nose. And this other gentleman is Sammy Wilberforce, formerly of Africa, I suppose, but at present residing at Seven Dials. Gentlemen, this is Major Kirtle Pomeroy.'

'You have the Calton Papers here?' asked Major Pomeroy, glancing apprehensively at Sammy, who stood leaning with his back against the door, grinning in a decidedly ferocious manner.

'They are here, sir, and ready for you to take away. Mr Molloy, would you kindly bring in that mahogany case from the next room? The business was done very discreetly yesterday, Major, and my agent was able to send a prying old professor about his business when he started to ask questions about you – but you know that, already, I expect.'

Molloy brought in the case containing the Calton Papers, and placed it on Mr Cottle's desk. Major Pomeroy immediately rose to his feet, and picked up the box, cradling it in his arms.

'I trust that our business is concluded, Mr Cottle?' he said. 'It would be convenient for me if I were to leave immediately. I have a train to catch within the next hour.'

'Of course, of course,' said Mr Cottle. 'You have a cab waiting outside, I expect? Sammy there will help you carry the case downstairs in a moment. But first, I want to congratulate you on your purchase, which you were able to make because of a loan from me of five hundred pounds, together with an agreement that I provided an agent to make the bidding for you. A very fine collection of papers, sir, if I may say so. All those letters and essays, that wonderful account of the voyage of the *Beagle*—'

'What? Have you opened the box? Have you been reading those papers? You had no right to do so.'

'Well, you see, Major Pomeroy, I wanted to make sure that you hadn't been cheated, so of course I checked the contents as soon as my agent brought the box to me here in Angel Lane. So, yes, I've read some of those documents, including the geological survey of the whole of England, dated 1880. Very interesting. Sammy, help Major Pomeroy down to his cab.'

Major Pomeroy smiled nervously, and made towards the door, but Sammy Wilberforce made no attempt to move out of the way. Instead, he produced a pearl-handled razor from his pocket, and flicked open the blade. Major Pomeroy turned white, and sat down again.

'There's just one more thing, Major,' said Barney Cottle. 'Yours is an unusual name, so I had the sense to look you up in the Army List. There you were, with all your postings, and all your promotions from subaltern up to major, and your tours of duty with the Royal Warwickshire Regiment, and then your transfer to the Indian Army, where you served in the Bengal Lancers.'

Barney suddenly sprang up from his desk, and stood threateningly over the man cowering in his chair, with the mahogany box of papers on his knees.

'And then I thought, what a clever man he is, this Major Kirtle Pomeroy! Because your last posting, according to the Army List, was to Putney Vale Cemetery, in 1890. You're a ghost, Major Pomeroy, and I have to be very particular when dealing with ghosts.'

By now, the two enforcers had stationed themselves on either side of the trembling visitor. Sammy still held the open razor.

'What it amounts to, Major,' Mr Cottle continued, 'is this. You took out a loan with me under an assumed name. I have no idea who you really are – no, no, don't tell me: I don't want to know. You declined to put your signature to a written agreement, and that was all right with me. All I did, was adjust the terms accordingly. But I don't like dealing with dead men, and so I am giving you due warning. The terms of our agreement stipulated that I would advance you five hundred pounds cash, in Bank of England notes, and that you would repay the loan, plus twenty per cent interest, in two months' time. You have to repay the principal and interest in one go: you can't pay off so much a week, or any nonsense like that. When the due date falls in, you come here, and you hand over six hundred pounds in Bank of England notes. If not – then, I'm afraid, my friends will come after you. I'll say no more than that.'

'You have no call to doubt my word,' said Major Pomeroy faintly.

'Let us hope not,' said Barney Cottle. 'But you have been warned as to what will happen if you try to evade your responsibilities. Good morning. Sammy, show the gentleman out.'

1

---•·•---

Sunlight and Shadows

The Warwickshire town of Copton Vale was a thriving, bustling place, determined to forget its origins as a country village, and very much insistent on its status as a county borough. It boasted a fine stone bridge spanning the River Best, across which lay the Parade, where the visitor could find the old stone Guildhall, the new redbrick Magistrates' Court, and Peel House, the imposing premises of the County Constabulary.

Early on the bright Monday morning of 4 June, 1894, in an office on the first floor rear of Peel House, Detective Inspector Saul Jackson of the Warwickshire Constabulary sat on one of Superintendent Mays' uncomfortable cane-bottomed chairs, waiting for his superior officer to finish re-reading the letter that was engaging his attention.

Superintendent Mays' hair was turning grey, and his face had the appearance of wrinkled parchment, so to some folk he looked older than his fifty years. Had he not been wearing the smart uniform of a senior police officer, he could have been mistaken for a distinguished barrister or surgeon. But on those rare occasions when he suddenly leapt from his desk and out into the passage in pursuit of an idea, he showed that he was still very much an active policeman.

'Ah! Jackson! Thank you for waiting. I wanted to be sure of my facts before I started to brief you.'

Superintendent Mays threw down the letter on to the table, and looked at the man who had been waiting politely for him to collect his thoughts. There was something disconcertingly civilian, he thought, about Inspector Jackson. With his penchant for brown suits of country cut, and those voluminous waistcoats adorned with gold watch chains and medals, he looked more like a prosperous seed merchant or corn-factor than a detective. Still, many over-confident villains had thought the same, with fatal results for either their liberty or their necks.

'I'm glad you were able to come across to the Vale this morning,' said Mays. 'Last thing on Friday night, I received this letter from Superintendent Rawsthorne at Coventry, warning me of a new villain who seems to have gone to earth in our corner of the county.'

'A new villain, sir?'

'Yes, his name's Joseph Ede, and apparently he's a more than competent safe-cracker.' Mays picked up the letter from his desk, and glanced through it. 'Joseph Ede, aged 44, round face, clean-shaven. Londoner by birth – like me – well spoken, but with traces of London accent – *not* like me. Uses very convincing forged references. Poses as a trained servant to gain access to likely houses.'

'What's he doing in our part of the world, sir?'

'He was released from gaol in Birmingham two months ago – he'd cracked a crib in Erdington, and made away with some silver spoons. Since then, he seems to have made himself scarce, and Mr Rawsthorne thinks he may be lying low in our part of Warwickshire.'

Superintendent Mays got up from his chair and crossed to the window. A few boys were playing on the sunlit recreation ground that sloped up behind the Parade to Hollis Hill, where the tall chimney of Sherman's Brewery was belching out smoke into the clear June sky. It was a brewing-day, and by noon the whole town would smell of hops. Mays closed the window, and sat down once more at his desk.

'Jackson,' he said, 'there's something that I want you to do today, as a personal favour to me. It's indirectly concerned with this business of Joseph Ede. I want you to visit Sir Nicholas Waldegrave, who lives at Langley Court, near the village of Abbot's Langley, a few miles beyond Hampden-in-Arden, and have a look at his safe.'

'Sir Nicholas Waldegrave? A very old Warwickshire family, sir,' said Jackson. 'They're related to the Essex Waldegraves, but have always shunned the limelight, so I'm told. Very private and unassuming, although they were quite prominent in these parts in the years before Cromwell. And you wish me to call on Sir Nicholas Waldegrave? Abbot's Langley is not a place that I've ever visited.'

Superintendent Mays stirred uneasily in his chair, and cast a wary but amused eye at his inspector.

'I *knew* you'd know all about them, Jackson,' he said. 'The Waldegraves I mean. You're a real native Warwickshire man, born and bred. You make me feel like an interloper! Anyway, let me tell you why I want you to call on Waldegrave in particular.

'I was playing bridge with Doctor and Mrs Savage yesterday evening, and I happened to mention this safe-cracker business. As you know, Arthur Savage is a retired police surgeon, and I see no harm in talking police business with him.'

'And what did Dr Savage have to say, sir?'

'He asked me to alert a former patient of his about this Joseph Ede, the patient being Sir Nicholas Waldegrave of Langley Court. He told me that Sir Nicholas had a rickety old safe in his bedroom, which looked very vulnerable to him. He described it as "one of those old single-lever safes that you can open with a piece of wire". It was painted a dull brown, he said, and the hinges were exposed very conveniently for the safe-cracker's hacksaw.'

'It sounds like one of Castle's "Fortress" safes, sir. A wonderful name. I thought most of them had gone to the scrap heap years ago. I'll be very happy to call upon Sir Nicholas Waldegrave, and advise him to buy a modern safe, provided, of course, that he's got anything of value to put in it! As you know, I've worked with Dr Savage on two cases in the past, and it's possible that I owe him a favour.'

'Ah, yes,' said Mays. 'The first occasion was in connection with that throat-cutting business at The Barns, and then, later, with the curious behaviour of Prebendary Arkwright at Ancaster.* Well, I'd be very grateful if you'd go out to Abbot's Langley this afternoon. There's a train leaving Copton Vale Central at eleven fifteen. It would be quite a pleasant excursion for such a nice day, and you'd be back in Warwick by the early evening. Have something to eat out there, and put in a claim for expenses when you return.'

'I'll do that, sir,' said Jackson, making towards the door of the office. 'And don't fret, Superintendent, just because you're a Londoner, and don't know all the byways of country life and custom, and the doings of all the old county families, it's not your fault—'

'Away with you, Jackson!' cried Superintendent Mays, laughing. 'Do as you're bid, and go out to Abbot's Langley. Who knows, you may catch this Joseph Ede red-handed!'

Just under one hour later, a fussy little single-carriage train deposited Jackson at Langley Platform, which he had been told was the nearest station for Langley Court. The train hurried off, clanked and clattered across a small bridge, and passed out of sight into a belt of dense woodland. An elderly uniformed porter standing at a sort of wicket gate clipped Jackson's ticket, and remarked that it was a nice day. That was certainly true: the weather had turned very warm and sunny, and far above the trees a single lark was warbling. Towards the west, though, a number of dark clouds had gathered, as though contemplating a concerted attack upon the fine weather later in the day.

'You'll be wanting to call on Sir Nicholas Waldegrave, I expect?' said the porter. He pointed to a narrow earth road just

* *The Haunted Governess; The Ancaster Demons*

beyond the railway line. 'Do you see that gap in the trees by the side of the road? That's the entrance to Sir Nicholas's carriage drive. It's only a short walk along that path to the house.'

Jackson thanked the man, and passed under a canopy of wild overhanging trees. There was not much to be seen from the drive, as the estate was evidently well wooded and, Jackson realized, cunningly landscaped

After a quarter of an hour, Saul Jackson began to feel hot and exhausted. A short walk, indeed! It was endless.... And then, to his growing relief, he heard the sound of a horse's hoofs behind him and, glancing back, he saw a gentleman's carriage approaching at a leisurely pace. One of the rear wheels was evidently not seated true on its axle, and was emitting an intermittent squeak.

The carriage was empty, and was being driven by a stolid-looking man dressed in a long coat adorned with many blue and red capes, which formed a fine setting for his round, stern face and close-cropped hair. On the driver's seat beside him reposed a high-crowned hard hat with a red and blue cockade. On seeing Jackson, he brought the carriage to a stop, put his hat back firmly on his head, and touched the rim in greeting.

'It's a warm day, sir,' he said, 'and not one for too much walking. If you'll get in the carriage, I'll take you the rest of the way to Langley Court.'

'That's very civil of you, my friend,' said Jackson, gratefully hauling himself up into the carriage. 'The porter at the station said it was just a short walk.'

'These station folk never know what they're talking about, sir,' said the coachman, urging the horse to resume its gently ambling pace along the drive. 'It's all part and parcel with what's wrong in the world today. There's a lot of folk, both high and low, who don't know what they're talking about.'

'You may well be right, Mr – er—'

'Cundlett, sir, Joe Cundlett.'

'My name's Jackson. I'm from Warwick.'

'Honoured to make your acquaintance, Mr Jackson,' said Cundlett. 'Warwick is a fine place, renowned for its doughty sons and beauteous daughters. I must apologize for that squeaking from the rear axle. They don't make things like they used to, sir. This carriage is not two months old, but that wheel will be off and spinning away into the hedge unless it's seen to. Which it will be, presently, when I've taken it round to the smithy. No, nothing's the same.'

The carriage turned abruptly to the left, and clattered on to a stone-paved drive, and there before them, brooding over an extensive lake, rose the mansion of Langley Court.

'I must leave you, now, Mr Jackson, sir,' said Cundlett, 'as I have to drive this carriage round to the stables behind the house.' The man surveyed Jackson critically for a moment before adding, 'The front door is behind the hedge on the opposite side of the lake. The tradesmen's entrance can be reached by going under the arch with the clock turret above it, over to the left of the house.'

Cundlett touched his hat once more, and presently the carriage with the squeaking axle lumbered away along a tree-lined carriage-road to the right.

Jackson smiled to himself. Gentleman or tradesman? It had been very kind of Mr Cundlett to give him the benefit of the doubt. In the days when he had been a raw village constable, he had worried about the correct way of calling on the gentry. Should he go to the front door, or to the servants' entrance? An old police sergeant in Kenilworth had put him right on the matter. 'When you call on the gentry, you're calling as a representative of the law, and the head of the law is the Queen. So front door it is.'

Saul Jackson stood on the carriageway, and contemplated the scene. It was very quiet, and as far as he could see there was no one about. In front of him lay the vast lake, its blue waters glinting in the morning sun. He could glimpse the occasional golden carp gliding through the water, which had become home to a colony of water lilies. Here and there, the half-submerged skeleton of a fallen tree formed a diving platform for a few mallards who had evidently made the lake their home. Thick banks of reeds obscured the edges of the expanse of water in such a way that it was impossible at first sight to ascertain whether or not the lake was natural or artificial.

On the left-hand edge of the lake stood a little architectural folly in the form of a sandstone chapel, with a Gothic door and pinnacles. It stood behind a miniature landing-stage to which a single rowing-boat had been moored.

On the far side of the lake rose the mansion of Langley Court, a long, three-storey house built of Cotswold stone, most of which was obscured by clinging ivy. Nothing very special, Jackson thought: just a good, solid, gentleman's residence put up about 1800, by the looks of things.

Quite suddenly, the sun was obscured by an errant cloud, and a dark shadow swept over the lake and its environs. At the same time, a man came into sight from the hidden side of the house. He was dressed in sober, dark-green livery, and was pushing another man who was confined to a wheeled chair. The crippled man sat quite upright, clutching a number of books which had been placed on his knees. The footman pushed the chair on to a small wooden bridge which gave access to the miniature landing-stage, produced a key, and opened the door of the Gothic folly. He wheeled his charge inside, and presently came out again, and quietly closed the door. As he did so, the sun shone forth again in all its glory.

It was almost as though the lake and the house beyond it, and the little folly, had constituted the scenery in a vast theatre, in which two mute actors had dutifully fulfilled their non-speaking roles. Jackson shivered. Why should that scene have disturbed him? Well, it was no time to be indulging one's fancies. Jackson quickly skirted the lake, crossed the front terrace, and knocked on the front door of Langley Court.

*

The door was opened by an elderly butler, a man well over seventy, with sparse white hair neatly brushed across his head.

'Detective Inspector Jackson? Good morning, sir,' said the butler. 'Sir Nicholas is expecting you.' There was a quaver to his voice, betokening advanced years, but there was also, Jackson thought, an edge of arrogance – or was it petulance? This old family retainer did not approve of the likes of Jackson coming in through the front door.

He followed the butler across a cool, marble-floored hallway, from which an elegant flight of stairs rose to the floors above. A sudden furtive movement on the first-floor landing caught Jackson's attention, and he saw the figure of a tall, soberly dressed man quickly retreating soundlessly and almost stealthily it seemed, into a corridor at the head of the stairs. As the figure disappeared, the sun, which had been shining steadily through a skylight, suddenly went in, and a dark shadow seemed to be sucked into the corridor as though to hide whoever had been watching from above.

The butler, too, had caught sight of the watcher and Jackson saw him frown, his lips puckered with distaste. They passed through an open arch into a short passage, and thence to a sort of antechamber, devoid of furniture, but with some old family portraits on the walls. He paused for a moment, and spoke confidingly to Jackson in a low voice.

'Sir Nicholas is an invalid, sir, on account of a damaged heart, and that's why he occupies a suite of rooms here on the ground floor, at the rear of the house. It's quiet, you see, and isolated from the more public corridors and rooms by this little vestibule.'

The butler opened one of two adjacent doors in the wall facing them, and preceded Jackson into what was evidently Sir Nicholas's sitting-room, a spacious apartment, solidly furnished, and with a wide modern bay window, draped with billowing lace curtains, looking out on to the wide rear yard of the house. There were many cabinets and tables, and a clutter of framed photographs, and pieces of china and porcelain. Books and newspapers were scattered around in comfortable untidiness, suggesting that Sir Nicholas spent most of his time in the suite of rooms.

Inspector Jackson looked at the man who rose from a high-backed chair to greet him. Sir Nicholas was a tall, spare man in his early sixties, with a full head of immaculately groomed grey hair. His face was gaunt and drawn, with a certain bluish tinge about the lips, but he sported a neatly clipped military moustache, and his blue eyes were bright and alert. When he spoke Jackson was startled at the power of his delivery.

'Thank you, Lincoln,' he said to the butler. 'Is Mr Lance back yet? I thought he'd be here by now.'

'Mr Lance is not back yet, sir, but I'm sure he won't be long. But Mr Garamond has just arrived back from his visit to London, and has returned to the cottage. Will that be all, sir?'

'Yes, that's all, thank you.' The old baronet waited for the butler to leave the room, and then turned to Jackson.

'Well, now, Inspector,' he said, 'what's all this about a new villain in the district?'

Jackson explained to the baronet the dangers of having an expert cracksman on the loose. While he was speaking, he became aware that a door in the wall to his right had been left half open, and that it was possible to see partly into a room beyond. There was no sound of anyone working in the room, but the daylight was intermittently interrupted, as though clouds were scudding across the sun. But there were no clouds.

'… And therefore, sir,' Jackson concluded, 'I'd be grateful if you would show me the disposition of your safe. It may be that I can give you some advice on security.'

'An excellent idea, Inspector,' said Sir Nicholas, 'though I keep nothing of value in it – nothing, that is, that a thief would want to steal.'

'Nothing, sir? No jewels, silver, sums of money in gold?'

'Heavens, no! Things like that are kept in a bank vault in

Birmingham. But come into the next room, and have a look at the safe.'

Taking a walking-cane from the side of his chair, Sir Nicholas led Jackson out of the sitting-room and into what proved to be a bedroom. The inspector took in his surroundings with a single sweeping glance. Doors, he said to himself, there are too many doors....

The bedroom, like the sitting-room, was heavily furnished. There was a large four-poster bed, a bedside table cluttered with medicine bottles, a couch, a couple of armchairs and a tall glazed bookcase. Directly facing the bed was a further door, standing ajar, and leading into a dressing-room. The window here was of the common sash type, covered with the same net curtain as the bay window in the bedroom.

Sir Nicholas Waldegrave walked over to a shady corner, and pointed with a certain amount of pride to a small but substantial safe. Dear me, thought Jackson, I'd know it anywhere. There's the trademark dull-brown paint, and the exposed hinges, inviting the safe-cracker's hacksaw, as Dr Savage had said. It's an antique Castle's 'Fortress', and a candidate for the scrap-heap.

'There you are, Jackson,' said Sir Nicholas. 'What do you think of that? I don't think this Joseph Ede could get through that steel door!'

'Well, sir,' said Jackson, smiling, 'I can assure you that an able cracksman could open that old safe in a matter of seconds. And don't forget: although *you* know there's nothing of value there, the thief wouldn't; so don't give him the chance to find out.'

Sir Nicholas took a key from his pocket, and opened the safe. It contained a neat array of buff folders, and two or three bundles of letters tied with tape.

'Nothing of value there, Jackson,' said Sir Nicholas. 'They're all copies of title deeds, land grants – things like that. My lawyer holds the originals. As for valuables, well, my late wife's jewellery is safely locked up in Coutts' Bank in London. I intend to present it all to my daughter Margaret when she marries in September.'

Sir Nicholas relocked the safe, and treated Jackson to an attractively humorous smile.

'Well, thank you for calling today, Inspector,' he said. 'I gather you know Dr Savage? He was a very good physician, you know, and I was sorry to lose him when he retired. Still, the man I've got now is a hearty, no-nonsense type of fellow, who knows his business, so I've much to be thankful for.'

Sir Nicholas's face became thoughtful, and he relapsed into silence. Inspector Jackson waited patiently for him to speak. He noticed that the changing shadows in the dressing-room had recommenced, as though someone was flitting about unseen in the depths of the room.

Sir Nicholas Waldegrave was counting his blessings. It had been a sad burden being a widower who had never felt inclined to marry a second time, but his late wife had given him three children, two sons and a daughter, and his older sister Letitia had been like a mother to them all. And he had always been fortunate in his servants. Lincoln in particular had always been there, so it seemed. Dear old man, frail, and at times irascible, he was utterly loyal and faithful to the Waldegrave family....

Suddenly the flitting shadows in the dressing-room seemed to rush together, and the silently watching figure whom Jackson had seen earlier on the first-floor landing came quietly into the room.

'Excuse me, sir, but all is ready now if you wish to take your morning rest.'

'Thank you, Skinner,' said Sir Nicholas absently. He was evidently still absorbed in his own thoughts, and the valet left the room.

The man's voice had been low and deferential, with just a touch of a southern accent. His pale, moon-round face betrayed no interest in Jackson, which was odd, to say the least. Most people were curious when a police officer visited the house. Was this cat-like man the elusive Joseph Ede? His accent suggested that he was a Londoner, but old county gentlefolk like the Waldegraves invariably made it their practice to employ local men and women as servants.

'How long has he been with you, Sir Nicholas?' Jackson asked.

'Eh? What?' The baronet sat up in his chair, and blinked his eyes. 'Dear me, Mr Jackson, I was wool-gathering! How long has … how long has he been with me? Oh, my goodness, years and years – more years than I care to remember! Well, Inspector, as Skinner's just reminded me, it's time for my morning nap. Thank you for calling. I'll think about getting a new safe eventually. Just pull that bell by the fireplace, will you, and Lincoln will come to see you out.'

Jackson walked thoughtfully around the margin of the lake towards the carriage road that would take him back to Abbot's Langley. He glanced at the little Gothic folly with its landing-stage, and wondered if the man in the wheeled chair was still inside it. It was still very sunny, and curiously still, but in a few moments a surge of dark shadow seemed to rush at him from behind, and sweep on ahead of him, faster than he could walk. Once more, the waters of the lake rippled as a sudden breeze disturbed their surface. Despite the warm day, Jackson shivered. In his mind's eye he saw the old baronet again, showing him the contents of his safe, while in the next room the shadows formed and re-formed.

Shadows....

2

---·•·---

Evening at Langley Court

While Jackson was talking to Sir Nicholas Waldegrave about the danger posed by the presence of Joseph Ede in the district, the old butler, Lincoln, was sitting at a long table in the servants' hall of Langley Court, pouring out his various griefs and troubles to a willing listener.

'Nothing's like it was, Mr Cundlett,' he sighed. 'That policeman who's closeted with the master knocked on the front door without a qualm. The front door! Years ago, in the good old days, he'd have come round here, to the servants' quarters. It's not right. It's not *decent.*'

Mr Cundlett sighed in turn, and agreed that nothing was the same these days.

'It's like that carriage,' he said. 'It's not two months old, but the rear axle's gone – squeaks something awful, it does. Nothing's properly made these days, Mr Lincoln.'

Mr Cundlett regarded his hard hat with the red and blue cockade, which he had placed on the table in front of him, and, for no particular reason, turned it round.

'As for that policeman,' he continued, 'I fancy that must have been the man I gave a lift to, earlier on. Jackson, his name was. He looked a decent sort of person, and I wondered at the time whether he wasn't a seed merchant come to see Mr Garamond at the cottage. So he was a policeman?'

'He was. And I don't like it,' said Lincoln rather petulantly. 'He's come to advise the master about security for his valuables – as if anyone here would touch any of Sir Nicholas's things! I don't know what's happening to the world today.'

'Well, now,' said Cundlett, 'don't you worry about it, Mr Lincoln. Just stick to the old ways, like I do, and you won't go far wrong.

> The rich man in his castle,
> The poor man at his gate,
> He made them, high or lowly,
> And ordered their estate.'

'How true that is, Mr Cundlett!' said Lincoln. 'And speaking of duty, I must bestir myself soon. Mr Beecham of Horton Grange is coming here for dinner tonight, and there'll be seven sitting down at table. A very nice gentleman is Mr Beecham, though I gather he's not one of the Beechams of Mount Royal—'

He stopped speaking as the green baize door from the house opened to admit Skinner, the valet. He spoke to neither of them, but averted his gaze, and hurried through to the kitchens. Mr Cundlett spoke.

'That valet – I'd keep an eye on him if I were you, Mr Lincoln. I've seen the likes of him before when I was with the army out East. Sly. You keep an eye on him.'

'So that's what you think, Mr Cundlett? Yes; you're right. He snoops, you know. I found him the other day in Mr Arthur's sitting-room, where he'd no right to be. That sitting-room is Williams's responsibility, as he well knows. Snooping, you see. I sent him about his business, and told him never to go in there again unless I told him to do so. But you know, Mr Cundlett, I could feel waves of insolence coming from him. Waves of insolence.'

'Snoops, does he? Well, just you keep an eye on the silver spoons. Perhaps it's a good thing that this Inspector Jackson has called today, though I don't think Sir Nicholas keeps any valuables just lying around in the house. Snoops, hey? You watch him. He's sly, that one, Mr Lincoln.'

Mr Cundlett stood up, and gave his many capes a swirl.

'Let's leave all this talk of safes and valuables to our betters,' he said. 'It's not for the likes of you or me to reason why. Ours but to do and die! I'll not detain you any longer. It's time for me to leg it back to the stables.'

Cundlett carefully placed his cockaded hat on his round head, gave old Lincoln a smart salute, and marched off into the stable yard.

Ever since the previous August, when he and Margaret Waldegrave had publicly announced their engagement, Jeremy Beecham had been a frequent visitor to Langley Court. For a while, he had behaved with a kind of brittle dignity born of nervousness, but then the unpretentious friendliness of Sir Nicholas Waldegrave had allowed him to emerge from that unwilling pose. Dinner had begun, and they had reached a little fallow period between the removal of the soup plates and the appearance of the entrée, giving Beecham time to observe his fellow diners.

At the head of the table sat Sir Nicholas, a man who was both impressive and friendly in his bearing. He spoke loudly but without arrogance, and Beecham wondered whether he was slightly deaf. Dear, decent man! He would make a good father-in-law.

To Sir Nicholas's right, and thus directly facing Beecham, was Arthur Waldegrave, heir to the title and estate. He sat looking down patiently at the tablecloth, as though waiting for someone to cover his portion of it with a plate. What would a stranger see, when first confronted by Sir Nicholas's elder son?

He would see a man in his early thirties, with a long, pale, clean-shaven face, which usually bore an expression of fastidious sensitivity. Yes, a shy, sensitive, shrinking violet – or so he liked to

appear. In fact, he was a man of overweening arrogance, endowed
with a vitriolic tongue.

What else would the stranger see? A man whose grey eyes
looked weak and strained, which was why he wore those gold-
rimmed spectacles. In striking contrast to his pallid face, his head
was crowned with an abundant thatch of ginger hair, an inheritance, apparently, from his late mother.

Arthur Waldegrave dressed at all times formally and precisely,
which gave him a certain impressiveness of bearing; but an expe-
rienced eye realized that his careful dress was the work of a
devoted servant, for Arthur Waldegrave was a victim of paralysis,
confined to a wheeled chair from the age of sixteen. One sympa-
thized with him for that; but he was still an arrogant and
impertinent fellow, whom he would have to tolerate for
Margaret's sake.

Margaret! Ever since their first meeting he had had no doubt
that she would one day become his wife, and only last week the
wedding had been fixed for 29 September. She was twenty-four,
slim and very fair, with light blue eyes. She was sitting at the far
end of his side of the table, with her brother Lance separating
them. Margaret Grace Waldegrave. Margaret had been her
mother's name. Grace had been her father's choice.

Facing Sir Nicholas at the other end of the long table was his
sister Letitia, known in the family as Aunt Letty. A handsome,
attractive woman in her late sixties, she had mothered Sir
Nicholas's two sons and his daughter ever since they were children.

And what of Lance? What should one make of him? He was a
good-looking man of twenty-five, with a haggard charm about
him that made one excuse his occasional abruptness, and his fits
of absent-mindedness. He sported a fine black military moustache, a relic of his three years in the army. Beneath the fine
moustache was a discontented mouth and a weak chin. Lance
wasn't a bad fellow, but he was too fond of drink, and not very
judicious in his approach to gambling. He'd declared his intention

of going up to London early the next day, but even the prospect of escaping to the capital for a day didn't seem to cheer him. He looked gloomy and preoccupied.

The seventh diner was an old family friend, Philip Garamond, who was sitting across the table next to Arthur Waldegrave. Garamond was a genial man in his mid-fifties, and a noted botanist. He was a man who laughed easily, and who commanded respect because of his learned achievements, and the modesty that went with them. For some reason, he seemed to be very fond of Arthur Waldegrave. One day, perhaps Beecham would find out why.

Garamond was a distant cousin of the late Lady Waldegrave, and he had lived for nearly thirty years in a house standing in a plantation of oaks known as Langley Grove. That house of his – the cottage, they called it – what an architectural gem it was! It was faced with white stucco, a narrow building rising to three storeys, and predated the mansion of Langley Court by a hundred years.

The entrée was brought in – an inviting saddle of lamb, served by two liveried footmen, working under the eagle eye of old Lincoln. Everybody did justice to the meal, and for a while the only sound was the tinkle of knives and forks on china plates.

All this, thought Beecham – the first-rate food, the footmen in attendance, the ornate dining-room with its gilded portraits of Waldegrave ancestors – all this was taken for granted by the people sitting around the table that evening. They had known no other kind of life. Was it logical to expect them to be grateful for their exalted lot in life? And was it reasonable for him to feel, deep down, almost hidden from consciousness, a smouldering resentment against them all?

Sir Nicholas laid down his knife and fork, and wiped his lips with his napkin.

'So, Philip,' he said, in his robust tones, 'you had no luck in London with the Calton Papers? You haven't said anything, but I know that look of yours when you've been thwarted – a kind of humorously rueful resignation.'

Philip Garamond laughed.

'You're quite right, Nicholas, I was beaten to it by a dark horse who bid through an agent – a Major someone-or-other. Much joy may he get from it. Still, my trip to London wasn't entirely a waste of time. I bought some Havana cigars for you, Nicholas, and lace shawls for the ladies – elegant affairs from Liberty's.'

Aunt Letty and Margaret were profuse in their thanks, and evidently delighted at Garamond's thoughtfulness.

'And for you, Lance, a couple of bottles of liqueur brandy. Ah! I thought that would cheer you up! You've been looking very sombre this evening.'

'Dashed civil of you, Uncle Philip,' said Lance Waldegrave. 'Thank you very much.'

'And for you, Arthur,' said Garamond, 'I have a book – something that I know you've wanted to possess for a long time. Why not come back with me to the cottage after dinner, and smoke a cigar? I'll give you the book then.'

'Thanks, Uncle,' said Arthur Waldegrave, his eyes shining. 'I'll look forward to that.'

Sir Nicholas spoke again, his voice carrying to the furthest ends of the room.

'You're very quiet, tonight, Beecham,' he said. 'I expect you're thinking about one of your landscape projects. I gather that your last commission was very lucrative.'

Jeremy Beecham found himself blushing. Really, these titled people were prepared to discuss the most intimate details of family life and private business in front of a roomful of servants! What was one to do? Before he could reply to Sir Nicholas's question, Arthur Waldegrave burst into speech.

'That was a huge conservatory for Sir Isaac Cohen at that vulgar villa he's building at Twickenham, wasn't it?' he said. His eyes behind their gold-framed glasses held a mocking glint. 'I wonder where he got his money from? I've heard a few odd things about Sir Isaac.'

He glanced down the table at his sister Margaret, who was blushing with vexation.

'When you and Beecham are married, my dear,' he said, 'you can invite Sir Isaac and his City friends to dinner. He'll be able to give you a few tips for the stock market.'

'Cut it out, you damned fool,' muttered Lance Waldegrave. 'Father's just asked Beecham a question, and he's waiting for an answer.'

Jeremy studiously ignored Arthur Waldegrave, and addressed himself to Sir Nicholas.

'Sir Isaac Cohen gave me three hundred pounds for that conservatory,' he said. 'You'll appreciate that ten such commissions in a year will bring in a very satisfactory income.'

'That's a tidy sum, Beecham,' said Sir Nicholas, 'but it's land you need these days: it's land that brings in the money.'

'I have twelve acres—' Beecham began. Everyone at the table, including Margaret, simply burst out laughing.

'No, man!' the baronet continued. 'I mean *real* land. I've got four thousand acres of good dairy and pastureland round here, and in Oxfordshire. That's what brings the money in.'

Was he making a grave mistake, marrying into this old, landed family? He would always be an outsider, someone to be indulged, apologized for....

Damn it! He was marrying Margaret, not the Waldegrave family. When he had achieved all his secret aims, perhaps he would dispose of Horton Grange, and take Margaret to London. Let them keep their thousands of acres, and their inbred attitudes. After all, were they such fine native stock as they boasted? The father ill with heart disease, his sister an old spinster, one brother a bitter cripple, the other a weak-chinned wastrel.... One day, they would all get their just deserts.

Philip Garamond watched as Williams carefully arranged a rug around Arthur Waldegrave's legs, and then positioned his wheeled

chair on the opposite side of the fireplace in the drawing-room of
the cottage. Williams, he supposed, was in his late twenties, and
thus a few years younger than Arthur. He wore the sober dark-
green livery of the Waldegraves, enlivened by red facings on the
lapels. From the way he went about his work, it was evident that
he was devoted to his crippled charge.

When Williams had gone, Garamond produced a tray on which
reposed two bulbous glasses, a bottle of Napoleon brandy, and an
open box of slim Dutch cigars. He saw Arthur visibly relax, and
knew that once again the peculiar spell of the cottage had exerted
its power over the young man.

'It's very kind of you, Uncle Philip,' said Arthur Waldegrave, 'to
let me come out here on occasion. These simple rooms, and the
sparse eighteenth-century furniture, give it a civilized atmosphere
which is all its own.' Arthur sipped his brandy, and then drew on
his cigar.

'I'm sorry you didn't manage to buy the Calton Papers,' he said.
'They sounded very interesting. I read the description of them in
Sotheby's catalogue.'

'Well, I must admit I was disappointed,' said Garamond. 'They
went for five hundred pounds to someone called Major Pomeroy.
I've no idea who he is, but he's evidently got money to burn. I
hope he enjoys his five hundred pounds' worth!'

Philip Garamond rose from his chair beside the drawing-room
fireplace, and opened a drawer in a bureau standing against the
far wall. He returned with an ancient calf-bound volume in his
hand, which he handed to Arthur.

'There you are,' he said, resuming his seat. 'My man at
Sotheby's procured that for you. *The Whole Historie of the
Waldegraves of Thanet*, by Silas Bolt. Anno 1594. That should fill
one of those annoying gaps in your research that you're always
complaining about!'

Arthur Waldegrave uttered a delighted cry of surprise, and his
rather austere features were radiated by a sudden smile.

'Uncle Philip! How very kind of you. I've nothing at all on the Waldegraves of Thanet. This old book will help me compose another chapter for my great *History of the Family of Waldegrave*. I knew about Silas Bolt's work, of course, but I never thought I'd own a copy of it.'

Philip Garamond sat in silence, watching Arthur as he began to dip into the old volume. The young man's cigar smouldered away unheeded in the ashtray, and his brandy remained unconsumed.

For the last two years, Arthur had devoted most of his waking hours to the composing of a vast detailed history of the various branches of the Waldegrave family. It was something more than a hobby for a man who could neither walk nor ride; it had become a consuming passion, arising from Arthur Waldegrave's intense family pride.

Garamond knew that Arthur's absorption in the family's history was a source of embarrassment to both Sir Nicholas and his other two children, who were essentially country gentlefolk, not grandees of the first order. But this genealogical study kept Arthur Waldegrave from brooding on his physical limitations.

Since the demise of winter, Arthur had left the house most evenings after dinner, and gone to work on his great book in the folly, which had been adapted for him as a kind of study. He would work there for a couple of hours, and return to the house soon after ten o'clock.

The family had become accustomed to the little procession: Arthur, sitting in his wheeled chair with a pile of books and papers balanced on his knees, pushed by Williams along the path to the little fanciful quay on the margin of the lake. Although built of sandstone, the folly, a relic of the house that had previously stood on the site of the present Langley Court, was panelled inside, and equipped with a tiny fireplace. It had proved to be a surprisingly warm and comfortable place in which to work.

'And now, Arthur,' said Philip Garamond, 'perhaps you'll put that book aside, and tell me why you were so confoundedly rude to Jeremy Beecham at dinner. Poor Margaret was mightily embarrassed. Even Lance roused himself sufficiently to make a protest.'

Arthur blushed, and Garamond knew that it was a blush of vexation as well as embarrassment. No doubt Arthur would produce a few spurious reasons for his behaviour, but eventually he would find himself compelled to tell the truth.

'You don't know what it's like to be helpless, Uncle,' he said. 'Physical restraint acts upon the will. I want Margaret to see what a mistake she's making in determining to marry that fellow, but all that comes out is the cheap sarcasm that you heard tonight – damn it all, I can *hear* myself being ridiculous, but there's nothing that I can do about it.'

'Why do you think that Margaret's making a mistake?'

'Because the man's got no background, no family! He's an upstart, with no pedigree to bring to the alliance. At first, I thought he must have been one of the Beechams of Mount Royal, but that proved not to be the case. Margaret should marry into the gentry, like all the Langley Waldegraves have done. This fellow's an upstart.'

Philip Garamond lit a second cigar, and smoked away for a minute or so in silence. Then he spoke.

'When you talk like that, Arthur,' he said, 'you sound like an upstart yourself. Your father has no objection to the match, and that should be enough for you. Besides, I don't believe you. I don't believe all this talk about pedigree, and family, and so forth. You're too shrewd a man to confuse your hobby of genealogy with the mundane facts of real life. There's something else about Mr Jeremy Beecham that you've found out, but haven't the courage to voice in public. I'm right, aren't I?'

Garamond saw his nephew's eyes grow troubled behind the lenses of his gold-framed glasses. On this occasion, as on most others, he had been able to read Arthur Waldegrave's mind like a book. In a moment, he would tell him what he knew about Jeremy Beecham.

'It was something Grimes told me, Uncle,' said Arthur at last. 'Oh, I know you think he's a rough, common fellow, good only for stoking the gas-house furnace in the yard, but he's a man with his ear to the ground, as the saying goes.'

'And what did Grimes tell you? You must have caught him in one of his periods of sobriety to get any sense out of him at all.'

'Uncle,' Arthur replied, 'do you remember the murder of Jabez Beecham at Horton Grange? It happened about five years ago—'

'Of course I remember it. It's not every day that a near neighbour gets himself murdered. Horton Grange is only a quarter of a mile from here, at Sheriff's Langley. It's a tumbledown old Tudor place, which poor Jeremy Beecham plans to restore to its pristine glory. I've been there on a number of occasions, together with Lance and Margaret. Well, what did Grimes tell you about it?'

'He was a recluse, wasn't he?' said Arthur Waldegrave. 'Jabez Beecham, I mean. He was found dead in the great hall, and the police discovered that he had died through the administration of cyanide.'

'Correct,' said Garamond. 'And but for an almost imbecilic mistake by the murderer, old Jabez Beecham's death would most certainly have been interpreted as suicide. But murder it was, Arthur, and the murder has never been solved.'

'Grimes told me that Jabez Beecham had been a convict in one of the Australian penal colonies,' said Arthur. 'He'd been found guilty of cheating honest prospectors out of their money, and it was widely rumoured that he had once committed a murder—'

'Yes, yes,' said Garamond drily, 'this is all hearsay and gossip, you know. Nothing definite was ever found out about Jabez Beecham's antecedents. And one can hardly ask his nephew Jeremy Beecham for details. One doesn't do that kind of thing.'

'There's more to it than that, Uncle Philip,' said Arthur. 'Grimes told me that it was this man Jeremy Beecham – the man who is going to marry Margaret – who administered that cyanide to his uncle.'

'Is that what Grimes told you? He'd better watch his step. There are laws of slander in this country, Arthur.'

'Listen, Uncle Philip. Five years ago, Jeremy Beecham was a penniless, struggling garden designer, and he coveted his old uncle's house and remaining money. Grimes has the proof that he murdered his uncle in order to inherit his property, and further his career. They're a family of Australian convicts, Uncle! And both uncle and nephew may have been murderers. Now you know why I'm so desperate to save my sister from this ruinous alliance. But what can I say to her? What can I do?'

Arthur struck the arms of his wheeled chair impotently, and writhed with some kind of inner fury. Philip Garamond looked at him. Poor, wretched fellow! What was to be done? What *could* be done?

'Of course, you'll say that all this is the fantasizing of a man with too much time on his hands—'

'I say nothing of the sort, Arthur,' Garamond replied. 'Although I wouldn't trust Grimes as a reliable source of information, I'll admit that people of his sort often do hear uncomfortable truths about their betters. Will you let me look into this matter for you? I'll be very discreet, so that Jeremy Beecham will not realize that I am playing the detective. If I find out anything positive, I'll inform you, but, more to the point, I will inform Margaret. Will that satisfy you?'

Arthur Waldegrave uttered a sigh of relief. Once more, his austere features were radiated by a smile.

'My goodness, Uncle Philip,' he said, 'you've lifted a great weight from my mind! I thought you'd dismiss my suspicions as the vapourings of an invalid. I'll leave the matter entirely in your hands. Meanwhile, I'll make a valiant attempt to be as civil as I can to the fellow.'

The evening had grown warm, and the atmosphere in the cottage was becoming oppressive and clammy. Philip Garamond rose, and began to guide his nephew's wheeled chair towards the door.

'Come on, Arthur,' he said, 'Williams won't be here to take you back to the house for half an hour yet. Let me walk you up through the oaks as far as the bridle road.'

They left through a rear door, and Garamond pushed his nephew's chair along the winding path that threaded its way through the grove of ancient oaks surrounding the cottage. To the left, a line of long glasshouses could be seen, the dying rays of the sun glancing from their many panes.

Here, over a period of twenty-five years, Philip Garamond had assembled his outstanding collection of exotic plants. Later in the season, various visitors would arrive to take a conducted tour, and to exchange knowledge and gossip with the renowned botanist. But now, in early June, both cottage and grove were his to enjoy alone.

High up among the oaks, at a point where the path began to emerge on to a little green containing a few humble dwellings, Philip Garamond and his nephew halted. This was as far as they would go: once out on to the green, and the magical atmosphere of the ancient grove would be dissipated. Philip Garamond leaned against a tree, and lit a cigar. Arthur Waldegrave pulled at the rug that covered his legs, tugging it with a kind of unconscious petulance.

'That fellow Beecham likes to pose as an independent spirit,' he said, 'but he'd be very happy to take the settlement that Father's making for Margaret after she's married him in September. He's going to present them with the four farms at Eaton Hill, together with ten thousand pounds in bank paper. Ten thousand pounds! The farms will bring them in four hundred or so. Jeremy will like that, I've no doubt.'

'Talking of settlements,' said Garamond, 'do you remember that old family joke about Margaret's Dowry? It was a bequest to Margaret made by a distant relative of her mother's in 1874, when Margaret was no more than four years old. Your father was still in the army in Bengal, stationed at Murshidabad, and some firm of lawyers in the Midlands telegraphed the news out to him there. I don't recall much of the details.'

'I do, Uncle,' said Arthur. 'This bequest becomes Margaret's absolutely when she attains the age of twenty-five, but if she's failed to marry before that age, then the property comes to *me*.'

'Well, I wish you joy of it, if you get it!' Philip Garamond laughed. 'Your father and I went up so see it, you know, about twelve years ago. It turned out to be a large tract of useless scrubland up beyond Nuneaton, adjoining a vast area of sour dereliction where factories and workshops were being built. It was all barren stuff, going up in a straight line beyond Coleshill and into Leicestershire.'

'I'm not worried about Margaret's Dowry,' said Arthur. 'If you can prove that Jeremy Beecham is innocent of the crimes alleged against him by Grimes, then he's welcome to a few hundred pounds' worth of useless scrubland, if he can find out who's administering it. It's not held by our family solicitors, and I've no idea who's holding it. Some provincial lawyer up in the Midlands, I suppose.'

A sudden strong wind began to throw the tops of the great oaks into an agitated frenzy, and the last rays of the dying sun fled from the sky. As Philip Garamond turned the chair round for the return journey, a great shadow, a kind of presage of ills to come, seemed to rush past them through the trees, charging like a demon on horseback down the twisting path. Garamond was more than relieved to see the figure of the faithful Williams climbing stolidly up the path from the cottage to take his stricken young master back to the warmth and light of Langley Court, before the night fell.

3

Incident at the Railway Arms

Lance Waldegrave turned up his coat collar against the sudden squall of rain, and hurried across the street in front of Copton Vale Central railway station. It was only half past nine, and the last train to Abbot's Langley wouldn't leave till an hour later. There was plenty of time for a glass or two of something stimulating before he set out for home.

It had been a smoky, depressing journey from London, as he had thought it prudent to save some money by travelling second class. The loss of cachet had been just another humiliation for him to bear. Humiliation.... Damn that sly, insolent moneylender! Not one penny more, the fellow had told him, until he had repaid some of what he already owed. On the way out of his office, some leering brutes on the stairs had jostled him, and then pretended to apologize. It had been a hint of brutalities to come if he failed to pay his debts. What was he to do?

He fancied that he'd recognized two of the rabble loitering on that dim staircase. Only a week earlier, he had been walking home from Abbot's Langley when they had accosted him as he made his way along the winding drive of Langley Court. One of them, a dangerous Irishman with huge scarred fists and a vicious mouth, had seized him by the throat and slammed him against a tree. His companion, a frightening black man wielding an open razor, had torn his wallet from the inside pocket of his coat, and abstracted his last five-pound note. The fellow had treated him to an insolent grin, and thrown his wallet into the grass.

'You know who we are, Waldegrave,' the man with the big fists had whispered – it was a hateful, chilling sound – 'and who we come from. He's getting impatient for his money, and this five pounds will be on account. We'll leave you in one piece, this time. Next time, though, you'll not be so lucky.'

And so he had gone up to London, and begged and pleaded with the usurer, but to no avail. And there, on the stairs, he was sure, were the two thugs who had accosted him in the grounds of his own home, and taken money from him by force. How much longer could he, a former army officer, put up with this frightful humiliation? What was he to do?

People assumed that he had been cashiered from his regiment for some dereliction of duty, or forced to resign to avoid a scandal. It never seemed to occur to them that he had handed in his papers for a perfectly legitimate reason. But whose fault was that?

He pushed open the swing door of the Railway Arms, and winced as he was assailed by the smell of warm beer and tobacco smoke from the public bar. It was a noisy, rough-and-ready sort of place, much frequented by market-traders and railway men, but it was handy for the station, and as welcome a berth as any on a dark rainy night.

The bar was crowded, and when Lance had been given his double whisky, he wove his way through the cheery, talkative crowd of customers, looking for an empty table.

'You can sit here with us, Mr Lance Waldegrave,' said a voice from the crowd. A hand pulled him firmly by the sleeve, and he gave a little cry of distress, as though he was in pain. God! On this night, of all nights, to be entrapped by that whining common girl and her two thuggish protectors! He thought he'd seen the last of them when he'd threatened them with the police a couple of weeks earlier. Would the terrors of this day never end?

'You remember, us, don't you, Mr Waldegrave?' said one of the two men, a young fellow in his mid twenties, with a clean-shaven face and a shock of fair hair. 'Steven Beamish, my name is, and I work in the wholesale vegetable market in Clive Street. Not quite the sort of company for a gentleman to keep, am I? And this is my friend Peter Pritchard. He's a time-keeper at one of the factories on the other side of the station.'

'What do you want?' asked Lance. He contrived to glance briefly at the young woman sitting with the two men at the table. She looked sick and pale, and her thin hands were trembling. Well, it was no longer any business of his. He'd done with her, and packed her away with a present long ago. How dare these common labouring men try to intimidate him! How much more of this persecution could he take?

This demeaning encounter had not gone unnoticed. Ever since he'd been forced to sit down with these people someone had been watching him, and contriving to listen to what they were saying. The watcher was sitting by himself at a table near the door, a big, shambling fellow wearing a mustard-coloured overcoat. He had deposited a battered brown bowler hat on the table at which he sat, beside a little nest of empty gin glasses. His homely face was flushed, but his shrewd grey eyes shone with intelligent interest. Why was he listening to their conversation? Damn it, why couldn't the fellow mind his own business?

'You know quite well what we want,' said the man called Peter Pritchard. 'We want you to do your duty by this poor girl that you've ruined and disgraced. You have a gentleman's name, Mr Waldegrave, but in my book, you're nothing but a common cur.'

Lance could not contain the cry of rage that rose to his lips. There came the clatter of a falling glass as he half rose from the table. His face flushed with anger as he tried, and failed, to free his arm from Peter Pritchard's retaining grip. Conversation in the bar became muted, and curious eyes were turned to look at them.

The man in the yellow overcoat picked up his hat and came

across to their table. Without more ado, he pulled up a chair and sat down.

'Now, sir,' he said, 'we don't want any kind of disturbance, or high words here in the Railway Arms. I suggest that you drink up, and leave the premises.'

'And who the devil are you, may I ask?' said Lance Waldegrave hotly. 'What do you mean, coming over here to breathe gin-fumes over us all?' His fine military moustache bristled with indignation, but his eyes could not meet those of the two other men, who viewed him with open contempt. The stranger produced a card from his overcoat pocket, and held it up for Lance Waldegrave to see.

'I'm Detective Sergeant Bottomley, of the Warwickshire Constabulary,' he said. 'I'd advise you to drink up and leave now, unless you'd like to spend the night with this evening's crop of drunks in Copton Vale Bridewell.'

Lance Waldegrave flushed with impotent anger, but he obeyed the police officer and rose to his feet. He looked at the two working men and the pale-faced girl with a kind of mean triumph.

'Certainly, Sergeant,' he said. 'I was just about to leave, anyway. I was incensed at what these rough fellows were saying, but they meant no harm, I dare say. I'll bid you good night.'

Sergeant Bottomley watched as Lance Waldegrave hurried from the bar, and then turned to look at the three people who had been sitting with him at the round, marble-topped table.

He was struck at once by the obvious respectability of both the men. One was a fair-haired lad in his early twenties; the other was older, and slightly stooped. They were dressed in the rough, home-spun suits of working men.

The young woman was certainly no older than eighteen. She wore an unadorned black dress, and had flung a thin shawl around her frail shoulders. A shapeless hat failed to conceal her luxuriant black hair. What ailed the lass? She was as white as chalk, and had scarcely glanced at Bottomley. The sergeant turned to the older man, and asked him a question.

'Would you like to tell me what kind of a row was brewing up before I came over to your table? I can see that you're all decent folk, and it may help to share your trouble with someone like me.'

The older man looked keenly at Bottomley for a few moments, glanced briefly at his companion, and then began to speak.

'My name's Peter Pritchard,' he said, 'and I work in one of the factories on the other side of the station. This here's Steven Beamish. He's a porter in the fruit market. We both live in Gashouse Lane, near the new railway bridge.'

Pritchard turned to look at the girl, and a spasm of anger passed over his rather gaunt face.

'And this is Mary Connor,' he said. 'She's an orphan, her mother dying when she was only three, and her father being killed on the railway soon after. She lives with her aunt – her father's sister – further along Gashouse Lane.'

'She's no one to look after her,' said the younger man, cutting his friend short. 'She's only a girl, and easily taken advantage of. That man you saw tonight—'

'That man,' resumed Peter Pritchard, 'seduced this girl, and then abandoned her. You can see the state she's in, Mr Bottomley. She can't even cry. She's going to have a baby, and her aunt won't have her in the house. She's got to go somewhere, and so I hit upon the idea of making that man part with a bit of money so as to help her. It wasn't extortion, or anything like that – we just wanted him to give her some money to rent a room until the business is over. We first spoke to him in the street near here last week, when he came down to catch a train to London.'

'And what did he say, this Mr Waldegrave?'

'He said that he hadn't any money,' Pritchard replied, 'and that in any case we couldn't prove that he was the father of Mary's child. To say that, was to imply that Mary was a loose woman, instead of someone little more than a child herself, who was led astray by the likes of *him*. I didn't know for certain that he'd come in here, but when he did, I grabbed him by the sleeve, and made him sit down with us. I don't know quite what I was going to do with him. Maybe I'd have frightened him into prising open his wallet.'

'This Mr Waldegrave,' said Bottomley. 'I've heard the name, but I can't place him. The landlord says that he's not a Copton Vale man.'

'That's right. He's the son of old Sir Nicholas Waldegrave, who lives out at Abbot's Langley, on the way to Knowle. Langley Court, that's what his house is called. I reckon I might go out there, and have a word with Sir Nicholas about his rotten son. Maybe I should have threatened him with that tonight—'

'No, Mr Pritchard,' said Bottomley, 'that could be interpreted as demanding money with menaces. If I were you, I wouldn't sully myself by seeing that man again. If poor Mary there is to be turned out by her aunt, I can give you the address of a lady living in the countryside a few miles from here who will take her in at any time of the day or night, and look after her until the ordeal's over. I'll write it down for you on this piece of paper, and you can keep it until you need it.'

The girl called Mary Connor suddenly burst into tears, and at once some natural colour returned to her cheeks. Herbert Bottomley's kindly concern had evidently penetrated through her carapace of misery and despair.

'It might be as well if you were to leave, now,' said Bottomley, handing the piece of paper to the older man. 'If you ever want to get in touch with me over this business, you'll find me at Barrack Street Police Office in Warwick. Remember the name. Bottomley. Detective Sergeant Bottomley.'

The two men stood up, and Peter Pritchard gently helped the girl to her feet. He muttered a word of thanks, and led her out of the bar. Steven Beamish, looking embarrassed, remained behind for a moment, and as soon as his two companions had left the premises, he spoke to Bottomley in low tones.

'I want to thank you personally, master,' he said, 'for being so very decent to us. I was at my wits' end over Mary. When all this is over, I'm going to marry that girl, and look after her – and her baby, too. It looks as though she'll find shelter, now, thanks to you.'

The young man knuckled his forehead, turned abruptly on his heel, and left the bar.

4

Morning at Horton Grange

Jeremy Beecham stood in the parlour of Horton Grange, and thought about his inheritance. This was not an ancestral home, for his uncle had bought it with hard-earned money on his return from Australia. At one time it had been the seat of an ancient family called De Greville, but they had died out centuries ago. Uncle Jabez had acquired it cheap when, empty and neglected, it had become a drag on the market.

There were times when he hated Horton Grange – hated its pervading air of dilapidation, its recalcitrant arthritic timbers, its twisted old brick chimney stacks. The house smelt of the decay of centuries, and stood as a living reproach to his lack of immediately accessible wealth in contrast with the family into which he was to marry.

Langley Court, the Waldegrave home, was less than a hundred years old, but it had been raised on the ruins of an ancient house, half manor and half palace, that had burned down in the closing years of the eighteenth century. The Waldegraves had been at Abbot's Langley for 500 years.

It was not wise to couple the idea of murder with the operation of Providence, but there could be no doubt that his inheriting of Horton Grange had come just in time to save him from ruin. His elegant, airy conservatories were just coming to the notice of the families who mattered, and the Prince of Wales had expressed an interest in connection with some new hothouses at Sandringham. And then, the landlord of his town house in Mayfair had demanded immediate payment of two quarters' rent, threatening to make a fuss if his demands were not met. Uncle Jabez's death had proved very convenient, and the crisis had passed.

Did he fear Uncle Jabez's vengeful ghost? No, ghosts were the product of ignorant imaginings and the creaking of ancient timbers in the dark country nights.

There were other times – and this was one of them – when he felt that the old Tudor house could well become his settled home, a place where he could raise a family, and it was for that reason that he had determined, a few months earlier, to reopen the rear part of the house, which had long been closed up and deserted. It contained many rooms, some quaintly named after various saints – a relic, apparently, of pre-Reformation times. A local firm of builders had proved to be excellent and sympathetic craftsmen, and work had already begun on the restoration of a number of the long-deserted rooms.

Very soon after coming to live at Horton Grange, he had caused this parlour where he now stood to be restored to something like its early glory. The oak panelling had been cleaned and repaired, the elaborate plaster ceiling carefully restored, and the windows, with their hundreds of tiny diamond-shaped panes, re-glazed. What the room needed now was some bright red and blue Turkey carpets. When he received payment for his last commission from Sir Isaac Cohen, he would order them from a man he knew in London.

Jeremy walked over to the long, low range of windows and looked out into the sunlit garden. Here they were, now – Margaret and her uncle, Philip Garamond, who must have walked the quarter-mile down the sunken road from Langley Court. No doubt Lance would turn up as the morning advanced. Later, their man Cundlett would arrive with the carriage to take them all back to Langley Court.

They were coming to see the latest curiosity to be revealed as a result of the restoration work. The workmen, in stripping the mildewed panelling from a length of wall near the kitchen passage, had uncovered a bricked-up stone archway. Jeremy had told them to open the arch, which they had done, revealing a narrow chamber behind the wall, in which had stood an old muniment chest. A flight of hidden steps had led the men down to a burial crypt beneath the house. It was a place worthy of a visit, if only to emphasize the truth of the old Latin saying, *Sic transit gloria mundi*.

'Come in, Garamond,' said Jeremy Beecham, as Philip appeared on the threshold. 'What's happened to Margaret? I saw her arrive with you, just now.'

'Margaret has been carried off by your housekeeper, Mrs Miller,' said Philip. 'She wants to show her the kitchens. Mrs Miller, apparently, has high hopes of a new coal range after you and Margaret are married! Are you going to show me this ancient vault? Or shall we wait for Margaret?'

'Let's wait for her, Garamond,' said Jeremy. 'I'm glad we've a little time in hand, because I've been wanting to ask you about the recent history of the Waldegrave family. Margaret has told me precious little, and I go in too much awe of Sir Nicholas to start pumping him about family affairs. Let's have a glass of sherry, shall we?'

Philip Garamond sat down on a settee, and sipped the sherry that Jeremy handed him. He was silent for a moment, ordering his thoughts.

'Sir Nicholas was a professional soldier,' he said at last, 'who served most of his time in India, where he was attached to the Bengal Lancers. Margaret was born out there. Nicholas, who was a major at that time, was supervising the construction of a railway line in Murshidabad, but his wife, Mary Jane, was up in Sikkim, nearly three hundred miles away. Margaret was born there, on 18 October, 1870.'

'Do you know,' said Jeremy, 'I had no idea that Margaret had been born in India. She's never so much as mentioned it!'

'Well, she was only six when Nicholas's tour of duty ended, and the family returned home. Nicholas thought it was time for him to devote more attention to the running of the estate, so he resigned his commission. He was forty-six, and Mary Jane was just thirty-four. Arthur had two years of normal life ahead of him before paralysis struck him down, and was still at Eton. Little Lance was seven, and living with one of his mother's elder sisters at Mortlake.

'And then, within a year, Mary Jane fell victim to galloping consumption, and Nicholas found himself a widower at the age of forty-eight. That was when Letitia – Miss Waldegrave – assumed the role of surrogate mother to them all.'

'A sad tale.'

'Yes, it was: very sad. Mary Jane was one of the Greggs of High Grove, near Nuneaton. She was a very beautiful woman, and adapted well to being the wife of an officer in the Indian Army. It was a terrible shock to lose her. I've never forgotten it.'

'Did the children get on well together?' asked Jeremy. 'They seem curiously detached from one another, to my way of thinking. I hope you don't mind my asking these questions?'

'Not at all,' Philip replied. 'Did they get on well together? Yes, I think so. Of course, Margaret was often left to her own devices, being a girl, while the boys romped about, and climbed trees, and so on. But after 1878, when Arthur was stricken with paralysis, he became very reclusive in his ways, and the two boys grew apart from that time. Oh, they're friends, of course, but they no longer have any shared interests. I sometimes think—'

Philip Garamond stopped speaking as his niece came into the room.

'Am I too late to see the new rooms?' she asked.

'You are not,' said Jeremy, smiling. 'Come along, let me show you both the latest wonders of Horton Grange.'

They left the parlour, and crossed a flagged passage which gave access to the long-shut-up side of the house. Uncle Philip and Jeremy went ahead of Margaret, and she saw them stop at the far end of the passage to examine the old muniment chest that the workmen had discovered. However, something else in the passage had claimed her own attention.

To her right, a little carved staircase of no more than five or six steps led up to a door, which stood half open to reveal a small, well-lit chamber. There was a tantalizing glimpse of an ancient fireplace, beside which, carved into the oak panelling, was to be seen a life-size image of a man, clutching a grid-iron in his arms. Margaret mounted the stairs, and saw inscribed in black and white painted letters above the lintel the words: 'Sanct Lawrens his Chambre'.

'Margaret! Come down from there at once!'

Jeremy's voice seemed uncharacteristically harsh and commanding, and Margaret felt compelled to do as she was told. But she felt vexed at being denied entrance to the mysterious room, and went to join her two companions in reserved silence. Jeremy seemed not to notice her subdued manner, but she was pleased when he ventured an explanation for his words.

'The floor up there isn't safe, Margaret,' he said. 'There's danger of collapse until the workmen have put it right. I thought they'd secured it with a padlock – I'll speak to them about that, tomorrow. But come along, my dear: your Uncle Philip's anxious to see the ancient crypt and its grim contents!'

The hidden part of Horton Grange, thought Margaret, contained some of the most charming rooms that she had ever seen. Presumably it was poverty, rather than choice, that had made Jeremy's old uncle shut up these spacious chambers, with their western aspect, in order to live in the gloomier rooms at the front of the house.

She could hear the two men talking as they descended the steps that led to the recently discovered burial vault of the De Grevilles, but her imagination was causing her to linger in the quaint old passageways, visualizing them newly decorated, their walls hung with portraits.

She glanced into an empty room, its floor thick with the dust of generations, but containing a long window brilliant with ancient coloured glass. She suddenly knew that, despite Jeremy's ambivalence towards the old house, she wanted to make Horton Grange her home.

Standing on the threshold, she began to furnish it in her mind as a dining-room, the coloured glass complemented by a bright Wilton carpet, upon which would stand a vast oak dining-table in the antique style, with matching chairs covered in Tudor embroidery. They would buy an authentic tapestry to hang on the wall opposite the window.... There would be a massive oak sideboard, and some dim old mirrors....

A noise somewhere in the house brought her back to the present, and the old room returned to its dust and dereliction.

She would have to satisfy Jeremy by peeping into this dismal vault that the workmen had unearthed, though such things held little interest for her. By the time she had reached the entrance to the vault, the two men had gone. Evidently, they had grown weary of waiting for her. Well, so be it. More to please her fiancé than to satisfy her own curiosity, Margaret ventured into the entrance to the tomb, and made her way cautiously to its further limit, where a steep stair went down to a square crypt, closed by a rotting wooden door.

The crypt smelt of damp earth. Two candles had been left burning on the stone floor, by the light of which Margaret saw four shallow stone chests, each containing a lead-wrapped corpse. Over the centuries, the lead had collapsed over the skeletons, producing four chilling reminders of the inelegance of death.

Who were these poor souls? Carved into the wall behind the graves was the coat of arms of the De Greville family, but there were no inscriptions on the lead-wrapped figures to announce to future generations who they had been. Margaret shuddered. If she had any sway at all with Jeremy, she would have this terrible place bricked up and the passage wall panelled again so that no hint of its existence would be apparent in the future.

Stooping, she blew out the candles, and then turned to make her way back to the light and air. She froze in sudden fear as the sound of heavy, deliberate footfall came from the steps beyond the door. At the same time a solemn voice, deep and hollow, intoned some chilling words as though they were an incantation:

> 'Fading is the worldling's pleasure,
> All his boasted pomp and show;
> Solid joys and lasting treasure
> None but Sion's children know.'

The door of the vault slammed shut, leaving her in the dark.

With a frantic scream of fear Margaret ran to the door, which was dragged open immediately, and she all but fell into the arms of Cundlett, her father's coachman. The man looked both horrified and contrite, and she knew in an instant that he had not been aware of her presence in the vault. She had clutched his arm when she had all but staggered out of the crypt, and she still retained it now.

'Oh, Cundlett,' she cried, 'take me out of this vile place. I thought for a moment that I was going to be left entombed with those ... those *things* down there!'

'Dear me, miss,' said Cundlett, 'don't take on so! Mr Beecham saw me arrive just now with the carriage, and told me to come down here and close the door, thinking that you'd made your way elsewhere. You may have heard me, miss, uttering some words of a poem that I felt suitable for the occasion; in fact, I believe it's a hymn. If I frightened you, miss, then I beg your pardon. Come, let me take you up into the light, for "Westward, ho! The land is bright!" '

There was something of the buffoon about Cundlett, thought Margaret, as, still clutching the big coachman's arm, she mounted the steps that would take her back into the house, but buffoon or not, his concern for her was obviously genuine and unforced. Why had she been so frightened? There was something strange and undefined about the atmosphere of Horton Grange, and Margaret was beginning to think that it emanated in some subtle way from its owner. Was that because Jeremy kept her a stranger to his innermost thoughts?

Jeremy Beecham watched his fiancée and her uncle as they walked across the lawns to the gate that would take them into the sunken road, where their carriage awaited them. Margaret had been very subdued, unwilling to talk to him about the new work in the house, and the discovery of the ancient vault. Philip Garamond was talking to her, his head bent gravely to hear her replies. What were they talking about? Why did she look so pale?

They were gone; and here was Lance at last, sauntering nonchalantly across the grass to the passage door. Poor fellow! It really was too bad of Sir Nicholas to keep his younger son so short of cash. There was nothing wrong with Lance that a few hundred a year would not put right.

Jeremy greeted Margaret's brother as he came into the parlour from the front passage. Lance always brought with him an air of faded gentility. His clothes were of the best London cut, but hung about his spare frame as though basically unwilling to clothe him. His military moustache was well trimmed, but it looked like the adornment of a man who had been cashiered, or drummed out of the mess, or whatever it was that the army did to a disgraced officer.

'It's dashed warm today,' said Lance, sitting down on a settee, and stretching out his legs. He glanced around the room, and Jeremy saw the expression of sad longing that crossed his face as he did so.

'It must be very satisfying to have a place of your own,' said Lance. 'You know, somewhere that isn't ultimately your papa's property. Do you like it here? You're not really a countryman, are you?'

'I like it well enough,' Jeremy replied, 'and after I've married Margaret, I'd be very happy to settle here. But when I'm fully established in my profession I will need a base of some kind in London. I have the lease of a small house there, in Mayfair, but I think I must surrender the lease this month. Like everything else, Lance, it's a question of money.'

Lance Waldegrave shifted uneasily, and dropped his eyes. Jeremy knew that he had been about to ask for a loan, but that the mention of money had precluded it for the moment.

'I don't suppose Arthur came down here today?' said Lance. 'I should have thought that discovery of yours would have interested him. He's very much taken with matters of ancestry, pedigree, and so forth. Well, of course, you know that. I hope you won't pay too much attention to his silly notions of caste. It's all nonsense, you know.'

'Well, Lance,' said Jeremy, 'I won't pretend that I'm happy with Arthur's innuendoes concerning my own particular ancestry, because, of course, I'm not. His little offering at dinner the other night was startling, to say the least. Startling and silly. But Arthur's in a very sad physical condition, and I'm more than prepared to make allowances. After Margaret and I are married, I've no doubt that Arthur will give up the struggle.'

Would Lance sense the cold anger behind his words? Perhaps, because he'd stood up, and was making a show of looking out of the window. No doubt he'd have the sense to change the subject.

'I don't suppose, Jeremy,' he said, 'that you could let me have five pounds on account? I'm keeping careful records of what I owe you, and as soon as ever I can, I'll repay my debt. Father's so confoundedly tight-fisted these days.'

Jeremy Beecham took five sovereigns from his purse, and

handed them to Lance without comment. Lance blushed as he slipped the coins into his pocket.

'Dashed civil of you, Jeremy,' he muttered. 'Much obliged.'

Moments later he had left the parlour in possession of the man whose independence he envied. Poor Lance, thought Jeremy Beecham. It's time that Sir Nicholas loosened his purse strings. The way things were going with Lance, there could be great trouble in store for the Waldegraves of Langley Court.

When Jeremy Beecham retired that night, he read a few pages of a novel before blowing out his bedside candle. After a while, the long rectangle of his bedroom window impressed itself on to his eyes, and he turned to watch the thin wisps of cloud crossing the face of the moon. He had never liked curtains drawn at night: he felt stifled by their very success in keeping out the light. The moonlight would ebb and flow across the room until the moon set, and the ancient house would come alive with the creaks and groans born of its antiquity.

Did he fear Uncle Jabez's vengeful ghost? Yes, he feared him at night, and would often imagine him lying dead and contorted on the floor of the great chamber, which lay directly beneath his bedroom. Sometimes, he imagined that he heard him shrieking in his final agony, but it was only the cry of some night creature in the woods. In the light of day, his uncle's death was something that could be recollected in tranquillity, but at night, it often seemed that his spirit was still present in the house, crying out soundlessly for justice.

5

---·•·---

The Lakeside Inferno

Sir Nicholas Waldegrave had grown very fond of the spacious sitting-room that had been created for him on the ground floor of Langley Court when climbing stairs had become too much of a burden. The furniture was the kind of thing he liked: cabinets of china and bric-à-brac, small tables holding collections of old family photographs, and a larger table on which were displayed a motley collection of newspapers and magazines.

He was reclining now in his favourite high-backed armchair, his eyes half closed, watching his old friend Dr Savage, who sat nearby, nodding off over a copy of that day's *Morning Post*. Savage had been a guest at dinner, where they had consumed fried cod and oysters, followed by mutton chops and brandy bread pudding. He and Savage had been served their coffee and brandy here, in Sir Nicholas's private retreat.

It had been a stifling, sultry day, this Monday, 11 June. Skinner, his valet, had told him that the temperature had risen towards the eighties by noon. In the afternoon the sky darkened, and there had developed one of those expectant stillnesses that herald a coming storm.

Savage was a marvellous physician, a man who knew a great deal about afflictions of the heart. A pity that he'd retired, and gone to live in Copton Vale. Savage had mild, grey, watery eyes and drooping grey moustaches, which covered his mouth so effectively that it was not always possible to know whether or not he was smiling when he uttered his witty, penetrating remarks.

Dr Savage suddenly jerked into wakefulness, the newspaper slipping off his knee on to the floor. Sir Nicholas opened his eyes.

'I saw Arthur being wheeled out to that folly place after dinner,' said Savage. 'He had a pile of learned tomes clutched on his knees. It's an odd fancy of his, to work in there. And speaking of learned folk, I thought Philip would have been at dinner tonight.'

'Philip wanted to potter about among his glasshouses this evening,' said Sir Nicholas. 'He received a consignment of plants from London yesterday, and he's anxious to put them in pots, spray them with soapy water, or whatever it is he does with them.'

'Well, he missed a good, honest dinner tonight,' said Dr Savage. 'A meal like that, Waldegrave, will do you more good than a whole battery of drops and nostrums. How are you getting on with Dr Radford?'

'Very well indeed. He's a cheerful, no-nonsense type of man, with a knack of getting his own way. And he's a dab hand at whist. He knows his business, too. I suspect that he has the rare ability of knowing how to prolong a fellow's life.'

Well, thought Savage, looking across the room at his old friend, he won't have much time to practise his magical arts on *you*. Another year, perhaps, and then....

'I had a detective here the other week,' said Sir Nicholas. 'He came to warn me that there was a safe-cracker in the district. I told him that all our valuables are safely locked up in banks. Jackson, his name was. The detective, I mean, not the thief.'

'Inspector Jackson? I know him well, Waldegrave. He's a very clever man. I worked closely with him over that murderous business out at Burton Viscount.* I know his sergeant, too. A man called Herbert Bottomley. He and I share a connoisseur's appreciation of gin.'

* *The Haunted Governess*

'Well, there's nothing much wrong with gin, I suppose, but I prefer a good brandy when I'm allowed to have it – I say! Did you hear that? Thunder, but nearer than before. Before the evening's out, Savage, we're going to have a storm.'

The billiard-room smelt of stale cigar smoke, and was falling prey to the lurking shadows of dusk. Lance Waldegrave threw down his cue on the faded green baize of the billiard table, and sat down on a wooden bench against the wall.

Damn it all, what was he to do? Father was unreasonable, and stubborn, too – maybe that was the result of old age. His allowance was to stay the same, and there were to be no more extra sums advanced for emergencies. He'd listened to Father's solemn lecture with what grace he'd been able to muster, successfully hiding his anger at the old man's parsimony.

That London moneylender was starting to turn ugly. If he didn't pay the fellow soon, worse things would happen to him than being jostled on the stairs by his hired thugs, or robbed in a country lane. No accommodation was possible: he had to pay the entire sum due by the end of the month, a little matter of £1200.

And then, that whining girl from the slums of Copton Vale – Mary something – was becoming importunate. She'd confronted him in the Railway Arms, supported by a couple of common, intimidating working-men, and disgraced him in front of a rough, red-faced bumpkin of a police sergeant. He'd seen the burning contempt in the man's eyes.

He would have to do something. Margaret would be all right, married to Jeremy. But as for Arthur – what use was he, now? Why should *he* inherit the title and estates, a man confined to a wheeled chair, growing more quirky and eccentric with the years? If Arthur were to die, everything would ultimately come to *him*, and the moneylenders would be happy to grant him unlimited credit on the strength of a *post obit*.

Hello! Surely that wasn't a thunder-clap? What was all that shouting? It came from the front of the house. Something was happening. Hastily burying his secret thoughts in his heart, Lance Waldegrave hurried out of the billiard-room.

'You're very quiet this evening, Margaret,' said Aunt Letty. 'I wouldn't ask you why until we'd come up here to my sitting-room. You haven't drunk your coffee, and it will be cold by now. What's the matter, dear? Is it Arthur's silly dislike of Jeremy Beecham?'

'No, Aunt,' Margaret replied. 'It's more than that. Just before dinner tonight, Arthur took me aside, and returned to the subject of Jeremy. He talked so earnestly that I had to swallow my anger, and listen to what he was saying. By the time he had finished, I was no longer angry: I was afraid.'

Letitia Waldegrave put her knitting down beside her on the settee, and regarded her niece. She looked pale and drawn. What nonsense had Arthur been telling her?

'Arthur begged me to find out more about Jeremy's background,' Margaret continued. 'He said that someone had told him that Jeremy was responsible for his Uncle Jabez's death – that it was Jeremy, in fact, who had poisoned him! It was an outrageous thing to say, Aunt, but he said it so earnestly that I could not help being impressed by his sincerity.'

'Sincerity fiddlesticks!' cried Aunt Letty. 'Arthur's become besotted with rank and station, and the imagined glory of his ancestors. He doesn't think Jeremy's good enough for you, and is seizing on idle tales and gossip to turn you against Jeremy. Well, your father's given his consent to your marriage, which is none of Arthur's business. Don't listen to him.'

'He'd already told Uncle Philip about it, Aunt, and when we called at Horton Grange the other day, Uncle hinted to me that all was not right there. I had to agree with him about that, because I had received a terrible fright while I was there. I thought that …

that somebody was trying to lock me away in that frightful burial vault. There's something horrible about that house.'

'It's nonsense, I tell you!' cried Aunt Letty. 'Good heavens, girl, have you no faith at all in your own fiancé? You're to marry him in September, and will go to live with him at Horton Grange. You told me that you intended to turn that old ruin into a home. And now – But what's that dreadful noise? Surely it couldn't have been thunder? What's all that shouting and running about? Something's happening outside!'

The two women had heard the sound of voices raised quite near to the house. The words were indistinct, but twice they heard frantic shouts of 'Fire!' Margaret rose, and pulled back the curtains in the bay window.

The sky was glowing with a ghastly orange light, and it was possible now to hear a hideous roaring and thundering sound from somewhere to the right of the house. Margaret turned away, white-faced, from the window, just as the door of the room was thrown open without ceremony to admit a frightened maid.

'Oh, madam,' she cried, addressing herself to Aunt Letty. 'There's a terrible fire in the folly – Mr Arthur....' The frantic girl ran from the room, and they heard the clatter of her feet as she hurried, sobbing, down the stairs.

The Gothic folly on the edge of the lake was burning fiercely, its narrow windows burst through by sinuous arms of flame. The landing-stage and the waters of the lake were bathed in orange light. In all that scene of fiery destruction, only the door of the folly held, a rectangle of darkness set in the front wall.

Margaret had run from the house and had joined Lance, who was standing with a band of indoor and outdoor servants, all of whom seemed virtually mesmerized by the hideous bonfire.

'Is Arthur still in there?' she whispered.

'Yes,' Lance replied. 'It's quite impossible for anyone to get near the building. It looks as though it will either explode or collapse at any minute. One of the grooms has gone off on horseback to alert the fire brigade at Copton Vale. As for Arthur—'

He stopped short as he saw Williams, the footman, run from the surrounding shadows into the lurid circle of light. He was wielding an axe and, as his pace increased and he raised the axe above his head, all the spectators realized what he intended to do. Disregarding the warning cries of the onlookers, he ran on to the landing-stage, braving the leaping flames, and smote the closed door with a mighty crash.

What followed remained in the memories of all those present at the scene for the rest of their lives. It would form the subject of many a nightmare for years to come. As Williams staggered away from the inferno, the door of the folly seemed to disintegrate. At the same time, the wheeled chair, with Arthur Waldegrave still sitting in it, rolled slowly out of the burning folly. They could all see him sitting securely in the chair, dead, enveloped from head to foot in crimson flame.

There were shouts and screams of horror, and at the same moment, the heavens were racked with tremendous peals of thunder. Torrential rain began to fall, though it was quite unable to quench the fire.

And then the wheeled chair and its burning contents began to slither slowly across the landing-stage. It teetered on the brink of the lake, and then unhurriedly toppled, with a hideous hiss and splutter, into the water. In this way, the crimson stage of lake and folly, which had so far held its captive audience in thrall, was robbed of its principal actor.

The pony drawing the trap was evidently enjoying the bright June morning. He trotted briskly along the carriage road from Abbot's Langley, responding eagerly to the light touch of the rein. Inspector Jackson glanced at his sergeant, and saw how his flushed, normally genial face had begun to assume an expression of anger mingled with despair. Herbert Bottomley felt some deaths keenly; evidently the grotesque fate of Arthur Waldegrave was to be one of those deaths.

They emerged from the trees, and there before them lay the lake, its surface glittering with a million bright reflections. A number of golden carp were swimming lazily near the surface, but there was nothing tranquil about the scene that met their eyes.

The folly was now a burnt-out and blackened ruin. Piles of salvaged debris lay on the little landing-stage, and also on the far edge of the lake, where the grooms had dragged it during the recovery of Arthur Waldegrave's burnt body. A smart fire engine stood on the path near the house; its horses had been released from the shafts, and taken, presumably, to the stable block.

Sergeant Bottomley turned the pony's head to the left, and brought the trap to a halt a few yards away from the ruin. At the same time, a man emerged from the interior of the building, and stood on the little wooden bridge, waiting for them to alight.

'Isn't that Mr Hawkins, the fire master from Copton Vale?' asked Bottomley, as he helped Jackson down from the trap.

'It is, Sergeant,' said Jackson. 'And a very unhappy man he is, if looks are anything to go by.'

The fire-master's uniform was rain-spattered and stained with smoke and soot. He looked tired and weary. When he saw Jackson and Bottomley, his face was animated by a glad smile of recognition.

'It was almost certainly a terrible accident, Mr Jackson,' he said, 'a fallen oil-lamp – something like that. But there was one detail about this tragedy that made me uneasy. That's why I alerted Superintendent Mays at Peel House. We arrived here with a fire engine just before ten o'clock last night. It took us half an hour to quench the fire, by which time some of the grooms had brought out flaring torches on raised stakes, and placed them along the path.'

'Did you leave the scene, once the fire was quenched, Mr Hawkins?'

'Yes, Inspector. One of the family had died in that blaze, but the body had toppled into the lake, and had been retrieved by some of the people from the yard. There's an old doctor here, Dr Savage, he's called. He was a guest here for dinner last night. Apparently he's taken charge of the remains. He's had them moved to a place they call the old tack-room, which is behind the house in the stable yard. My business was to put the fire out, which I did. We returned to Copton Vale just after twelve, but I came out here this morning with an engine in case the fire had rekindled. That happens, sometimes.'

'You said that there was something that made you uneasy?' said Jackson.

'Well, Inspector, it may be nothing, but I'll mention it to you all the same. This building, this folly, as they call it, was a thin shell of sandstone over a single thickness of brick: it wasn't really built to be a real house, or anything like that. Inside, it was divided into two little panelled rooms by a wood and plaster partition – you can still see the charred wooden beams that formed its framework. It was like – like a flimsy wooden doll's house, Mr Jackson, but the flames coming out of it were dark red, and all capped with palls of thick black, oily smoke.'

He held out the sleeve of his coat, and picked off a small patch of feathery ash, which he smoothed out between finger and thumb.

'You see? That's what you expect to be covered in when you're called to a fire of this nature. But now look.' This time, he smeared his hand along his sleeve, and showed them an oily black smudge. 'Earlier this morning I penetrated into what was the back room of the folly. Mr Jackson, I found the remains of three oil drums there, the type of drum used to store lamp oil or paraffin. I've mentioned that to no one but you.'

'And do you want to draw a conclusion from that discovery, Mr Hawkins?'

'It's not for me to draw conclusions, Mr Jackson – not conclusions of that kind, anyway. But the thought did cross my mind that someone may have primed the building with a great deal of oil for some … some sinister reason of his own. Just a thought, you know. Now, if it's all right with you, I'll get back to Copton Vale.'

Jackson and Bottomley stepped carefully over the ruined threshold of the folly, and found themselves standing on a hot, sodden paste of rain-water and wood-ash. Above them rose a number of bulbously charred and blackened roof beams that had fallen during the fire, but had not been wholly consumed. Sergeant Bottomley picked his way cautiously over the debris, stooped low beneath a fallen beam, and was lost to sight in the rearmost of the two burnt-out rooms.

Jackson made his way gingerly to the centre of the floor, and began to sift through the rain-clotted ash. In a few moments he had uncovered the remains of three books. They had been virtu-ally consumed by fire, but, with the curious resilience of bound paper, some parts at least of the pages had survived. Buried near to them under the ash was a shapeless mass of fused glass, which had once, perhaps, been a wine bottle. It lay near another piece of glass, a cracked and discoloured rod, which Jackson thought may have been the stem of a shattered wineglass. Returning to the door, he carefully placed the three volumes and the salvaged pieces of glass on the flags of the little landing-stage.

Jackson clambered over the charred timbers and joined his sergeant in a windowless chamber at the back of the building. A rectangular gap in the rear wall where a door had once stood showed a patch of bright green grass on the sward behind the folly.

'Look at those, sir,' said Bottomley. He pointed to three twisted and flattened metal containers. 'Oil drums. This one's still got some of the painted name surviving on the outside: "Parsons' Paraffin Oil".' He smeared his hand across the wet floor, and held it up for Jackson to see. It was covered with a thick, black, oily deposit.

'This place seems to have been used as an oil store,' said Bottomley. 'Maybe they were nervous of storing oil in the main house, and kept it out here. But you can see for yourself that there was once a rear door to this room. Someone could have got up to mischief in this second room without poor Mr Arthur Waldegrave knowing about it.'

'It's like a theatre, Sergeant,' said Jackson. 'Poor Mr Arthur was the principal attraction, but there was someone else – someone unknown – controlling the scenery and the special effects from this little back room. There's nothing more we can do here for the moment. We need to question the family and the servants before we start drawing conclusions. Let's find Dr Savage, and hear what he's got to say.'

Leaving the ruined folly, the two policemen walked under the archway leading to the stable yard. The clock in the turret above the arch showed that it was ten past nine. The yard was a wide expanse of flagged paving, stretching the whole length of the house, from the turret arch to a set of wrought-iron gates at the far end of the mansion.

Whereas the front of Langley Court had been all but deserted, the stable yard seemed to be full of people. Little knots of grooms and indoor servants were engaged in excited conversation, but when they saw the two police officers enter the yard, they dispersed as though by some kind of unspoken agreement.

The rear of the great mansion rose to their right; like the front elevation, it was covered in luxurious green ivy. A large bay window, and two flat sash casements adjacent to it, showed Jackson that he was standing near Sir Nicholas Waldegrave's suite of rooms. He could see various white-painted doors let into the walls further along the yard, and guessed that these would lead to the kitchens and other domestic quarters of the house.

Near to where they stood was a modern, redbrick gas-house, with a squat chimney-stack rising up from the side of it. A wiry, stubbly, wild-eyed man in a moleskin suit stood at the open door, looking at them with baleful eyes set in a grimy face. Jackson wondered who he was. In a moment the man had pulled the door shut. Evidently, his curiosity had been satisfied.

From the gas-house to the far end of the yard, a continuous line of irregular buildings stretched away to their left. They housed what appeared to be workshops and harness rooms. Where the iron gates rose at the far end of the long yard, they could see the imposing gabled entrance to the main stables of the house.

A door some way along the left-hand range of buildings suddenly opened, and a man whom they both recognized as Dr Savage stepped out on to the flags. They would remember for years to come how oddly sinister he looked on that sunny June morning. He stood in his shirt sleeves, with a rough apron of coarse sacking tied round his ample waist. Elderly and stooping, his face half-concealed by his thick drooping moustache, he looked clumsy and untidy, but any idea that this old physician was maladroit was dissipated when one saw how delicately he held a bloodstained scalpel in his right hand.

'Jackson!' he cried. 'We meet again. And you, Sergeant Bottomley. How are you? You'd better come in. This place is called the old tack-room, and I've been working on poor Arthur Waldegrave in here since early light.'

They entered the dim brick building, which was swept clean and whitewashed, but evidently not in everyday use. They could smell the sickening odour of charred flesh. On a trestle table in the centre of the room lay the body of Arthur Waldegrave, roughly covered with a horse-blanket. There were a number of benches against the walls and Savage motioned to the two men to sit down while he laid aside the scalpel and began to wash his hands in a tin basin. Sergeant Bottomley fumbled in one of the capacious pockets of his yellow overcoat, and produced a battered hip flask. Presently, the perfume of gin joined that of charred flesh in the gloomy chamber.

'I hope, Sergeant Bottomley,' said Dr Savage, drying his hands vigorously on an old towel, 'that you're going to exercise that hospitality for which, I'm sure, you are renowned. All they've brought me in here this morning is weak tea.'

Herbert Bottomley treated the old doctor to a lopsided smile, and placed his silver flask on the edge of the trestle table, beside the blanketed remains. He recalled a time of crisis in the case of the accused governess Mary Grant, when he and the old doctor had sat together in the saloon bar of the Prince Albert Hotel at Copton Vale, with a battery of gin glasses in front of them, discussing the nature of poisons.* The doctor helped himself to a hearty swig, wiped the neck of the flask with his sleeve, and returned it to the sergeant with a mocking bow.

'Thank you, Sergeant,' he said, sitting down on one of the benches. 'London Dry, if I'm not mistaken. You're a man of impeccable taste. Now then, Jackson, what do you think happened here last night? I was a dinner guest, you know, but I stayed here all night when this business happened. It's a very peculiar feeling, to dine with a fellow in the evening and then dissect his corpse the next morning.'

'From what I can see,' said Jackson, 'this young man, this Arthur Waldegrave, who was crippled, knocked over a lamp while he was studying or writing in that little building, the folly, as they call it. Unable to help himself, he sat there helpless, while the burning lamp ignited a store of oil kept on the premises. As a result of all this, young Mr Waldegrave was burned to death. That's what the fire master thinks.'

'A worthy man,' muttered the old doctor, 'and no doubt an ornament of his profession. Now, I always have my doctor's bag

---

* *The Haunted Governess*

with me, which is why I was able to open poor Arthur up this morning. There were a few knives in my bag, though of course they're not proper post-mortem scalpels. Anyway, I opened him up, and what do you think I found?'

'Smoke in the lungs,' said Jackson, 'showing that he died in the fire.'

'There was *no* smoke in the lungs,' said Savage, 'showing that it was not the fire that killed him. And, of course, there was no water in his lungs after that dowsing he got in the lake. What I *did* find, Jackson, was a large quantity of cyanide in the stomach, and it was *that* which killed Arthur Waldegrave.'

'Suicide?'

'Dear me, Jackson,' said Dr Savage, springing up from his bench and sweeping the blanket off the blackened corpse. 'Just look at that appalling ruin! Couldn't an intelligent gentleman find a more convenient way of doing away with himself? All his main organs are sound. The only thing wrong with him was the paralysis which had atrophied his lower limbs, and he'd lived well enough with that for half his lifetime. He was heir to a very wealthy estate, and everybody deferred to him. One day he would have been a baronet. And all you can do is say "suicide".'

'Asking your pardon, sir,' said Bottomley, half-heartedly knuckling his forehead, 'but maybe poor Mr Arthur suddenly tired of being a helpless cripple, and decided to end it all, whereby my guvnor here, meaning Mr Jackson, could be right in his suggestion, meaning no offence, sir, and not wishing to speak out of place.'

Dr Savage laughed, and the sound spread from his throat to his racked lungs. The dim tack-room echoed to his harsh coughs as he gasped for air.

'Listen, Sergeant,' he said, at last, 'let's imagine that you are Arthur Waldegrave. "I will end it all!" you cry. "Where is my cyanide? Here, in this little blue bottle. Let me drink it. Ah! That's better! And now, let me set fire to all this oil". Or maybe he said,

"I'll end it all. I'll throw this lamp to the floor, and burn myself to death. Very good! Now, let's have a swig of this cyanide, just to make sure—" Suicide? You know as well as I do, both of you, that it was murder!'

Dr Savage pulled the blanket roughly over the remains, and began to struggle into a tail-coat which he had retrieved from a dark corner of the room. It was only then that Jackson realized that the old doctor had not been able to change into more suitable dress for the grim work that he had been carrying out.

'I felt it in my bones, Jackson,' said Savage, 'that something like this might have happened one day soon. That's why I took charge of the body as soon as the men dragged it out of the lake. There are others in this house who are going to profit mightily from Arthur's death. Do a bit of digging and delving, and you'll soon find out what I mean. And have a look in that ruin for the remains of a bottle and glass – something of that sort. Cyanide acts almost immediately, as you know. It could only have been given to him in drink, moments before he died.'

'You may be quite sure, Doctor,' said Jackson drily, 'that I will do all the delving that's necessary – in fact, I've already started. But I take your advice kindly.'

'I suppose the killer meant poor Arthur to be burnt to a cinder, so that no autopsy would have been possible,' Dr Savage continued. 'When you start asking questions, be sure to put a young footman called Williams on your list. It was his brave but foolish attempt to save Arthur from the inferno that brought the door down, making it possible for me to retrieve the body, and find that telltale poison in the stomach.'

'How has the family reacted to this tragedy?' Jackson asked. 'I've met Sir Nicholas Waldegrave before. I thought he was a most pleasant, unassuming gentleman. I'm more sorry than I can say about his loss.'

'They all think it's an accident,' said Savage. 'When Sir Nicholas heard the news, he suffered a heart spasm, and I saw to it that he was confined immediately to his bed. Dr Radford's been, and had prescribed complete rest. He made sure that he was obeyed by giving Sir Nicholas a powerful sleeping-draught. He said that he'd call again this morning.'

'What about the other members of the family, sir?' asked Sergeant Bottomley.

'Well, Lance seemed frozen with shock, but I've no doubt that he'll unfreeze himself with a few stiff whiskies when he realizes that he's got to take command of things while his father's *hors de combat*. As for the ladies – well, they're coping with the business as ladies of quality should. They all think it was an accident, of course, because nobody knows about this devilry with cyanide, except for us, and the one who used it.'

'Will you see to things here, Dr Savage?' asked Jackson. 'It's time that Sergeant Bottomley and I went across to the house.'

'I'll arrange for the body to be taken to the police mortuary in Copton Vale,' Savage replied. 'I wish you well in your investigation, Jackson. Somehow, I think this case is going to be a tough nut for you to crack.'

6

Responses to Murder

Inspector Jackson stood on the threshold of the drawing-room in Langley Court, and noted that it was sumptuously furnished, but in the heavy styles of the sixties. Evidently the master of the house saw no reason for sacrificing solid comfort to the demands of nineties fashion.

The occupants of the room seemed to be frozen where they sat or stood, like so many waxworks. Jackson knew that they were waiting for him to speak about the unspeakable. Seated on a couch near one of the windows were two ladies, one elderly and distinguished in appearance, the other young and attractive. They were both pale, and their eyes were red with weeping, but they comported themselves with commendable calm.

Beside them stood a young man of military bearing, sporting a fine moustache. That, Jackson supposed, would be Lance Waldegrave. Sergeant Bottomley had told him of his encounter with Lance in a public house at Copton Vale, and he recalled now Bottomley's tale of a desperate girl, her two stalwart friends, and this man, Lance Waldegrave, who had not denied that he had been her betrayer. Jackson saw how he gave a kind of guilty start when he saw and recognized Bottomley.

It was Lance Waldegrave who broke the frigid silence.

'Inspector Jackson, is it not?' he said. 'And Sergeant Bottomley. I am Lance Waldegrave. This lady is my aunt, Miss Waldegrave, and the younger lady is my sister, Miss Margaret Waldegrave. I have not thought it right that my father should be present at this interview. His heart is very weak, and he has been confined to bed on doctor's orders since last night.'

'Well, thank you, sir,' said Jackson, 'for receiving us at this sad time. You will all by now know that Mr Arthur Waldegrave has indeed perished, and before I begin my investigation, I want to assure you of my true sympathy and sadness. I am very sorry.'

'I can't think why Arthur wanted to coop himself up in that hateful place!' cried Aunt Letty. 'Why did we allow him to sit alone in there, with a naked lamp, knowing that he could not move out of his chair if anything happened? This accident is partly our fault, for taking Arthur's quirks and oddities too much for granted.'

Margaret took her aunt's hand in hers, and murmured some words of comfort. Jackson looked at them and realized that the two women had not had time to adjust to the reality of Arthur's death. They had only reached the stage of self-reproach and self-accusation.

'Now, Miss Waldegrave,' said Jackson, 'and you, Miss Margaret, I am about to mention very distressing things, unpleasant things, not, perhaps, fit for ladies' ears. I shall quite understand if you wish to leave the room now.'

His words seemed to recall Letitia Waldegrave to her position as the chatelaine of Langley Court.

'I can assure you, Inspector,' she said, drawing herself up, 'that Miss Margaret and I are quite capable of hearing unpleasant things without going into hysterics. Pray continue.'

'Very well, ma'am,' said Jackson. 'Sergeant Bottomley and I have just returned from consulting with Dr Savage, who has conducted a post-mortem examination of the body of the late unfortunate Mr Arthur Waldegrave. It is part of my sad duty to advise you that Mr Arthur's body has been partly consumed by fire, and that it would be inadvisable for either of you ladies, or indeed any other members of the family, to look at those remains.'

'Yes, yes, of course,' said Lance. Jackson caught the tremulous tone of Lance Waldegrave's voice: the strain of the nightmare evening was beginning to take its toll. 'The fire was extremely violent,' Lance continued, 'and I think that we all feared that Arthur, once he was trapped in the folly, would be … would …'

'Yes, indeed, sir,' said Jackson quickly. 'I knew that you would have thought along those lines. But now I must tell you that Mr Arthur Waldegrave did *not* die in the fire. He was killed by the administration of a lethal dose of potassium cyanide. If it's any consolation to you, he would have died within seconds.'

There was a moment of stunned silence, and then Lance said, very quietly, 'Are you suggesting, Inspector, that my brother Arthur committed suicide?'

'Oh, no, sir,' said Jackson, 'I am suggesting nothing like that. Mr Arthur Waldegrave was deliberately killed. He was murdered, Mr Waldegrave, and the fire was started intentionally by the murderer. He hoped that no trace of the crime – murder by poisoning – would be detected because of the intense fierceness of the conflagration. However, he was unsuccessful.

'You have told me, Mr Lance,' Jackson continued, 'that Sir Nicholas is unwell, and that he has taken to his bed. Nevertheless, it is my duty to inform him immediately that his son has been murdered. May I suggest that you come along with me, now, while I break the news? Sir Nicholas should have his family present on such a melancholy occasion.'

Sir Nicholas Waldegrave lay in his four-poster bed, propped up by pillows. He looked drawn and ill, but unexpectedly composed, considering that he had just suffered the tragic loss of his elder son. When he saw Jackson, his eyes were animated by a glint of recognition, and he half raised a hand in greeting.

'Well, Inspector,' he said, 'we meet again. How kind of you to call. I never thought for one moment that I would outlive poor Arthur. But there: Providence decreed otherwise.'

He had vaguely acknowledged the presence of his sister and daughter in the room, but his eyes now sought out Lance, who was standing hesitantly near the door of the room.

'Lance,' said Sir Nicholas, earnestly, 'you realize, don't you, what your brother's death means to the family? You are now my heir, and common sense tells us all that I will not last much longer. I want you to mend your ways, discard your dissipated cronies, and prepare yourself to take charge of this estate when I'm gone—'

'Father,' said Lance, glancing uncomfortably at Sergeant Bottomley, 'this is neither the time nor the place for a conversation of this sort. Let it wait. Inspector Jackson here has some serious news to impart.'

Gently and gravely, Saul Jackson told Sir Nicholas that his son had been poisoned with cyanide, and that his death was not accident, but murder. The baronet lay back on his pillows, and gave vent to a prolonged sigh.

'Murdered?' he whispered. 'Who would want to murder a harmless fellow like Arthur? He hardly ever left the estate.... Cyanide? That stirs a memory. Now, what was it? Well, Jackson, if you say it's murder, you'd better find out who did it, and why.'

As he finished speaking, the silent figure of Skinner, the valet, appeared in the doorway of the adjacent dressing-room. Impassive as ever, he loaded a tray with the remains of the baronet's breakfast, and left the room as silently as he had entered it. No doubt the news that murder had been committed would now spread like wildfire through the house.

There was something alien about the man, thought Jackson, something that makes him seem almost like an intruder in the house. And yet he had been in Sir Nicholas's service for 'more years than he cared to remember'. Skinner was an enigma.

There was a sudden brisk footfall in the anteroom, heralding the arrival of the Waldegraves' physician, Dr Radford. He was an energetic little man whose features seemed to have moulded themselves into a wrinkled, humorous kindliness. He greeted the family, nodded amiably to Inspector Jackson, and then approached the bed.

'How are you now, Sir Nicholas?' he asked.

'Well, that's for *you* to say, Radford!' Sir Nicholas's voice had regained some of its strength, and there was a flicker of amusement in his eyes. 'If you mean how do I *feel*, then I'll tell you. I feel decidedly shaky, but I expect I'll be all right again by evening. You'll have heard about Arthur, I expect. I never thought that he'd live to advanced years, which softens the blow, I expect. But murder! What a world it is!'

Dr Radford said nothing. He took Sir Nicholas's pulse, and then applied a short stethoscope to the baronet's chest, putting his right ear down on the ear-piece. After this, he addressed his patient once again.

'I'm going to give you a dose of your digitalis,' he said, 'and then you must get some sleep.' He turned to the bottle-laden bedside table, and chose one of the bottles.

'My goodness, Sir Nicholas,' he cried, 'you've made away with a goodly quantity of this stuff! I'll have to send you another bottle of it today.'

' "Made away" with it?' replied Sir Nicholas. 'D'you think I *like* your foul brews? I'd rather "make away" with a half-bottle of brandy!'

Dr Radford laughed. 'Well, brandy in moderation won't harm you at all. Or brandy in coffee. Now, sir, come: do as you're bid.' The doctor administered the digitalis, and Sir Robert composed himself to rest. Soon, he was asleep.

Dr Radford left the bedside, and motioned to the family and the two detectives to come out into the anteroom. He closed the door of Sir Nicholas's bedroom quietly behind them.

'Miss Waldegrave,' he said to Aunt Letty, 'I'll get a nurse to come first thing tomorrow, and she can stay with Sir Nicholas during the daytime. I don't think there's need for a night-nurse at the moment, but it would do no harm if someone were to sit up with him, at least for tonight.'

As they made their way along the passage to the front of the house, Jackson pulled Bottomley by the sleeve, and waited until the members of the family, and Dr Radford, were out of sight.

'Sergeant,' he said, 'there's nothing more that we can profitably ask the family about at present. It's time for us to interview that footman, Williams. I expect Mr Lance will give us some little room where we can do so. After that, I suggest we go back to Warwick, and do some serious thinking. I don't like the feel of this crime at all.'

Lance Waldegrave had shown Jackson and Bottomley into a little-used writing-room, which was situated in a dark corner at the front of the house. A single barred window looked out on to the gaunt ruins of the folly. Jackson sat down at the writing desk, while his sergeant chose an upright chair on the darker side of the room. Jackson looked up from the desk as Williams came into the room.

The footman was a slight, sandy-haired young man in his late twenties. He seemed nervous and ill-at-ease, but that, Jackson mused, was only natural. He wore a suit of sober green livery, with dull red facings at the collar. The young man's eyes were red-rimmed: here, thought Jackson, was another person, beside the two Misses Waldegrave, who had shed tears at Arthur Waldegrave's passing.

'Williams, sir,' said the young man. 'Mr Lance says that you wish to ask me some questions.'

'I want to talk to you about poor Mr Arthur,' said Jackson, smiling kindly at the young man. 'I understand that it was your custom to wheel Mr Arthur out to the folly in the evenings. Was this a usual thing? I mean, have you always been doing it?'

'As you can see from my livery, sir,' said the young man, 'I am a footman, not a valet, but Mr Arthur always regarded me as his confidential servant. For the last three months, he had ordered me to push him out in his chair to the folly, because he'd taken a fancy to studying out there in the evenings. He'd been working for the last two years on a great book, all about the Waldegrave family, and most evenings he'd take a few books out with him to consult. I know that he liked me, and I was hoping that one day he would engage me as his valet, but now ...'

'Tell me the routine of the thing, Williams. What exactly did you do on these occasions?'

'Well, sir, I'd unlock the door with the key that I always carried, and then I'd wheel Mr Arthur into the front room of the folly. It was quite comfortable, though very cramped. I'd manoeuvre his wheeled chair up to the table and, when he had everything he wanted, he would say "good night", and I would leave him there until ten o'clock, or occasionally half past ten, if that was what he had ordered.'

'And then you would return to wheel him back to the house?'

'Yes, sir.'

'I want you to cast your mind back carefully and calmly to last evening,' said Jackson. 'You wheeled Mr Arthur into the folly, and settled him at his table. Did you place his books on the table? Can you tell me the titles of those books?'

'I took the books from Mr Arthur's knees, and put them on the table. I'm afraid I can't tell you what the titles of the books were. They were books from Mr Arthur's big bookcase in his rooms. I checked that there was a sufficient supply of writing paper and a number of sharpened pencils in the tray. Mr Arthur liked to write in pencil.'

'So there was a writing-tray there. Was there anything else on the table?'

'Yes, sir. There was a lamp – an ordinary paraffin lamp with a glass shade. I lit the lamp, and trimmed the wick. Then Mr Arthur bade me "good night", and I left the folly, closing the door behind me.'

'Was the fire lit? I gather that there was a little fireplace in there.'

'The fire wasn't lit, sir. It was quite warm in there, as you'd expect in June.'

'Now, you've described to me what you generally did when you accompanied Mr Arthur to the folly. You've told me that there was a pencil-tray and a lamp on the table. Was there anything else on the table yesterday night, anything that you'd not seen there before?'

'I don't think so, sir. Oh, there was a bottle of wine and a glass. I wondered at the time how they had got there, but then I realized that Mr Garamond must have brought them. I said nothing about the bottle, and Mr Arthur didn't, either.'

'Mr Garamond? That's a name that's unfamiliar to me, Williams,' said Jackson.

'Mr Garamond is the uncle of the family, sir. I gather that he was a relative of the late Lady Waldegrave. He lives in the cottage at the foot of the grove. He was particularly close to Mr Arthur, sir, and I gather that he's taken his death very badly.'

'And you reckon that this Mr Garamond could have placed that bottle of wine in the folly?'

'Yes, sir. He and Mr Arthur often gave each other bottles of rare French wine, and then they'd spend some time discussing them. Although I only glanced at the bottle, I saw the little label bearing Mr Garamond's crest stuck on the neck.'

'I must say, Williams,' said Jackson, 'that you make an excellent witness. You've helped me enormously with my investigation. Now, I gather that you made a very valiant attempt to rescue Mr Arthur last night. In fact, you ran at the door of the folly with an axe. Tell me about that.'

The young man glanced involuntarily out of the window at the ruined building at the edge of the lake.

'It was terrible, sir. The folly was blazing like a torch, and everybody was just standing about, mesmerized, as it were. The two ladies of the house were clinging to each other, and one or other of the kitchen women was howling like a banshee. Everybody was lit up crimson by the flames, but no one seemed prepared to do anything. Mr Lance.... I saw Mr Lance calmly lighting a cigar while his brother was burning to death.'

'And so you decided to do something?'

'I did, sir. I ran to the store beneath the clock turret, and took an axe. I ran back on to the landing-stage, and attacked the door with all my strength. Well, it seemed to fall to pieces at the first blow – perhaps the timbers had been attacked by wood-rot. Huge flames billowed out at me and I ran for my life. And then, and then....'

'Yes, Williams, I've heard what happened after that, and there's no need for you to dwell on the matter. You've done very well. I think that's all I want to ask you.'

'Thank you, sir,' said Williams, moving towards the door. 'I hope you soon catch the fiend who murdered poor Mr Arthur.' His voice shook as he added, 'What harm had he ever done to a single soul?'

Williams, evidently very upset, bowed, and hurriedly left the room.

'Well, now, Sergeant,' said Jackson, as Herbert Bottomley turned the pony's head towards the drive that would take them back to the Abbot's Langley road, 'who do you think murdered Mr Arthur Waldegrave?'

'Well, sir, the man who benefits directly is that scapegrace Mr Lance, who's now the heir to the title and the estate. Very convenient for him, I expect. He'll have debts, sir – that sort always have – and now he can borrow money readily on the strength of his expectations.'

'So you definitely think it was Lance who murdered his brother?'

Sergeant Bottomley permitted himself a kind of strangled hoot of mirth.

'Well, of course, sir,' he said, 'it might have been a demented tramp who rushed into the folly with a bottle of cyanide that he kept for occasions of that sort, and—'

The sergeant uttered an oath and pulled at the rein as a man ran out on to the carriage drive, holding up both arms in an attempt to stop the trap. The pony whinnied and shied away, but Bottomley quickly got him under control.

'Thank goodness! I thought I'd miss you. Tie up the horse to the paling, and come into my house. It's vital that I talk to you.'

Jackson, who had climbed down from the trap, retrieved a satchel from under the seat, and surveyed the man who had so dramatically brought them to a halt. He was a gentleman in his mid fifties, with thinning grey hair, and a face that would normally have been genial, but was now contorted with some kind of desperate grief. He wore round gold-framed spectacles, and was dressed in a rather shabby frock coat.

'And who are you, sir?' asked Jackson.

'My name is Philip Garamond. I'm a second cousin of the late Lady Waldegrave, and I've lived here, in this house, from the time that Nicholas Waldegrave married. The children call me uncle, though I'm not their uncle, really— Must we stand here, talking, in the open road? For God's sake, come into the house, and let me tell you what I know about this terrible business.'

Jackson and Bottomley followed Philip Garamond into the cottage and found themselves in an elegant, high-ceilinged drawing-room. Neglecting to offer them seats, Garamond stood before the fireplace, wringing his hands, and literally writhing under the influence of some powerful mental anguish.

'It was the most frightful thing that I've ever beheld,' he said. 'Forgive me, Officers, I'm not myself today, and scarcely know what I'm saying.... There, in the devilish glow of that conflagration, the door of the folly collapsed, and Arthur came out, blazing, in his chair, as though to utter an accusation.... I fancied that I heard his voice echoing in my ears – I arrived late and was standing at the back of the crowd – and the words that I imagined that he uttered were: "Behold, there is the man who slew me".'

'One moment, Mr Garamond,' said Jackson. 'You speak of an accusation. But at the time of which you speak, it could only have been thought that Mr Arthur had perished in an accident.'

'No, no, you don't understand – how could you? There, I'm a little more settled, now. It was the thought of missing you and having to spend another night of torment, that drove me frantic out there on the path. Sit down, gentlemen. Will you take a glass of brandy with me?'

Garamond crossed to a sideboard, and began to pour brandy from a decanter into three glasses, His hand shook so badly that Sergeant Bottomley got up and finished the task for their badly shaken host. Presently the three men were sitting around a table in the centre of the room. Garamond drank some of his brandy, and then began to talk. Gradually, his voice and manner returned to normal.

'Last Monday – it was 4 June, the day on which you called on Sir Nicholas about a potential jewel thief – Arthur Waldegrave joined me here, in the cottage. He was wheeled here, you understand, by the footman, Williams. He came here often, to talk to me about intellectual matters, and to sample a glass or two of wine. That evening, though, it was brandy that we drank – not this one, but a fine Napoleon brandy.'

Philip Garamond stopped speaking for a moment, cradling his brandy glass between his hands. Then with an effort of concentration, he resumed his story.

'Arthur had been extremely rude and discourteous at dinner to Mr Jeremy Beecham, my niece Margaret's fiancé. She's to marry him in September, but maybe this vile tragedy of Arthur's death will make them postpone the wedding. Arthur had always been opposed to the match, and that evening I was to find out why.

When I upbraided him for his rudeness, he told me an extraordinary tale involving Jeremy Beecham and his late uncle, Jabez Beecham, who had been murdered some years ago at Horton Grange, not far from here.'

'Ah! Now you're entering familiar territory, Mr Garamond,' said Jackson. 'I wasn't myself involved with that case, which was in Superintendent Spengler's time. I must refresh my memory about it. But there, I'm interrupting. Please continue your story.'

'Arthur told me that Jeremy Beecham's uncle, Jabez, had been a convict in one of the Australian penal colonies, and that at one time he had been suspected of having committed murder. That, of course, was only ever hearsay, and until that day when Arthur spoke to me up in the grove I'd given no credence to it. Of course, I could easily understand Arthur's dislike of his sister's marrying into a family that may have included a murderous convict, but apparently there was more to Arthur's objection than that. Jabez had been poisoned with cyanide, and someone – I think it was an old former servant of Jabez's – had told Arthur that it was the nephew, Jeremy Beecham, who had given him that poison. According to Arthur, my niece Margaret was about to marry a murderer!'

'Who told Mr Arthur this?' asked Jackson sharply. 'Hearsay is no basis to accuse a man of murder.'

'He was told by a man called Grimes, a rough, common fellow who's in charge of the gas-house in the yard at Langley Court. He's rude and uncivil and sometimes he's obviously drunk, but he works hard. He does work for me here, too, at the cottage, tending the heating-plant for my glasshouses further up the grove, among the trees.'

'How did this Grimes know about the murder of Jabez Beecham?'

'I don't know, Inspector, and Arthur never told me, but I believe he must have heard it from an old servant who'd retired from work at Horton Grange. People of that sort often meet in the ale house to gossip about old times. No doubt you'll speak to Grimes yourself, and hear the story at first hand.'

'Mr Arthur evidently believed the story,' said Jackson. 'Did *you* believe it, Mr Garamond?'

'Yes, I do, Inspector. Poor Arthur's vehemence in the matter convinced me that Grimes had been telling the truth. Here was a penniless, struggling landscape designer, who, according to Grimes, coveted his old uncle's house as well as his remaining money – coveted them enough to murder the old man in order to acquire them. And now, poor Arthur himself has been murdered with cyanide by a man who hoped that the fire he had started would obliterate all trace of poison. Yes, I believe it.'

Philip Garamond began to wring his hands again, and the haunted, desperate look came back to his face.

'What am I to do? Like Arthur, I am desperate to save my niece from this ruinous alliance. There's not much time left. Will you look into the matter? I promised Arthur that I would make enquiries, but the police have much greater resources than I have. Will you, at least, speak to this fellow Grimes?'

'I will,' Jackson assured him. 'In fact, I would say that it's imperative for Sergeant Bottomley and me to do so. Thank you for telling me all this, Mr Garamond. I can see that you were keenly affected by your nephew's murder. Let me assure you that I will not rest until I have brought that murderer to justice.'

Jackson opened the satchel that he had brought with him from the trap and produced the charred remains of the books that he had found in the burnt-out ruins of the folly.

'Could you tell me anything about these books, sir?' he asked. 'They were with Mr Arthur in the folly at the time of the fire.'

Philip examined the books in silence for a while. Jackson noticed how his hands trembled. It would be a very long time before this man's horrific memories of his nephew's death were blunted.

'Two of these books are genealogies – lists of the various

members of ancient families. I can't put a title to either of them, but that's what they are. This third book is one that I gave to Arthur that very evening. It was a present that I'd bought for him on a recent trip to London. It was a history of another branch of the family dwelling in Kent, in the Isle of Thanet.'

'Did you at any time that day leave a bottle of wine in the folly as a present for Mr Arthur? Williams said that he saw such a bottle there.'

'Yes, Inspector. I'd promised him a bottle of a new claret to sample. I left it there on the table, with the cork already drawn, and a wine glass for him to use. I don't know whether he had the opportunity to drink any of it before … before—'

'Try not to think too closely about that terrible event, Mr Garamond,' said Jackson, rising from his chair. 'Will you leave the business of Mr Jeremy Beecham with me? What this man Grimes told Mr Arthur may be nothing more than an appalling slander, but I can't ignore the possibility that his tale may contain something more than a grain of truth.'

7

—•◦•—

Murder Remembered

Saul Jackson glanced up at the big railway clock hanging over the fireplace in the quiet back room of Barrack Street Police Office. It was a quarter past eight on the morning following his visit to Langley Court. Sergeant Bottomley would be in from Thornton Heath in ten minutes' time, and at nine o'clock old Jacob Pendle would call.

It was always a relief to get back from Copton Vale to his native town of Warwick. Barrack Street Police Office was a kind of home-from-home. The front of the premises was occupied by Sergeant Hathaway and his three uniformed constables, but the back room, with its scrubbed and sanded floorboards, was the undisputed territory of himself and Detective Sergeant Bottomley. A laconic notice, pinned on the door, read: Detectives. Knock and Enter.

The echo of a horse's hoofs came to him from the alley leading to the stables. Jackson glanced out of the window and saw Herbert Bottomley, still wearing his flapping yellow overcoat and battered bowler hat, sitting high on a grey pony, which he brought to a halt at the narrow gate to the stable yard. Presently a clattering of boots in the passage announced the sergeant's arrival in the office. He struggled out of his overcoat, hung it on the peg, and added his bowler hat. Then he sat down in a chair opposite Jackson's desk, and looked at him with the eager gaze of an affectionate terrier.

'You were right, Sergeant,' said Jackson, resuming his seat at the desk. 'Old Jacob Pendle, retired constable of Sheriff's Langley, has been living with his married daughter at Hill Wootton, a stone's-throw from here, for the past three years. He's coming here this morning to tell us all he knows about the murder of Jabez Beecham at Horton Grange, five years ago.'

Sergeant Bottomley had been rummaging around in one of his capacious overcoat pockets, from which he produced a half-smoked cheroot. He lit it carefully with a wax vesta, and placed the match on the edge of Jackson's desk.

'Coincidence is a fine thing, sir,' he said, 'but everything has its place. This Jabez Beecham was poisoned with cyanide, and so was Arthur Waldegrave. All that land around the Langleys is famed for its root crops, especially potatoes, and swedes, some of them the size of a pig's head. But it was never renowned for potassium cyanide.'

'Horton Grange is only a quarter of a mile's walk from Langley Court,' said Jackson, removing Bottomley's spent match from the desk, and throwing it into the fireplace. 'Too near for comfort, as they say. And this Mr Jeremy Beecham, nephew of a murdered man, wants to marry the sister of another murdered man. Food for thought, Sergeant.'

'Yes, sir. The murder of old Jabez was the only unsolved crime that old Superintendent Spengler left lying on the file when he retired. Mr Mays moans about it, sometimes. He doesn't like unsolved crimes.'

'No more do I, Sergeant,' said Jackson, 'and in this case— Ah! Here's old Jacob Pendle now. He's just climbing the steps to the front office. They'll show him through here in a minute.'

The door opened, and a uniformed constable came into the room, followed by a gnarled, cheerful old man, much bent with age, and with a weather-tanned face.

'Mr Jacob Pendle to see you, sir,' said the constable, and left the room, closing the door behind him.

'Well, sir,' said the old constable, lowering himself into a chair that Jackson drew forward for him, 'this is a wonderful experience, being back in a police station again. It knocks years off my life, seeing you, sir, all blooming like, and that other gentleman – Sergeant Bottomley? Please to meet you, Sergeant.'

Jacob Pendle removed a small black notebook from one of his pockets, and laid it on Jackson's table. He cleared his throat, looked intently at both the detectives as though to command their attention, and launched into speech.

'Well, gentlemen,' he began, 'the murder at Horton Grange was committed over five years ago, which, as you'll appreciate, is a long time in the country! Most folk have forgotten all about it, if the truth be known. Sergeant Bold was still alive then, but then he died of sugar, and they never sent another sergeant to the Langleys. Of course, we never had any detectives there at Sheriff's Langley, where our little police station was.

'Have you ever visited Horton Grange, Mr Jackson? No? Well, it's been mouldering away in the hollow at the bottom of Gorse Lane for over four hundred years. It was always a neglected kind of place, and everything about it was crooked and crazed, though there's some as think it would make a handsome dwelling for a gentleman if it was properly restored. Mr Jeremy Beecham, the gentleman who lives there now, is making a real effort to put the place in good repair, so I've heard, but I'd say he's got his work cut out.'

'Mr Beecham was the nephew of the man who was murdered, wasn't he?'

'That's right, sir. He's a distant nephew, and he's been living there at Horton Grange for the last three years. He's a landscape designer by profession, a man who builds glasshouses and conservatories for the gentry. He's doing very well, by all accounts.'

'And Horton Grange had been derelict for years?' asked Jackson.

'That's right, sir. Centuries ago, there used to be a little hamlet called Horton where Gorse Lane runs now, and the owners were a family called De Greville. Well, the De Grevilles are long gone, and Horton disappeared under the plough a hundred years ago. Various people bought the place, but there were long periods when it was empty, and fair bidding to become derelict.

'And then, about eighteen years ago – yes, 1876, it was – it was acquired by this man called Jabez Beecham, an Australian. He had quite a bit of money, and had made enough at the diggings to buy Horton Grange outright. And there he lived, until he died.'

Jackson was content to listen to the old man's account and to ask the occasional question. Sergeant Bottomley, though, had opened his own notebook, and was making brief notes as Jacob Pendle continued his story.

'He was a dour, black-bearded man,' said Pendle, 'civil enough, but a man who kept himself to himself. He was what they call a recluse, and he lived there alone all those years, apart from a succession of menservants, who always left him after a year or so. He was a peculiar, solitary sort of man – morose, you know. It doesn't do to be so stand-offish in the country, Mr Jackson. When he died, no one missed him, because he'd never been a true neighbour.'

'What about the present Mr Beecham?' asked Jackson. 'What kind of a man is he?'

'Oh, well, he's a very nice gentleman, sir, very handsome, you know. I dare say you've heard that he's going to marry Miss Waldegrave up at Langley Court in September. It's quite a romance, Mr Jackson. Sir Nicholas is happy about it, so we've heard, and so is Mr Lance Waldegrave, though poor Mr Arthur didn't really approve.'

The old constable leafed through his notebook for a while, then began to give the two detectives a careful account of the murder that had occurred at Horton Grange five years earlier.

'It was a Friday as I recall, Mr Jackson,' he said, '22 February, 1889. You'll remember the snow we had that year, sir. The whole village was covered with a white blanket. Mr Beecham – Black Beecham they called him round there, on account of his huge wild beard – used to live off the produce in his small kitchen garden, but once every fortnight the shopkeeper from Abbot's Langley, a man called Truscott, would come over in his trap with a box of provisions.

'Well, on that particular Friday afternoon, Truscott arrived at Horton Grange, and found the front door open and a drift of snow lying across the threshold. The upshot of it was, that he found Mr Beecham dead, and ran for Sergeant Bold. He and I accompanied Truscott back to the Grange. And now, sir, I'll tell you in detail what we found.

'We ventured into the great chamber of the house, which is an old, warped, panelled place rising through two storeys to an open-beamed roof. In the centre of the room, lying face down on the floor, we found the body of Jabez Beecham. We turned the body over on to its back and saw the look of agony imprinted on the features. Some inches away from the dead man's out-flung right hand there was a small damp patch, which smelt of spirits – whisky or brandy – but there was also the telltale aroma of peaches, sir – the hallmark of cyanide.'

'I suppose,' said Sergeant Bottomley, looking up from his note-book, 'that you assumed it was suicide?'

'Well, it certainly looked like it, Sergeant. The local doctor hummed and hawed a bit, but later, when the police surgeon came, he confirmed that it was death by cyanide poisoning and that Jabez Beecham had died that very morning. "Murder", he said, and that was that. You see, there was no drinking glass or cup near the body, only that little damp patch where some liquid had obviously been spilt. But in the parlour, a room across the passage from the great hall, we found a small tumbler standing on a table – or maybe it was a sideboard, I can't remember exactly. It still held traces of whisky, and when it was examined by the forensic specialist at Birmingham, it was found to contain cyanide as well.'

'So what do you think had happened?'

'Well, sir, I think that someone had given Mr Beecham what he imagined was a glass of whisky, which he drank. As you know, sir he'd have been dead within the minute. Now, all that this murdering third party had to do to make it look like suicide, was to leave the glass where it had presumably fallen – where we found the damp patch. Instead of which, he picked up the fallen glass, and put it in the next room, thus ensuring that Sergeant Bold and I, and the police surgeon, too, knew that Jabez Beecham's death was murder.'

'And nothing else was discovered?'

'Nothing, sir. No one had seen any strangers in the district all that week. Mr Truscott, the shopkeeper, was entirely eliminated from the case. Enquiries were made in Australia about the dead man, but no one seemed to have heard of him. There were no letters or papers of any significance in the house. Jabez Beecham was a mystery, sir, and his death remains a mystery.'

'This tumbler, Constable – what was it like? Was it, in fact, a whisky glass?'

'No, sir, it was the type of little glass that you'd take medicine from.'

'Were there any proper whisky glasses in the house?'

'Yes, sir. There were six whisky glasses on a shelf in the kitchen – very nice lead crystal, they were. And there were two bottles of whisky, one unopened, and the other a quarter full. They were both Sherman's Highland Maid Scotch Whisky, bought locally from The Coach and Horses. I remember that, well enough.'

'But the victim had been content to accept a medicine glass from his killer,' said Jackson. 'Strange…. Did you find another glass? And had there been whisky in it? You see, Constable, as Mr Beecham was the master of the house, it would be he who would have proposed a drink – perhaps a toast to celebrate some kind of agreement or compact. The killer would then have introduced the cyanide into poor Mr Beecham's glass in some way…. Perhaps the killer offered to pour the drinks himself. So was there another glass?'

'Yes, sir. It was standing on the mantelpiece in the great chamber, where the body was found. It was a proper whisky glass, taken from those standing on the shelf in the kitchen, and there were still a few drops of whisky remaining in it.'

'I take it that there were no servants at Horton Grange at that time?'

'That's right, sir. Poor Mr Beecham was quite alone, apart from a bit of help from a couple of women in the village.'

'That medicine glass.... Were there any medicines in the house?'

'Yes, sir; there were a number of bottles of cough mixture and patent medicines made up in packets in a cupboard in Mr Beecham's bedroom. They were all examined by the forensic expert at Birmingham and found to be harmless.'

'And you didn't find a poison-bottle anywhere: blue glass, with fluted sides?'

'Well, no, sir,' the old constable replied, smiling. 'If the murderer had brought such a bottle with him, he was very careful to take it away with him when he left. Sergeant Bold and I searched the whole house from attic to cellar, and found no trace of a poison-bottle. The murderer must have taken it away with him, and disposed of it later.'

'So what it amounts to, Constable,' said Jackson, 'is this. Some time on the morning of Friday, 22 February, 1889, Mr Jabez Beecham received a visitor, a man whom he seems to have known. At some stage in the morning, either Beecham or the visitor proposed a toast, to be drunk in whisky. The visitor succeeded in introducing cyanide into Beecham's drink for reasons unknown to us, missed a golden opportunity to make his murder look like suicide, then retired from the scene, never to be seen again.'

'That's about it, sir,' Pendle agreed. 'It's a dark mystery, and I don't suppose it'll ever be solved. It's five years ago, Mr Jackson, and the trail has long gone cold.'

'This Jabez Beecham came from Australia, didn't he, Mr Pendle?' said Bottomley. 'Maybe someone came to England from out there, to seek revenge for some past wrong. You do hear of such things.'

'Well, that's true, Sergeant,' said old Pendle. 'And now I come to think of it, I once heard him talk about some kind of a threat that was hanging over him. It was just about a year before he died. I'd gone down to Horton Grange to take him news that he'd been successful in closing a footpath that crossed his land. The magistrates agreed that there was no right of way and I went to tell him their decision.

'The front door was open, and I went straight into the great chamber. There he was – Mr Jabez Beecham, I mean – standing quite alone in the centre of the room, staring into space. Suddenly, he spoke, but it wasn't to me, it was to himself. "If I'm not careful," he said, "the old devil will do for me one of these days". And then he sighed. A moment later, he realized that I was there, and he spoke to me quite civilly. But I've often wondered what he meant by those words.'

' "The old devil will do for me one of these days". What did Jabez Beecham mean by that, Sergeant?'

Jacob Pendle had finished his tale, and departed, having left behind him his notebook. His daughter had brought him into Warwick, and would make sure that he returned safely to Hill Wootton.

'Maybe he was the kind of man who made enemies, sir,' said Bottomley. 'As far as we're concerned, he was a man without a history. But whoever the "old devil" might have been, it's our business to investigate the nephew, the man who came into all Jabez Beecham's possessions. Someone we haven't seen yet – a man called Grimes – has already pointed the finger of suspicion at this Mr Beecham, if what Mr Philip Garamond told us was true.'

'Yes,' said Jackson, 'the elusive Mr Grimes. It was he who told

95

poor Mr Arthur Waldegrave that Mr Beecham of Horton Grange had murdered his uncle.... There's a train from Warwick to Langley Platform at eleven-thirty. Are you game to go out there this morning, Sergeant, and beard this man Grimes in his den?'

'I am, sir. I'm quite anxious to see a man who blithely accuses another man of murder, without thinking of informing the police of his suspicions. I don't think we'll find him to be a very nice man, to my way of thinking.'

The gas-house in the yard at Langley Court was a gloomy, sulphurous place, windowless, and lit by a dim, flaring gas-jet. It was stiflingly hot. The wall to the right of the chamber was occupied entirely by the retort and furnace of the gas-making apparatus; the rest of the available space was filled with heaps of coal, shovels, rakes, and a couple of wooden benches.

In the midst of this hissing, fume-laden cavern stood Mr Grimes, whom Jackson immediately recognized as the wiry, stubbly, wild-eyed man in a moleskin suit whose smutty face had scowled at him from the doorway on the previous day. His grey hair stuck up from his head like a flue-brush and, as he moved about his sooty kingdom in a series of vicious jerks, little puffs of coal-dust shot from him hither and thither.

'So you want to know what I told Mr Arthur about this precious Beecham, do you?' snarled Grimes, after Jackson had stated his business. 'It would have suited Mr Garamond better to have kept his own counsel. This is a family matter, a Waldegrave matter. You tell me you're Inspector Jackson, and you'll be his sergeant, I expect,' he added, looking venomously at Bottomley, who had sat down on one of the benches. 'Policemen always hunt in pairs, so I've heard. Well, what d'you want with me?'

'What we want, friend,' said Sergeant Bottomley, treating Grimes to a rather fearsome smile, 'is a bit of common civility, and less of your lip. With that as the basis for our little conversation, we should get on very well together. Yes, I'm his sergeant,

Detective Sergeant Bottomley. Perhaps you'd better remember the name.'

'No offence, guvnor.' Grimes's voice dropped to a kind of ingratiating whine, but he eyed both men with what seemed like an expression of inner glee. 'If I spoke out of place, it's because I'm upset in my feelings. Mr Arthur was always very civil to me and wasn't above giving me a shilling whenever I helped him in and out of doors in that chair of his. Just imagine, him being all burnt up. And poisoned, too. Terrible, it is.'

He leered at both men, and turned his attention to a dial on the retort, which he tapped with a bulbous knuckle. If this man is upset in his feelings, thought Jackson, he has a very peculiar way of showing it.

'You seem very vexed with Mr Garamond—' Jackson ventured, but the stoker interrupted him.

'Vexed? I'm not vexed with him. He's another gentleman of a kind that's fast disappearing in these days. Always a civil word and an open hand. Very fond of Mr Arthur, he was.'

'Yes, he was,' said Jackson, sitting down beside Bottomley on the bench. 'And Mr Arthur was very fond of *him*, because he confided to Mr Garamond some damaging secrets that he'd learnt from *you*, Mr Grimes. You told Mr Arthur that the man who's going to marry Miss Margaret, a gentleman called Jeremy Beecham, had poisoned his old uncle with cyanide. Who told you that?'

'Who told me what?' snarled Grimes, making a dart at a pile of furnace-rakes, and setting up an intimidating rattle.

'Who told you that Mr Jeremy Beecham, of Horton Grange, had poisoned his own uncle with cyanide? It's a very serious business to accuse a man of murder without concrete evidence.'

Mr Grimes aimed a kick at the fire-hatch door, wincing and mumbling as the cast-iron seemed to retaliate in kind. He regarded both men with the same enigmatic expression of something amusing ruthlessly suppressed, and then suddenly sat down on the bench beside them.

'I'll tell you everything, Mr Jackson,' he said in an ingratiating tone. 'What's the use of beating about the bush, now? Mr Garamond's let the cat out of the bag. Here's what happened.

'About four years ago, I struck up a bit of a friendship with a man called Owen Stubbs, who'd been a servant of Jabez Beecham's at Horton Grange. Jabez never kept servants long, but one or two of them turned up to help him when he asked them, and Owen Stubbs was one of that kind— Why are you writing in that notebook?'

'I'm writing in it,' said Jackson, 'because whatever you're going to tell me needs to be recorded. Get on with your story.'

'I won't have to go to gaol, will I?'

'Not if you tell me everything about this Owen Stubbs,' said Jackson, 'and what he told you.'

'Owen Stubbs came to drink a couple of bottles of ale with me in my cottage outside the paling. This was about four years ago, as I said. Owen told me that his conscience was troubled because he'd witnessed the murder of Jabez Beecham. He said that it had happened one day in February, 1889. He was working upstairs in the house, when he heard voices coming from the great chamber. He tiptoed out on to the gallery, and saw old Jabez talking to a young man.'

'Talking? Did he say that they were quarrelling?' asked Jackson.

'They weren't exactly quarrelling,' said Grimes, 'but their voices were raised, so he said, as though they were having a disagreement about something. But then they both quietened down and the young man picked up a bottle of whisky from a sideboard. "Come, Uncle", he said, "let's bury our differences. I'll drink a toast to your good health." The young man busied himself at the sideboard for a while, said Owen Stubbs, and then turned round, holding a little tumbler, which he'd filled with whisky.

'Owen was about to turn away and go back to his work, when Jabez Beecham took the little tumbler, and tossed back the contents. He gave a kind of strangled shriek and dropped dead on the spot. The young man calmly picked up the tumbler, took the whisky bottle off the sideboard, and passed from sight into the parlour next door. Later that day, a shopkeeper arrived with some provisions, and found poor Jabez dead. And that's the story that Owen Stubbs told me.'

'Did Owen tell you in so many words that the murderer was Mr Jeremy Beecham?'

'He did. He whispered it, his voice shaking all the time, as though he feared his turn was next. He said that Beecham had glanced up at the gallery for a moment, and he wondered whether he'd seen him standing there. But I reckon he didn't, because poor Owen died of natural causes when his time came.'

Grimes's tale seemed to have all the verisimilitude of an eye-witness account. It was definitely not some fantasizing culled from the bad-tempered stoker's imagination. Grimes would have been incapable of concocting such a convincing story. Grimes, or rather this man Owen Stubbs, had seen the unknown murderer hand Jabez a tumbler – a medicine glass, according to PC Pendle's account – full of whisky, which he had drunk. For some reason of his own, he had failed to make the murder look like suicide, removing the fatal glass, and taking it, together with the whisky bottle, into the next room. The killer had then furnished himself with a whisky glass from the kitchen, drunk a grim toast to his own success as a murderer, and fled the scene. Owen Stubbs had witnessed the murder of his master, but fear had silenced his tongue.

'And this Owen Stubbs is dead, is he?' asked Jackson.

'He is,' said Grimes. 'He died of natural causes eighteen months ago. I kept my own counsel; but when Mr Arthur, too, was poisoned with cyanide, I decided to tell Mr Garamond, but apparently he already knew: Mr Arthur had told him. Well, it's in your hands from this moment, Mr Jackson, and I'll have nothing more to do with it. Now, if you don't mind, gents, I'd like to get on with my work.'

Margaret Waldegrave, her mouth set in a determined line, walked swiftly across the yard and flung open the door of the gas-house. The action was so abrupt that Grimes dropped the rake that he was using in alarm.

'Miss Margaret! What can I do for you, miss? Don't touch that retort door, you'll burn your fingers. This is no place, miss, for a lady—'

'Grimes,' cried Margaret imperiously, 'you have been regaling all and sundry with fairy-tales about my fiancé, Mr Jeremy Beecham, of Horton Grange. You will now tell *me* the substance of these tales.'

The stoker suddenly grew strangely quiet, and looked at Margaret with something approaching fear. He licked his dry lips nervously, and tried to avoid her gaze, but her eyes seemed to mesmerize him.

'Very well, miss,' he said at last. 'I've just told the story to two policemen who came nosing in here, so it's all fresh in my mind. And it's no fairy-tale, miss, asking your pardon.'

From some dark recess of the room Grimes fetched an old towel, which he used to dust the more presentable of the two benches, and motioned Margaret to sit down. Standing almost motionless beside the gas retort, Grimes repeated almost verbatim the story that he had told to Jackson and Bottomley. As he spoke, he saw how Margaret became pale and subdued. His words were as barbed spears, he thought, but they had to be spoken.

When he had finished his tale, Grimes reached up to a shelf, and took down a rusty tin box, which he opened. From it, he removed a dirty scrap of paper which he handed to Margaret, who sat silent, and somehow shrunken in stature, on the bench.

'I never told that policeman about this, Miss Margaret,' said Grimes. 'Soon after old Mr Jabez Beecham was murdered, Owen Stubbs gave me this bit of paper with writing on it. He said that he was afraid to tell anything else that he'd seen at Horton Grange that day, but that he'd written down the key to the whole thing.'

Margaret read the words written on the scrap of paper, while Grimes watched her closely. Her face betrayed no emotion, but her hand trembled as she slipped the piece of paper into the pocket of her dress. She turned to the door, which Grimes hastened to open for her. Margaret gave him a curt acknowledgement and walked out into the yard.

8

The Secret of Horton Grange

Margaret stood in the shelter of the trees at the end of the sunken road, and watched Jeremy Beecham as he climbed into his carriage. The young lad who acted as coachman sprang up on to the seat and, in a moment, master and man had begun their morning's journey. How disturbing it was, to hide like this from one's own fiancé! Jeremy was meeting a potential client who was staying at Sheriff's Langley, so he would be away for all of that morning.

It was a beautiful June day, and the grounds of Horton Grange were showing themselves at their best. The lawns had been neatly trimmed and the beds were bright with early summer flowers. What a gracious home it would have made! She would have been supremely content to bring the old grange back to life, to put down roots there with Jeremy, founding a new family.

But now, the baleful Grimes had placed a piece of paper in her hand upon which were written words that threatened to turn her dreams to nightmares. *The answer lies beneath St Lawrence's feet.* To most people those words would have been an enigma, but, to her, their meaning was as clear as day.

She recalled her previous visit to Horton Grange, when, lingering behind Jeremy and her Uncle Philip, she had discovered the little carved staircase of five steps, leading up to a small, well-lit chamber. She had glimpsed an ancient fireplace, and beside it, carved deeply into the panelling, a life-size image of a man with a grid-iron in his arms. It was a medieval figure of St Lawrence, and above the door, in quaint old characters, had been carved: 'Sanct Lawrens his Chambre'. When Jeremy had caught sight of her, he had ordered her peremptorily to come down from the staircase immediately. What was it that he had not wanted her to see? Later, he had claimed that the floor of the little room was unsafe, but was that the truth?

The answer lies beneath St Lawrence's feet.

Horton Grange seemed deserted that morning. The doors had been thrown open in order to freshen the rooms which still held the heat of the night. Margaret walked along the corridor leading to the old De Greville vault and paused when she reached the little flight of stairs. The door of St Lawrence's room still stood temptingly open: evidently, Jeremy had not, after all, ordered it to be padlocked. She mounted the stairs, and stepped over the threshold of the room.

The old boards creaked, and a fine cloud of dust rose to form little moving motes in the slanting rays of the sun. There was a not unpleasant smell of old, sun-bleached timber. It was evident that the little unfurnished room had not been inhabited for many years. It would have made an ideal sewing-room....

There was St Lawrence, clutching the grid-iron of his martyrdom to his chest. He was wearing the slashed doublet and hose of Tudor times, and his round wooden eyes regarded Margaret with supreme disinterest. She knelt down on the bare boards, and examined the area of the floor beneath St Lawrence's feet.

Yes; here, directly before the feet of the carved figure, was a short section of floorboard that formed the lid of a small cache. With mounting excitement, Margaret carefully lifted out the section of wood to reveal a space between the joists. The space was thick with dust, and in its centre lay a small, rusted tin box.

Margaret's heart pounded with a sudden fear. Did she really

want to open that box? What if it contained something inimical to her peace and wellbeing? Would it not be better to replace the boards, and leave the Grange at once? But then she remembered her Uncle Philip's words about murder, the story dragged unwillingly from Grimes, and knew that she must open the box.

It was rusted shut, but with the aid of a pair of scissors from her reticule, Margaret succeeded in prising up the lid. It contained a blue glass bottle, lying on a pad of cotton-wool, and secured by a leather stopper. A label affixed to the bottle read:

Potassium Cyanide
Poison! Not to be Taken, Poison!

Beneath these words was printed an address:

James Anstruther, Apothecary.
6 Old Town Square, Ancaster.

Poison! The box was rusted, but the glass bottle was clean, and free of dust. Was this the secret hoard of a poisoner?

Why ask such a silly question? Five years earlier, Jeremy's old uncle had been murdered in this house by the administration of cyanide in a glass of spirits. Her own brother, poor silly Arthur with his antiquated notions of caste, had died in the same way. Both Arthur and their uncle, Philip Garamond, believed that Jeremy was a killer, and Grimes's story of an unseen witness to Jabez Beecham's death, an old servant, now dead, seemed to affirm the truth of her fiancé's guilt.

What was she to do? She still held the tin box with its grim contents in her hand, and she realized that she was clutching it, as though fearful that someone would take it from her by force. Had Jeremy used this deadly poison to murder her brother Arthur? Arthur had opposed her engagement from the start, and Jeremy had been quite unable to conceal his sullen resentment.

The atmosphere in the little room suddenly became choking and oppressive. She must get out into the air as soon as possible, and show her find to Uncle Philip. He would counsel her as to what she should do.

Margaret had just reached the door when she heard a heavy but cautious footfall in the passage at the foot of the little staircase. Her heart pounded with fright and she looked desperately around the room for a hiding place. But the room was unfurnished, and there were no closets built into the walls in which she could conceal herself. The footsteps came slowly up the stairs and, as the door swung open, Margaret was quite unable to suppress the shriek of fear that burst from her lips.

She closed her eyes, as though the action would banish the terror, and when she opened them again, she saw the police sergeant who had come to investigate Arthur's death – what was his name? – standing motionless on the threshold. She stood looking at him for what seemed an age, but was, in fact, merely a few seconds. He was wearing his mustard-coloured overcoat open to reveal a dark suit of homespun grey worsted and, instead of a tie, he sported a red scarf tied into a wide knot at his neck. He wore heavy boots, which bore traces of moist soil, as though he had just come from working in a garden. His heavy face was flushed and there came from him the unmistakable scent of gin; but his rather fine grey eyes were alert and questing and, when he spoke, his voice was quiet, and almost refined, though it would have been impossible to mistake him for anything other than a born countryman.

'Well, miss,' said Herbert Bottomley, 'fancy finding you here in St Lawrence's room! It looks as though you've come to Horton Grange on the same errand as myself.'

'What do you mean?'

It was a blunt question, but it held no arrogance. Margaret Waldegrave reminded him very much of his second eldest girl, Nan, who had the same abrupt, defensive way with her when she was nervous.

'I mean, miss, that we've both come to find out what lay at St Lawrence's feet, and it looks as though you've beaten me to it.' Bottomley smiled, and held out a big, square-fingered hand. Margaret gladly relinquished the tin box and its lethal contents.

'I've forgotten your name.'

'Detective Sergeant Bottomley, miss. And now we've encountered each other again, I wonder whether you'd like to come for a little drive with me? I'm on my way to visit a lady who lives near here, and if you'll come with me, I'll be able to bring you safely to the gates of Langley Court after I've paid my call.'

Margaret knew that this was an invitation to talk about her find away from the intimidating atmosphere of Horton Grange. She had noted the word 'safely' that the sergeant had used, and it had sent a little thrill of fear through her body; what she did not know was that Sergeant Bottomley had used the word quite deliberately, and was secretly pleased with its effect.

She followed him down the little flight of stairs, along the passage, and out into the reviving air. The garden was full of summer smells, a welcome contrast to the dusty oppression of the old house. A little way along the sunken road a small, yellow-painted pony cart stood against the hedge, the horse tethered to a fence and quietly grazing. The sergeant helped Margaret up into the cart, where she settled herself on the rough wooden rear seat. Bottomley untethered the horse, climbed up on to the driver's bench and drove them slowly along the sunken road.

Margaret looked around her. On one side of the trap she saw a straw basket, full of bunches of carrots and long, succulent radishes, the soil still clinging to them. Perhaps this rural policeman, like others of his kind, kept a smallholding? And there in front of her was the broad back of the curiously comforting and reassuring Detective Sergeant Bottomley. She knew that the tin box containing the bottle of poison rested securely in one of the capacious pockets of his yellow overcoat.

They came to a little crossing, where Bottomley left the sunken road, and drove the cart along a narrow track bordered by high thorn hedges. Memories stirred. Surely, thought Margaret, she had been along this road before, years back, in her childhood? It was part of a well-wooded tract of land lying some mile or two beyond the village of Abbot's Langley, a sparsely inhabited corner of the shire, where the roofs and gables of a few large houses could be glimpsed occasionally above the trees. Yes, of course! She had been along this road when she was small, riding in a trap with Lance and Arthur, in the days when poor Arthur could still walk....

'You're going to visit the Lavender Lady!' cried Margaret. Herbert Bottomley turned briefly to look at her, and smiled.

'Yes, miss,' he said. 'I'm calling on Miss Cecily Hargreaves to make her a present of those carrots and radishes. It's by way of being a little "thank you" for favours received.'

They had reached a small clearing where the thorn hedges yielded to well-tended privet. Above the trees Margaret could see the grey tiled roof of the Lavender Lady's house. Sergeant Bottomley brought the cart to a halt, and turned full round on the seat.

'Do you feel better now, Miss Waldegrave?' he asked. 'You had two nasty shocks back there at Horton Grange: finding that bottle of cyanide, and being frightened by me. I shall only be a few minutes talking to Miss Cecily Hargreaves – the Lavender Lady, as you call her – and then I'll come out to the summer-house standing in the grounds. You and I can have a conversation there, undisturbed – that is, if you want to talk to me about Mr Jeremy Beecham, and his uncle, the late Mr Jabez Beecham.'

'Yes, I do, Sergeant,' Margaret replied. 'And will you tell me how far you've got in solving the mystery of my brother Arthur's murder?'

Bottomley gave her a shrewd glance. He knew what had lain behind that question.

'I know what you're thinking, miss,' he said. 'Mr Jabez Beecham died through the administration of cyanide, and so did

Mr Arthur Waldegrave. Today, you discovered what could well be the very bottle of poison used to commit those crimes. Appearances point the finger of guilt in one direction, but appearances are not evidence, Miss Waldegrave, and it's early days yet for drawing firm conclusions. I'll be gone about fifteen minutes. You could sit in the summer-house until I return.'

Margaret watched as the sergeant, carrying the basket of garden produce, walked to the front porch of the two-storey brick-built house. He knocked on the door, and presently it was opened by a tall, commanding woman in her fifties, dressed in black, and with gold pince-nez fixed on the bridge of her nose. She beckoned the sergeant to enter the house and the door closed behind him.

How pleasant it was in this cheerful enclosed garden! There was a well-tended lawn fronting the house, with wide flower-beds alive with many-coloured antirrhinums and white stock. A number of standard rose trees, their flowers just coming into bloom, rose from semi-circular beds arranged along the front wall. It was still very hot, and a number of bees moved indolently among the flowers.

A kind of grass alley passed along the left-hand side of the house towards what appeared to be another extensive garden to the rear and, as Margaret ventured along this alley, a flash of white told her that someone had just emerged from the back of the house into the rear garden. It proved to be a young girl, no more than eighteen, wearing a dove-grey dress over which she had tied a coarse white linen apron. She wore no hat, and her luxuriant black hair fell free over her shoulders. She stood still for a moment, looking uncertainly at Margaret as she approached, and then gave her a small, tentative curtsy.

'Good morning!' said Margaret, walking further into the rear garden. 'What a glorious day it is! This garden – it's quite different from the one at the front. Is this where the Lavender Lady grows her plants?'

The young girl smiled, and nodded her head. She seemed very timid, but evidently Margaret's cheerful greeting had put her at her ease.

'Yes, miss,' she said, 'this is Miss Hargreaves's lavender garden.'

Six long parallel beds stretched the whole length of the back of the house, each containing a line of sturdy shrubs, about two feet high, rising on thick stems of ragged bark to a broad, bushy head. Growing up from among their grey-green slender leaves, long erect spikes already bore their expanding clumps of mauve flowers. The pungent but pleasing smell of lavender hung in the air.

'When they've done flowering, miss,' said the girl, 'the blooms are plucked and dried, and then they're sent to the London perfumiers. They distil them, so Miss Hargreaves says, and then they're turned into lavender water.'

'I came here, once, when I was a little girl,' said Margaret. 'I was told that a lot of lavender was grown at a place called Mitcham, in Surrey, but that Miss Hargreaves decided to open this garden here, in Warwickshire. Are those bee hives? It's really a very quiet, embracing kind of place, isn't it? It has the feeling of a sanctuary, a place where you could hide yourself away from the troubles of life. Do you work here, my dear? What is your name?'

'Mary Connor, miss.' The girl's initial timidity seemed to have returned, and she spoke now with a renewed nervousness. 'I've not been here long, and as well as helping in the house, I'm learning something of the lavender business. It's wonderful here in the country. I don't think I want to go back to the town, miss, ever again.'

It was time to leave the girl to her work. It had been a pleasant, exhilarating interlude from the troubles and trials of the Waldegrave family.

She was turning to go, when the girl asked her a question.

'Asking your pardon, miss, but are you calling on Miss

Hargreaves? If so, I'll show you the back way in to the house and introduce you.'

'No, I'm not calling, Mary,' Margaret replied. 'In fact, I'm waiting for Mr Bottomley to come out. But it was remiss of me not to tell you my name. I am Miss Margaret Waldegrave of Langley Court.'

The girl's face turned as white as chalk, and her hand flew to her mouth to suppress a cry of distress. She turned on her heel and ran, stumbling, to a door at the back of the house, which she pulled open. In a moment, she had gone.

'So you met Mary Connor, miss, and she ran away from you? Well, that doesn't surprise me. Mary's had a great deal to put up with, you see, and her nerves are all shot to pieces, as they say. She's here not just to make herself useful to Miss Hargreaves, but to settle her mind.'

Sergeant Bottomley had finished his business in the house, and was sitting in the secluded summer-house in the front garden.

'Miss Hargreaves is something more than just a lavender grower, isn't she?' asked Margaret. She watched Bottomley give a little frown of vexation, which soon turned into a rather bashful smile.

'Do you remember the old fairy-story, miss,' he asked, 'the one about Cinderella? There was a fairy godmother, as I recall, a good lady who could make a young woman's dreams come true. Well, Miss Cecily Hargreaves is by way of being a fairy godmother, and poor Mary Connor has had the good fortune to become part of her fairy-tale. I can't tell you more than that, because there are confidences that I can't break. But perhaps you'll understand what I'm talking about without me spelling it out word for word.'

They sat in silence for a few moments, and Bottomley stole a glance at his companion. She was, he knew, only twenty-four, a slim, very fair young lady, with light-blue eyes. That white linen

dress and wide-brimmed summer hat became her. Had she under-
stood that Mary Connor was a girl in trouble? Yes, surely; but it
wouldn't do to tell her why the girl had run away from her in
fright on hearing her name.

He carefully removed the tin box from his pocket and opened
it, revealing the sealed blue glass bottle and its deadly contents.

'As you can see, miss,' he said, 'this cyanide was dispensed by a
chemist in Ancaster, which is a good twenty miles away from here.
Now, in order to obtain deadly poisons of this sort, you have to
sign the poisons register, so I propose to go over to Ancaster and
ask this chemist – James Anstruther – to show me that book. It
would be very interesting to see who signed for this cyanide.'

'You think it was Jeremy, don't you?' said Margaret.

'Don't *you*, miss?' asked Bottomley, quietly.

'How did you know that I was coming here today?'

'I didn't, Miss Waldegrave. But the other day, after my guvnor
and me had interviewed that man Grimes, you went in to see him,
didn't you? Well, I cornered Grimes later in that smoky den of his,
and made him tell me what you'd said to him. He told me about
that paper, and what it said about the answer being at St
Lawrence's feet. So when I saw you there today, miss, I knew what
you were up to.'

'What should I do, Mr Bottomley?' asked Margaret. 'About
Jeremy, I mean? These accusations against him are becoming an
open secret.'

'I'd like you to give him the benefit of the doubt for the
moment, Miss Waldegrave. As I've told you, rumours are not
proofs. But don't mention your discovery to him on any account,
because that would complicate matters.'

Bottomley rummaged in one of his pockets and produced a
dented old silver watch.

'It's nearing twelve,' he said. 'I'll take you back now to Langley
Court, and then I'll have a bite to eat at the village inn. This afternoon, miss, I'll call on Mr Jeremy Beecham at Horton Grange,

and have a little talk with him. I've never met him, you see, and it's about time that I did.'

'Sergeant Bottomley?' said Jeremy Beecham. 'Come in, won't you? This is what they are pleased to call the "great chamber", though, as you can see, it's not really great at all. Notice the ugly Jacobean screen at the far end: bereft of beauty it may be, but it hides the kitchen door and keeps out the draught. It was just there, where you are standing, that the body of my Uncle lay, poisoned with cyanide. Later, we'll go across the passage to the parlour, and there I'll show you the very sideboard upon which the wicked assassin placed his empty whisky glass, after he'd celebrated poor Uncle's demise with a reviving tot of spirits.'

'Mr Beecham—'

'The very same, Sergeant, though I must point out to you that I am not one of the Beechams of Mount Royal.'

This gentleman, thought Bottomley, is deliberately taking on the role of a curator of some stately pile, rather than behaving as the owner of Horton Grange. Poor man, why can't he be comfortable with his own station in life? There was no point being resentful against his betters. But it was an encouraging sign: this handsome, well-set-up man didn't behave like a guilty assassin. It was social rank that preoccupied him.

The centre of the great chamber was occupied by a number of writing-frames, over which Jeremy Beecham had draped delicate drawings of soaring palaces and pavilions of glass. Despite the business in hand, Bottomley was attracted to the work. Here, he saw, was a very talented man, a man who could transform glass and iron into airy buildings designed to look as though they were to be set in the magical landscapes of a fairy-tale.

Beecham suddenly gave a good-humoured laugh, and threw down the pencil that he had been clutching. He motioned to some chairs drawn up before the great fireplace.

'There, don't mind me, Sergeant Bottomley. I'm talking

nonsense. Sit down, won't you? I had no doubt that you, or the inspector – Jackson, isn't it? – would want to see me. I expect you'll ask me questions about the tragic demise of Arthur Waldegrave, although there's not much of value that I can tell you.'

'I expect you find it a change, sir, living in the country? A change from London, I mean.'

'Yes, Sergeant, I— Ah! So you've been checking up on me, I see! Well, it's no secret. Why live in an expensive house in Town when one can live here at what was once called Horton, in one's own spacious property? I've lived here since '91 and, as you probably know, I am engaged to Miss Margaret Waldegrave of Langley Court. It was our intention to marry in September, though Arthur's death may interfere with that plan. One must observe the niceties, Sergeant Bottomley.'

Bottomley said nothing for a moment or two. He looked quizzically at Beecham, and then said, 'What you have told me is very interesting, sir, but may I ask you *why* you are telling all these family details?'

Beecham gave him a shrewd glance, followed by a slight, amused smile.

'I should imagine, Mr Bottomley,' he said, 'that you already know the answer to that question. In this affair of Arthur's death, I'm the outsider, and I feel that I have a duty to myself to show you that I am putting down roots in this neighbourhood. I am liked and fully accepted by the Waldegrave family, and will soon be allied to them in marriage. That, I may say, will compensate me amply for not being one of the Beechams of Mount Royal.'

Bottomley saw Beecham's face suddenly flush with anger.

'For the last thirty years or so, Bottomley,' he said, 'the aristocracy and gentry have tried to slam their collective door in the faces of such as I. But I have my foot firmly in that door now, Sergeant, and there I intend it shall remain.'

Herbert Bottomley was quiet for a moment. He glanced around

the great chamber. It was here that old Jabez Beecham had breathed his last. The present Mr Beecham, to judge by the flippant way he talked, did not seem to have shed many tears for his murdered uncle. He thought of the little room at the top of the stairs and of the tin box, with its sealed poison bottle, hidden beneath the floorboards.

'You say that the Waldegraves have accepted you into their circle,' said Bottomley, 'but that wasn't true of all the family, was it, sir? Mr Arthur, I gather, was very much opposed to the match.'

'Arthur was an arrant snob, who had determined to render my fiancée as miserable as possible by constantly referring to our difference in station. I pretended to make light of it for Margaret's sake – but it rankled, Sergeant, it rankled. Arthur made a number of wounding assertions about me and my antecedents that were difficult to forgive. Indeed, I have not forgiven him, even though he is dead, and dead in a most tragic manner. So there, Mr Bottomley, you have my heart conveniently pinned for you to read on my sleeve. I did not like Arthur. But it's only fair to myself to say that I didn't murder him.'

'Were you here, at Horton Grange, sir, on the night that Mr Arthur was killed?'

'I was. My housekeeper was here, too, and prepared an evening meal for me, which I ate alone in the parlour. I can't prove that I never left the house that evening, but then, no one can prove that I did. I was not informed of Arthur's death until the following morning.'

There was nothing more to be learned from this man, thought Bottomley, rising from his chair. Jeremy Beecham accompanied him to the front entrance of the old grange, where the yellow cart and its patient horse stood in the shale path.

'There's just one little point I'd like to make, Sergeant Bottomley,' said Beecham, with a sudden impish gleam in his eyes. 'I did not murder my uncle and I did not murder Mr Arthur Waldegrave. But had I done so, I would have contrived very subtle means, which neither you, not your good inspector, would ever have been able to detect. Good day to you!'

'Good day, sir,' Bottomley replied, raising his battered bowler in salute. Subtle means, hey? he thought. Would they have included a secret cache beneath the floor of St Lawrence's room, and the possibility of access to Mr Garamond's bottle of wine, left ready for Mr Arthur in the folly? Perhaps. The time had come for him to pay a visit to Mr James Anstruther, Apothecary, of 6 Old Town Square, Ancaster.

9

Death on a Hot June Morning

Nurse Stone, a neat, capable young woman of twenty-five, had been at Langley Court for nearly a week. She had arrived early on the Wednesday morning following Arthur Waldegrave's death, and Dr Radford had introduced her to her new patient. 'Aha!' Sir Nicholas had said, with a good-humoured twinkle in his eye. 'So you've brought a hospital dragon to bully me, hey?'

'This young lady is no dragon, sir,' the doctor had said. 'Nurse Stone is very quiet and very kind. Nevertheless, she'll stand no nonsense from *you*. She's devoted to *me*, and will carry out my instructions to the letter, whatever *you* may think!'

The doctor's reply had amused her, though it contained more than a grain of truth about her own personality and professional code of conduct.

It was the bright, very warm morning of 18 June. Rose Stone had settled herself in an armchair near Sir Nicholas's grand four-poster bed. He seemed to be sleeping peacefully and by lunch time would be strong enough to take some refreshment in the adjacent sitting-room. It was not good practice to leave patients languishing too long in bed.

It had been a busy morning for her patient. Miss Waldegrave, and Miss Margaret had come in after breakfast, and made themselves comfortable around Sir Nicholas's bed. They'd chatted about family matters and she had felt obliged to withdraw from earshot while they did so. Not that titled people cared who was listening to their private business, but *she* cared and acted accordingly! Then, just as she had settled Sir Nicholas quietly in bed, his old friend Mr Garamond had arrived to talk about botany. He was a pleasant, good-natured man, who lived in what they liked to call the cottage, just outside the gates of the estate. Finally, Mr Jeremy Beecham had called, but he had stayed only for five minutes. No doubt he'd really come to see his fiancée, Miss Margaret.

But now they were all gone and she and her patient could have a bit of peace. What a great number of photographs and ornaments there were! She passed a professional eye over the various bottles and measures on the bedside table. There was the vital digitalis: a new bottle, sent up the day before, and another bottle two-thirds empty. There were other medicines, and boxes of pills and powders. She smiled at some of these. 'Professor Neilson's Dyspeptic Drops', 'Atterbury's Bile Compound'. *They* won't do him any harm, she thought; or much good, either.

There was also a carafe of water, and beside it a beautiful small tumbler of ruby glass etched with delicate gold flowers. Rising quietly from her chair, Nurse Stone picked it up.

'You like it, do you, Nurse?' came Sir Nicholas's voice from the bed. Rose was so startled that she almost dropped the tumbler.

'Yes, sir. It's so very pretty.'

'I suppose it is, my dear. It's Venetian, you know. One of a pair. I don't know where the other one is – there are so many ornaments and pictures in here that you can't find anything! My late wife and I bought those glasses on a trip we made to Italy, the year after our marriage. That's the glass I take your Dr Radford's foul brews from, or sometimes a drop of water from that carafe.'

Just as suddenly as he had awakened, Sir Nicholas went to sleep again. Rose was still holding the tumbler. She returned it quietly to the table, and sat back in her chair. When *she* administered medicine to her patients, she used a no-nonsense plain glass tumbler, which she took with her to every case. Evidently Sir Nicholas favoured something more elegant when taking medicines himself!

Like most skilled nurses, Rose Stone was careful always to convey an air of optimism to her charges, though inwardly she allowed the realism born of experience to form her judgements. Dr Radford had left her in no doubt of the seriousness of Sir Nicholas's condition. 'You understand, Nurse,' he had said, 'that he's received a great shock very recently, and the nature of his case is such that he could easily have died as a result of it. However, he's survived and, hopefully, with care, we should be able between us to ensure his recovery. In the long term, of course ...' He had pursed his lips, and then sighed.

Sir Nicholas, she knew, was a very sick man, with little future ahead of him. She looked at him as he lay quiet in sleep. He reminded her of other cardiac patients who had been in her charge, old Mr Povey of Cross Acre, or Mr Lanchester of Kenilworth. Patient and cheerful, but doomed....

She was shaken from these melancholy thoughts by the sound of footsteps in the adjacent sitting-room. In a moment, Mr Lance Waldegrave appeared at the bedroom door. What a handsome man he was – handsome, but haggard. Of all members of the family, Mr Lance seemed the most affected by the ordeal of the last week.

'Good morning, Nurse. I didn't know you were here. How's your patient?'

'Much better, I think, sir,' said Rose brightly. Sir Nicholas opened his eyes.

'Ah, Lance! I'm glad you've come. There's something I want to talk to you about. It's to do with those renewable mortgages on the outlying farms. There are two of them falling in soon, and we don't want any boundary disputes breaking out. Old Walker's going to cause trouble....'

More family talk! Could the poor man not have a moment's peace? Rose got up from her armchair, and walked discreetly out of earshot into the dressing-room, where she stood by a tall cheval-glass standing against the far wall. She leafed over the pages of a magazine that she had brought with her that morning. The murmur of voices continued for a minute or two, and then stopped. She glanced in the mirror, which gave her a full view of Sir Nicholas lying in his bed. Mr Lance was leaning over him, holding the Venetian tumbler to his lips.

Sir Nicholas drank from it and Mr Lance settled his father gently on his side. As he did so Rose heard him say, 'Try to rest now, Father. Don't worry, I'll see about Walker.' At the same time, Mr Lance caught sight of Rose in the mirror and beckoned to her to join him in the bedroom.

'Nurse,' he said, taking her by the arm, 'come through into Sir Nicholas's sitting-room for a moment. There's something I want to ask you.'

They passed quickly from the dressing-room into the sitting-room and Rose heard Lance Waldegrave make a sudden inarticulate sound of annoyance – a swift drawing in of breath. In the far corner of the room the ever-silent valet Skinner was busying himself setting a small table for luncheon. The man stood in an unnatural, frozen attitude, as though he had been detected in some misdemeanour.

'Come out into the anteroom', said Lance, opening the outer door. Together they stood in the quiet, picture-lined vestibule. Lance looked pale, and Rose felt that he was controlling some powerful emotion only with the utmost difficulty.

'Now, Nurse Stone,' he said, 'I'm speaking to you in confidence. I have a high opinion of Dr Radford, but I am minded to call in a specialist from London. Are you personally satisfied that Radford is doing all that is possible for my father?'

Rose bit her lip and her face became suffused with a blush of vexation.

'Really, Mr Lance, it is not for a nurse to question the competence of the physician in a case. These things are not always clear to the layman, if I may say so without impertinence, and I can assure you that Dr Radford—'

Her words were dramatically interrupted by the sudden and violent opening of Sir Nicholas's bedroom door. The valet Skinner, his face ashen and his eyes almost mad with fear, stood on the threshold. He looked wildly at Lance and Rose for a second, as though not recognizing them. Suddenly he found his voice.

'Oh, my master!' he cried. 'My poor master! He's dead! Go in and see! Oh, the sorrows of this house!'

Before they could reply he had hurried past them and away down the passage. Nurse Stone made towards Sir Nicholas's door, but Lance seized her arm in such a strong grip that she almost cried out.

'Did you see the look on that fellow's face?' he asked. 'What devilry has he been up to? It's as though—' Suddenly recollecting himself, he released her arm and waited in the passage while she went into the bedroom.

It took her no more than a moment to ascertain that the old baronet had died, and that he had done so peacefully, to judge from the expression on his face. It had been a quiet end, she mused, and had occurred on a quiet, pleasant morning, with gentle sun streaming in through the window. Rose rejoined Lance in the anteroom.

'I'm sorry to say, Mr Lance,' she said, 'that Sir Nicholas has indeed passed away. It would have been a quiet and totally painless death.' Lance gave a long sigh and his shoulders drooped, as though he were crushed by a burden of trouble and sorrow. For a while he seemed lost in thought or reflection.

At that moment Jeremy Beecham appeared from the short passage leading into the front part of the house.

'Lance,' he said, 'I'm so very sorry. I've just passed Sir Nicholas's valet in the passage and he has told me the news.'

Lance inclined his head by way of reply, then turned to Nurse Stone.

'Nurse,' he said, 'I want you to go back into my father's bedroom and lock the door. Don't open it to anyone except Inspector Jackson, who's here in the house today. I think you mentioned to my sister that you knew him?'

'Yes, sir. Mr Jackson's a neighbour of ours in Warwick, though he doesn't know that I'm working here.'

'Good, good. Well, do as I say, and lock yourself in until Jackson comes.'

Rose passed into Sir Nicholas's bedroom and closed the door. The two men heard the key turn in the lock.

'Now, Beecham,' said Lance, 'I want you to find Jackson and tell him to come along here. I think he's with his sergeant, examining the ruins of the folly. There's something sinister in all this. That valet fellow looked far too agitated to be an innocent man.'

'Surely you don't think—'

'I don't know *what* to think. But there's something wrong, which is why I've asked Nurse Stone to stay with Father's body until Jackson arrives. I must go, now, to break the news to Aunt Letty and Margaret.'

Lance hastened away down the corridor, and Beecham went off in search of Inspector Jackson.

Jackson, accompanied by Sergeant Bottomley, hurried with Jeremy Beecham along the stable yard. So poor old Sir Nicholas had succumbed at last to heart disease. Why, he wondered, had Lance Waldegrave sent for him? Presumably because, in a house where murder had been committed, it was as well to make sure that any subsequent deaths were natural....

The whole of the rear wall of the house was bathed in sunshine. The yard seemed to be empty, save for a young groom who was hurrying towards the stable carrying a bucket of water. Evidently the news of Sir Nicholas's death had not yet spread through the house.

'Come through here, Jackson,' said Jeremy Beecham, laying his hand of one of the many doors in the rear wall of the mansion. 'It will take us straight to Sir Nicholas's suite – but hello! Here's Lance Waldegrave now. Perhaps he has something to tell us.'

A door further along the wall had opened and Lance Waldegrave had hurried out into the yard. He looked totally preoccupied and failed to see the hurrying groom on the path. In a moment the two men collided, the bucket fell clanging to the flags, and Lance was sent staggering against the wall. Jackson and Beecham saw a frightful spasm of agony pass over his face. He clutched his side, as though in pain.

'Damn you, Barlow, damn you!' Lance gasped. He peered around him in a sort of daze, scarcely seeing the white-faced groom, or hearing his stammered words of apology. 'Damn you,' he repeated, 'oh, damn, damn!' His voice, harsh and laboured, died away in a kind of gasp, Jackson and Beecham watched him dart back into the house, still clutching his side. Did Lance Waldegrave, too, suffer from heart disease?

The groom, shocked and frightened, stared at the closed door for a few moments before retrieving the fallen bucket and walking away along the path.

Jackson and Bottomley parted from Beecham in the vestibule. Jackson went swiftly to the bedroom door and gave a low knock. He heard the key grate in the lock as the door was opened from the inside.

'Why, it's Rose Stone!' he exclaimed. 'I didn't know that you were working here. This is my colleague, Sergeant Bottomley. But whatever's the matter, girl? You look pale and you're trembling.'

Rose pointed towards the bed, where the body of Sir Nicholas lay. She had turned him on to his back, composed his limbs, and pulled up the sheet over his face.

'Inspector,' she whispered, 'as you know, Sir Nicholas has just died. Mr Lance behaved very oddly, suggesting that all was not well about the death, and told me to remain here until you came. I want to have a few quiet words with you about Mr Lance.'

Sergeant Bottomley, who had been standing at the foot of the bed, his battered bowler clutched against his chest, moved away into the adjacent dressing-room. Jackson sat down in one of the armchairs. He seemed to relax and Rose, without quite knowing why, began to grow calmer. She, too, sat down.

'Tell me all about it, Rose,' said Jackson.

'I can't be exact as to times, Mr Jackson, but about twenty minutes to half an hour ago Mr Lance Waldegrave came in here and began to talk private business with Sir Nicholas. I moved away into the dressing-room over there, and stood near the big cheval glass against the wall. They stopped talking after a while and I looked into the glass. To my surprise, I saw Mr Lance holding that little Venetian tumbler there on the bedside table to Sir Nicholas's lips, and saw Sir Nicholas drink some of the contents. It was an odd thing for him to do, with a trained nurse in the next room. Mr Lance must have known that the nurse acts under the doctor, and that she has control of all medicines and treatment in his absence.' She added, 'I just felt uneasy about it, you see.'

Inspector Jackson sat quietly for some time, and Rose could sense that he was arranging a series of questions and clarifications of her story in his mind. Presently, he stirred in his chair and smiled kindly at the girl. From the depths of one of his pockets he brought out a black notebook and a stub of pencil, which he moistened with his tongue.

'You did right to tell me, Rose. Well done. Now: you said that they began to talk private business. Was it Mr Lance or Sir Nicholas who started the conversation? About the private business, I mean.'

'It was Sir Nicholas. He wanted to talk about mortgages, or some such matter.'

'I see. And when Mr Lance held the tumbler to his father's lips, did he know that you had seen him in the mirror?'

'Yes. I heard him say that he'd see about something for Sir Nicholas. Then he looked up, saw me in the mirror and beckoned to me to come back into the bedroom.'

'Well now, Rose,' said Jackson kindly. 'From what you tell me, Mr Lance seemed to be quite at ease in his manner, as though he were doing something quite innocent, if you see what I mean. Has anything in the room been touched since Sir Nicholas died?'

'Nothing, Mr Jackson. No one has entered the room since I locked the door on Mr Lance's orders.'

Inspector Jackson pointed to the ruby Venetian tumbler on the edge of the table.

'Is that the tumbler in question? Is it still where Mr Lance placed it before you both left the room?' Rose answered in the affirmative to both questions.

'Now, one final question, Rose. You told me just now that it's a Venetian tumbler. How did you know that, my dear?'

'Well,' said Rose, 'Sir Nicholas told me. I was admiring it and he said it was one of a pair of Venetian tumblers.'

Jackson stood up, crossed to the table, and sniffed delicately at the tumbler which contained about a quarter of an inch of clear liquid. He dipped his finger in it, and gingerly tasted it. Rose expected him to make some comment. Instead, he said to her, 'Will you examine Sir Nicholas's medicines, Rose, and tell me whether or not they have been tampered with since you came?'

Rose took up the two bottles of digitalis and examined them closely. She looked rather crestfallen. One bottle was still about one-third full as she had seen it on her arrival, and the other, full, still had its paper seal intact. 'Oh, dear,' she said quietly.

'Tell me, Rose, this little fancy glass – it's not really a medicine glass, is it? Was it used for any other purpose?'

Rose considered for a moment. 'Why, yes,' she said slowly. 'I remember now that Sir Nicholas told me he liked to have a drop of water from it. There's a carafe just there, as you can see.'

Jackson, who had sat down again, pointed to the little glass.

'And that's what's in it now, Rose,' he said. 'Water. All that Mr Lance was doing was giving his father a drop of water.'

Rose gave a sigh of relief. 'Oh, Mr Jackson, I feel so foolish and wicked, especially as I knew that Sir Nicholas might die suddenly at any time.'

'No, Rose,' said Jackson, rather sombrely. 'It's what can easily happen in a house where there's been some devilry going on. You'll have heard all about the murder of Mr Arthur in the folly, and people will have voiced some of the suspicions that such a wicked deed can set in motion. It's always like that, you see.'

'But I should have known better, Mr Jackson. After all, it was Mr Lance who told me to stay here and lock the door until you arrived.'

'Have you any idea why he did that, Rose? What made him think that Sir Nicholas's death was not natural? Tell me exactly what happened before I came to see you.'

As Rose was telling him about the dramatic appearance of the valet Skinner from the bedroom and Lance's reaction, the door opened, and Lance Waldegrave himself came in to the bedroom. He had already changed into a formal black suit with a matching frock coat. His voice came tremulous and low, but he seemed now to be in full command of himself and there was no sign of the frantic panic that he had shown in the stable yard.

'Nurse,' he said, 'will you please go along to the butler's pantry, where Mr Lincoln will make you comfortable for a while? I wish to talk to Inspector Jackson alone.'

'Now, Jackson,' he continued, when Rose had left, 'did Nurse Stone explain to you that I suspect that valet Skinner of having been up to no good? He was skulking around in Father's sitting-room just before he died. I hesitate to make an open accusation, but—'

'Nurse Stone said nothing definite about Skinner, sir,' said Jackson. 'But I doubt very much that a servant who has been in your household for so many years would wish to harm his master. Why should he?'

'What do you mean, so many years?' asked Lance. 'Skinner has only been with us about two months.'

'What? But Sir Nicholas told me—'

Jackson's mind raced back to his first meeting with the elderly baronet. He saw him lost in recollections of the past, and half-listening to the question that Jackson had asked him about Skinner. 'How long has he been with you, Sir Nicholas?' he had asked, and the old baronet had replied, 'Oh, my goodness, years and years – more years than I care to remember.' He had been speaking not of Skinner, but the faithful old butler, Lincoln. Nevertheless, it seemed inconceivable that the skulking valet, Skinner, had murdered his master. Going after Skinner, he felt, would lead him dangerously astray.

Sergeant Bottomley suddenly appeared from the dressing-room, dusting what looked like dried whitewash from the skirts of his long yellow overcoat.

'Sir,' he said, turning to Jackson, 'in that dressing-room next door, there's another door in the corner leading out on to a servants' staircase, a narrow affair, closed in by newly white-washed bare brick walls. If murder's been done here, then the murderer could have come in through that door, entered this bedroom, done the wicked deed, and returned the way he came.'

Murder.... The fact of murder seemed to be a tangible entity in that still room of death. Too many doors, thought Jackson. He had felt that on his first acquaintance with this suite of rooms. It was theoretically possible for anyone to come and go as he pleased without being seen. Whatever the truth might be about Skinner, Sir Lance Waldegrave's suspicion about foul play could not be ignored. Sir Nicholas Waldegrave could not be consigned to the grave until his body had been examined by a police surgeon.

'Sir Lance,' said Jackson, 'I want you to send a groom on horse-back to Kingston Lacey, where he will find the police surgeon, Dr

James Venner. He is to bring Dr Venner back with him. I'm sure you'll want to summon Dr Radford as well. Say nothing as yet to the family. We need to hear Dr Venner's expert verdict before we move in the matter.'

Sir Lance Waldegrave uttered what sounded like a sigh of relief.

'I'm very relieved, Inspector,' he said, 'that you've decided to make certain about Father's death. I'll send a groom over to Kingston Lacey immediately.'

'Sergeant,' said Jackson, when Lance had left the room, 'go and find out what's happened to the valet, Skinner. He'll have made a bolt for it, but you'd better search his quarters. I'll stay here until Dr Venner arrives.'

Jackson walked into the sitting-room, and surveyed the relics of a life that had been suddenly extinguished. Here was a large table holding a selection of magazines and newspapers. *The Daily Telegraph, The Standard, The Morning Post* – all London papers, supporting the aristocratic and conservative interests, as befitted a country gentleman. And beside them, much thumbed, were piles of back copies of the illustrated journals, *The Illustrated London News, Black and White*, and *The Graphic*.

What a lot of china ornaments and statuettes! And here was a small round table, covered with a velvet cloth, exhibiting a whole collection of framed photographs. That young lady in old-fashioned Court dress was clearly Miss Waldegrave in her youth. This one is Miss Margaret, not a posed portrait, but a picture taken in the grounds of Langley Court.

Jackson picked up a rather faded vignette portrait of two army officers in the splendid dress uniform of the Bengal Lancers. They were both men in their late twenties or early thirties, one sitting rather stiffly on a camp stool, the other sprawled in dignified discomfort at his feet. The man on the camp stool was easily recognizable as Sir Nicholas Waldegrave.

Jackson lingered for a few moments. He looked again at the faded photograph, and at the proud young man sitting on the camp stool. He was oppressively aware of the sadness of things. Idly he turned the photograph over and saw a faded label on the back of the frame. On it was written, in faint black ink, the words 'Nicholas with Kirtle Pomeroy at Camp, June 1862'. Two young soldiers with their professional lives stretching before them. Now one of them was dead. Jackson wondered idly what might have happened to his officer friend.

10

Digitalis

Old Lincoln, fortifying himself with a cup of strong tea, looked up eagerly as a burly figure passed the kitchen window.

'Here he is now, Mr Cundlett!' he cried. 'Perhaps he'll tell us what he's found out.'

'He will if you pour him out a cup of this excellent tea, Mr Lincoln,' said Cundlett. 'There's nothing like the fragrant brew for loosening a bobby's tongue. "The cup that cheers", that's what they call it.'

The door from the yard opened, and Herbert Bottomley came into the kitchen. He looked crestfallen, but his eyes brightened noticeably as Lincoln poured tea into a large china cup, and set it invitingly in front of him.

'Come and sit down for a while, Mr Bottomley,' he said. 'Oh, what wicked times we're living in! First Mr Arthur, and now the master – what does it all mean?'

'It means villainy, Mr Lincoln,' said Bottomley, helping himself to three spoonfuls of sugar. 'I'm minded to tell you all about it, and you, Mr Cundlett. Why not? You know already that Mr Arthur was murdered by a person or persons unknown, which is why we've got to be careful about Sir Nicholas. He may have died of a heart attack, but perhaps he died of something else—'

'Surely not another murder, Mr Bottomley?' quavered the old butler.

'We'll have to find that out, Mr Lincoln, which is why we've sent for Dr James Venner, the police surgeon. He'll have a look inside poor Sir Nicholas, in order to find out for certain what he died of. He may have been poisoned, you see, especially today, when everybody seemed to have visited him in his rooms. Sir Lance believes that there was foul play involved, and the guvnor and I are inclined to agree with him.'

'Sir Lance…. Of course, we must all be careful to address him by that title from now on. But who could possibly have poisoned dear old Sir Nicholas? He hadn't an enemy in the world.'

'When you're investigating a murder, Mr Lincoln,' said Bottomley, 'the first thing you have to consider is opportunity, followed by motive. Or to put it another way, who could have done it and why? So, in theory at least, Sir Nicholas could have been poisoned by Nurse Stone, or by any member of his family. And we mustn't forget Mr Garamond, and Mr Jeremy Beecham from Horton Grange. They were all here this morning, and they all paid a call on Sir Nicholas. It was a very convenient day for a murder.'

'Or it might have been that sneaking valet, Skinner,' said Cundlett. 'He had the opportunity, hovering around all the time like a bird of ill omen. And he's run off, so I've heard in the yard.'

'I never liked him, as you well know, Mr Cundlett,' said Lincoln, frowning. 'He never fitted in here. Oh, he was a good enough valet, but he held himself aloof. We weren't good enough for him, you see, with his London ways, begging your pardon, Mr Cundlett, you being a Londoner, too, but a very different kind of person.'

'No offence taken, Mr Lincoln,' said Cundlett. 'I warned you about that fellow, didn't I? Sly, that's what he was, flitting around like a ghost all day, poking and prying where he wasn't welcome. But for the life of me I can't see why he'd want to murder his master. Whatever could his motive have been?'

'Well, as a matter of fact, Mr Cundlett,' said Bottomley, 'I don't think he did anything of the kind. He wasn't a killer, to my way of thinking. But the fact remains that his room in the attic storey is empty – I've just finished searching it – and he'll have made his way across country to some little station, by now, and caught a train to London.'

Old Lincoln got up from his chair at the kitchen table, and took down a tin box from a shelf. He opened it, rummaged through its contents for a minute, and then extracted a single sheet of paper which he handed to Bottomley.

'It was the master who engaged Skinner directly,' said Lincoln, 'and that was the reference that he handed me for safe-keeping. You see, Sir Nicholas's previous valet died quite suddenly, and Sir Nicholas secured the services of this man Skinner through a friend as a temporary replacement. As you can see, it's a very fulsome testimonial signed by a gentleman called Julius C. Stanton of Albany, New York State. He says there in the letter that he wouldn't require Skinner's services again until September.'

Herbert Bottomley got up from the table, drained his mug of tea, and handed the letter back to the old butler.

'Well, Mr Lincoln,' he said, 'perhaps that reference is a forgery. We'll have to find out. But for the moment I think the guvnor's got more important things on his mind. This business of Skinner will have to wait.'

'Hey, you, mister, what the blazes are you doin' in that midden?'

Mr Grimes was not in a good mood and, in any case, he resented strangers in the yard. His sooty features contorted with passion, he rushed furiously to a remote enclave behind the gas-house, where a number of tall iron receptacles stood against a wall. There was a strong smell of refuse, and a great number of well-fed flies and bluebottles hovered expectantly in the air.

Standing on a short set of steps was an enormous man clad in the leather-patched garb of a midden-shifter. His back, which was turned to Grimes, was more reminiscent of a cliff-face than part of the human anatomy. In his great left hand he held a bundle of clothes roughly tied with string. He slammed down the lid of the midden into which he had been delving, and slowly descended the steps. Then he turned round to face the irate stoker.

'I reckon you'll be Grimes, the furnace man,' he said. His voice was like an echo ascending from a fathomless cavern. 'I've been warned about you. You think this yard's your own little kingdom, don't you? Well, while I'm here, you're deposed, see?'

A pair of steely-grey eyes looked at Grimes from a wide face almost covered in hair. A massive spade beard entirely concealed the top parts of the man's leather jacket.

'But who are you? I've never seen you before.'

'This is Monday, isn't it?' said the big man. 'And Monday's the day Langley Court's middens are emptied. Well, your usual man's off sick today, and the gaffer's sent me in his place. The cart's drawn up by the stable gates, so you'd better give me a hand with the trolley, so I can get these middens up there and empty them.'

'What are you holding there, in your hand?' asked Grimes. 'You've no right to go rooting through our middens. It's stealing, that's what it is. You give that to me, do you hear?'

The big man threw the parcel of clothing at the stoker, and spat in contempt.

'You calling me a thief, Grimes?' he demanded.

'Well, what if I am? You've no right to—'

The midden-shifter looked carefully and slowly around him, to ensure that no one else was in sight, and seized Grimes by the collar, which he twisted until the unfortunate stoker felt that his eyes would pop out of his head. He felt himself being raised several feet from the ground before he was slammed against the wall.

'If I get one more uncivil word from you, little man,' said the midden-shifter, 'I'll take you apart, slowly, limb from limb. Now, are you going to help me with these middens, or would you like me to put you into one of them, head first?'

Grimes knew when he was beaten and when the giant had released him, he wriggled himself straight in his clothing and followed the victor out into the yard. But he was careful to stash the bundle of clothes away in a convenient corner before he did so. When this big stiff and his muck cart had left the premises, he'd have a close look at that bundle. It could prove very interesting, to his way of thinking. And very profitable, too.

'Sir,' said Sergeant Bottomley, 'Dandy Jim's carriage has just stopped at the bottom of the street. I expect he's bringing us the results of the post-mortem.'

It was the morning of Wednesday, 20 June, two days after the suspicious death of Sir Nicholas Waldegrave. Jackson and Bottomley were working in the back room of Barrack Street Police Office in Warwick. Whenever Dandy Jim paid them a visit, they felt compelled to give their office a frantic tidying before he came in from the passage. Jackson straightened the mass of papers on his desk; Bottomley hastily hid several unwashed cups in the stationery cupboard.

'Here he is, now,' said Bottomley, and the door opened to admit Dandy Jim. Dr James Venner, MD, the police surgeon, was a distinguished grey-haired man in his sixties. Fastidious to a fault where dress was concerned, he was wearing an elegant grey frock coat complemented by a black silk stock, in which he had placed an opal pin. He wore pale-mauve kid gloves and sported a gleaming silk hat.

'Well, Jackson, and you, Bottomley,' he began, after he had sat down in front of Jackson's desk, 'it was murder right enough. First, poor Arthur Waldegrave with cyanide, and now, Sir Nicholas Waldegrave with digitalis. There's a ruthless killer on the prowl at Langley Court.'

Dr Venner had placed a cardboard folder on the desk. He now peeled off his gloves, and deposited them in his top hat. He opened the folder, and gazed in silence for a few moments at the single sheet of paper that it contained. Then he spoke.

'Digitalis, gentlemen,' he said, 'is very valuable in certain forms of heart disease. You get it from the dried, powdered leaves of the foxglove. You can administer it as the dry powder, or, more usually, as an infusion or tincture prepared from the leaves. That's what Sir Nicholas was given for his very serious heart complaint. It had been prescribed by his physician, Dr Radford, and also by Dr Savage before him, and I would agree that it was the best treatment for his condition.'

'There was a bottle of digitalis present in Sir Nicholas's bedroom,' said Jackson. 'I remember Dr Radford remarking on how much of it had been consumed.'

'Yes, he told me,' said Venner, 'and I'm sure you'll see the sinister implications of that. I know you don't like me playing detective, Jackson, but I would suggest that someone had carefully abstracted a quantity of that tincture of digitalis to use later as a weapon of murder.'

'I certainly agree with you, Doctor,' said Jackson. 'This was evidently a cold, premeditated killing. This digitalis – how does it act upon the heart?'

'Well, it can slow down or increase the force of the heart's beat, and it is the business of the physician to know in what quantities to administer it in order to achieve either of those results. It's a very careful business and should not be done by anyone who is not a physician, or a fully trained nurse. But let me tell you now about the post-mortem.

'After I'd answered your summons to Langley Court on Monday, I arranged for the body of Sir Nicholas Waldegrave to be transferred to the police mortuary at Copton Vale. Dr Savage had been quite right to examine the remains of Arthur on the premises, but I felt that in Sir Nicholas's case I needed to have certain instruments and substances immediately to hand, as his death, as far as we knew at that stage, could have been from natural causes.

'I performed the post-mortem yesterday. The internal organs, other than the heart, were in very fair condition. The left leg was arthritic. The heart – my examination of the heart confirmed the earlier diagnoses of Savage and Radford that the left side was gravely diseased, particularly in the area of the mitral valve between the left auricle and the left ventricle. Digitalis, properly administered, was exactly right for this condition.'

'But in this case, sir,' said Jackson, 'it had *not* been properly administered?'

Dr Venner stirred uneasily in his chair and flicked a minute piece of fluff from the sleeve of his frock coat.

'These things are not always clear-cut, Jackson,' he said. 'That's why I've brought you a written report of my observations which you will be able to read at leisure. What I can say with certainty is that the stomach was awash with digitalis, and there was certainly enough present to have produced an immediate and fatal heart spasm. Someone – someone who was neither doctor nor nurse – administered a fatal dose. You will need to ascertain for certain whether that administration was by accident or design.'

'Can digitalis be administered over a long period of time?' Jackson asked. 'I'm thinking of the way arsenic is used by murderers to produce the symptoms of acute gastritis—'

'Well, of course, digitalis *is* administered over a long period of time: it's for use in certain forms of chronic heart disease, as I've explained. It can accumulate in the patient's body and produce symptoms of poisoning, but the physician recognizes them as arising from such an accumulation. There is vomiting, a weak, slow pulse, giddiness and a characteristic slow, sighing respiration. You give the patient brandy and coffee and wash out the stomach. But nothing like that had ever happened to Sir Nicholas. His death was the result of a sudden large overdose of digitalis, administered orally.'

Dr Venner began to draw on his gloves. He stood up, reached for his hat and then thought better of it. He sat down again at the table.

'Gentlemen,' he said, 'I expect you will be seeking a link between the murder of Sir Nicholas Waldegrave and that of his son. It looks very much as though someone in that family is bent on eliminating anyone who stands between him and the Waldegrave fortune. The prime suspect is very obvious, but it would be imprudent of me to mention his name—'

'There's no need to be prudent between these four walls, Dr Venner,' said Jackson. 'The prime suspect is Sir Lance Waldegrave, a man with an unsavoury past, who is in thrall to moneylenders. It's evident to Sergeant Bottomley and me that Lance was in quite desperate straits. Now, of course, with his father and elder brother out of the way, he's a man with great expectations. Those money-lenders will be all smiles, now. They'll be more than willing to extend his credit to the crack of doom.'

'Moneylenders?' said Venner. 'How did you find that out? Or is it merely an intelligent guess?'

Sergeant Bottomley emitted a sound that was something between a cough and a hoot of mirth. Saul Jackson smiled to himself.

'Lance Waldegrave makes frequent visits to London,' he said, 'and for the past ten days his movements there have been observed and noted. There's an old colleague of mine from my uniformed days who's a sergeant in the Metropolitan Police, stationed at the headquarters of "G" Division, in King's Cross Road. This old colleague found out for me that Lance Waldegrave visits a money-lender called Barney Cottle, who has premises above an undertaker's parlour in Angel Lane, a little alley not far from Finsbury Pavement. Mr Cottle's not a very nice man, Doctor, but then, neither is Lance Waldegrave.'

Dr Venner looked rather abashed. 'Well, well,' he said, 'how very clever of you, Jackson. But what was it I wanted to say? Oh, I know. I agree with you that Lance Waldegrave is your chief suspect, but it's the means of encompassing those two deaths that worries me a little. You know as well as I do that poisoners usually stick to one successful poison, often, in these terrible times in which we live, white arsenic. But at Langley Court we have two poisons used: cyanide and digitalis. It seems – well, it seems rather extravagant to me! I'm just wondering whether there may be two different murderers involved here.'

'Well, you see, Doctor,' said Jackson, 'it's ultimately a question of motive: who benefits from those two deaths? The answer can only be Lance Waldegrave, even though I have more or less ascertained that he could not possibly have murdered his father. He was under observation all the time that he was in his father's rooms, and it was he, in fact, who first suggested foul play. So we find ourselves in a bit of a quandary, if that's the right word. I'm right, am I not, Sergeant?'

'You are, sir,' said Bottomley. 'No one else in the family has anything to gain by risking the gallows, but there are two outsiders to consider. One of them is the family's uncle, Mr Philip Garamond, but then again, what possible gain could he receive from the death of either of those gentlemen? None. But the other man—'

'The other man, Dr Venner,' said Jackson, 'well, suffice it to say that there *is* another man, but this time it would indeed be indiscreet to mention his name. Let's just say, sir, that our enquiries are proceeding.'

'Sergeant,' said Jackson when Dr Venner had left, 'now that Lance Waldegrave is under observation, I think it's time for us to pursue some enquiries about Jeremy Beecham and this accusation of murder made against him by Mr Garamond and that man Grimes. Go over to Ancaster today and see if you can turn up anything interesting at that chemist's shop – what was it called?'

'James Anstruther, Apothecary,' said Bottomley, 'of 6 Old Town Square, Ancaster. There's a train from Warwick at twenty past one. I'll go out there straight away.'

Jackson picked up a letter which lay open on his desk.

'Mr Mays sent this over from Copton Vale first thing this morning,' he said. 'It seems that Joseph Ede, safe-cracker, was apprehended in Evesham last night. It looks as though he'd never strayed on to our patch at all. It was just another of Charlie Rawsthorne's periodic panics. So that's another nagging little problem out of the way.'

The ancient cathedral town of Ancaster was one of the hidden gems of Warwickshire. To Herbert Bottomley it was a magical sort of place, one of those old towns that seemed to have a breathing, living spirit of its own. It was not so very long ago that he and the guvnor had come there to investigate the horrific murder of the cathedral's dean.*

The apothecary's shop stood basking in the sun on one side of Old Town Square, a quiet backwater of tall sandstone buildings in the complex of narrow streets lying to the north of the cathedral. The sign above the door read VOKINS, LATE ANSTRUTHER and, when Bottomley entered the premises, a young fair-haired man standing behind the counter assured him that James Anstruther, Apothecary, was no more.

'He died over two years ago, sir,' he said. 'Atrophy of the liver, I believe. My name is Vokins, the present proprietor. What can I get for you, sir?'

Sergeant Bottomley removed from one of his overcoat pockets the tin box that Margaret Waldegrave had found under the floor-boards of St Lawrence's room in Horton Grange. He put it on the counter and opened it, revealing the blue glass bottle lying on its bed of cotton wool.

'I am Detective Sergeant Bottomley of the Warwickshire Constabulary. This bottle, as you can see from the label, contains potassium cyanide, sold to a customer by the late Mr Anstruther. I'd be obliged if you'd show me the poisons book for the year 1889.'

* *The Ancaster Demons*

Without a word, young Mr Vokins disappeared through a bead curtain into a room beyond the shop leaving Bottomley to savour the pleasant balsamic odour of the various preparations arrayed for sale. In a minute Vokins returned, carrying a slim, bound ledger. He wiped the dust off it with his sleeve, and placed it on the counter.

'I don't suppose, Mr Bottomley,' he said, 'that you'd let me look at the contents of that bottle? I realize that you're investigating a suicide or a murder, and I'll not ask you any questions, but I would like to ascertain whether that really is potassium cyanide in the bottle.'

Bottomley nodded his assent and the young man carefully prised off the leather cap. He spread a clean sheet of notepaper on the counter and carefully shook out some of the contents. It proved to be a clear white powder, produced by crushing what had originally been crystals. Vokins nodded his head in evident satisfaction.

'It's cyanide right enough, Mr Bottomley,' he said, carefully replacing the powder into the bottle and resealing it, 'and it certainly came from this shop.'

Bottomley had opened the ledger, and was examining the entries for January, 1889. His square, stubby finger hovered over one or two items, and then moved on down the column of entries. He turned the page and gave a little sigh of satisfaction.

'Here it is, Mr Vokins,' he said, and pointed to an entry under the date 21 January, 1889. It had faded to a light brown, but was very clear to read, having been entered in a bold, flowing hand.

Potassium Cyanide, 8 oz. Purpose: To kill vermin in a barn.

Purchaser: Mr Beecham, 2 Farm Cottages, Abbot's Langley, Warks.

The last line of the entry consisted of the purchaser's signature, J. Beecham, witnessed by the apothecary, J. Anstruther, 21 January, 1889.

Jeremy's uncle, Jabez, had been murdered by the administration of cyanide just a month later, on 22 February.

Bottomley thanked the young proprietor for his trouble, cautioned him not to mention his visit to anyone, and walked thoughtfully out into the sunshine.

11

—•◦•—

A Madman's Confession

The joint funeral of Sir Nicholas Waldegrave and his son Arthur was held on the morning of Thursday, 21 June, the bodies having been surrendered by the coroner on the previous Tuesday. The old parish church lay only 200 yards behind Langley Court, and the family had walked solemnly to the church from the mansion.

Sir Lance and his aunt Letitia had both agreed that the funeral should be private, with a memorial service to be held at a later date, but a number of gentlemen's carriages were to be seen in the vicinity of the churchyard, including those of Sir Nicholas's old friend Dr Savage, and Sir Frank Devereaux of Walton Manor, the Deputy Lord Lieutenant of the county.

The Waldegrave family plot lay at the rear of the churchyard, shaded by three stately yews and, after a rather sombre ceremony in the church, the procession made its way slowly through the paths to the graveside. Inspector Jackson, standing with Sergeant Bottomley behind the respectful line of servants flanking the main path, observed the members of the family as they followed the two coffins.

Sir Lance Waldegrave, clad entirely in black, and with a long crape mourning band falling down his back from his silk hat, looked pale but dignified; the features of Aunt Letty and Margaret, who were also in full mourning, seemed frozen into expressions of aristocratic hauteur beneath their veils.

'Sir,' Bottomley whispered, as the cortège passed them on the path, 'there's the uncle, Mr Philip Garamond, bringing up the rear. He looks very smart and upright, doesn't he? But look at his eyes, sir. He's frantic with grief.'

'Frantic?' muttered Jackson in reply. 'Deranged, more like. There's something very wrong with that man, Sergeant. Do you remember how disturbed he was that day, when he rushed out of his house to stop us on the path? It's time we looked more closely at that gentleman.'

The procession had just reached the graveside and the minister was turning the pages of his book to find the words of the committal, when Jeremy Beecham appeared from among the trees. He, too, was dressed in full mourning, though Jackson noticed that there was a hesitancy about his gait which suggested that he was uncertain of his welcome.

Jeremy made as though to join the family party, but as he took a step forward, Philip Garamond suddenly erupted in a frantic denunciation.

'You villain!' he cried. 'Have you come here to gloat over your handiwork? Everyone knows that these deaths are *your* doing. Be off with you!'

Jackson was to remember that appalling scene for many years to come. He saw Sir Lance, bewildered, physically restrain Garamond, who suddenly became calm, allowing himself to be led away from the graveside by Dr Savage. The two ladies seemed to have been turned to stone. They stood perfectly motionless, looking in Jeremy's direction, but apparently not seeing him.

Jeremy Beecham stood speechless with shock for a few seconds, but his wild eyes looked at them all as they stood, silent and expressionless, opposite him. Then he appeared to emit a kind of soundless snarl before turning his back and plunging blindly away into the trees. Soon, the minister had regained his equanimity, and proceeded to consign the two murdered men to the grave. Wreaths were placed on the grass and, as the family turned away to begin their walk back to Langley Court, the gravediggers came from behind the church, wide spades ready in their hardened hands.

'In God's name, Uncle,' said Sir Lance Waldegrave angrily, 'what was the meaning of that insane outburst? To accuse my sister's fiancé of murder at the very moment of her father's interment – and in the presence of the Deputy Lord Lieutenant—'

'I could not contain myself,' said Philip Garamond, 'and I've no regrets. It's time that that man's villainy was brought out into the light of day. I should think that you are the only person who does not know the truth about Jeremy Beecham.'

Uncle and nephew were standing in the lane that led from the parish church to the rear gardens of Langley Court. Margaret and Aunt Letty, accompanied by their friends and a little knot of indoor servants, had already returned to the house.

'What truth?' demanded Lance hotly. 'Are you saying that Jeremy Beecham murdered Arthur in the folly, and then made away with my father on that day when we were all present in the house? I am the head of the Waldegrave family now, Uncle Philip, and I think that you owe me an explanation.'

'I will give you one, here and now. The facts that I am about to impart were revealed to poor Arthur by Grimes. It was Arthur who told me all about it. Inspector Jackson knows, too, and he's already investigating Beecham's antecedents.'

'And Margaret?'

'Oh, yes, Margaret, too, has heard the story of that man's perfidy, and I think she may have discovered something that confirms all that I am about to tell you. Perhaps you yourself have noticed a growing coolness between her and Beecham? Do you want your sister to marry a triple murderer? No, of course you don't. Then listen carefully to the tale that I've got to tell.'

They stood in the lane for nearly half an hour. During Philip's account of the murder of Jabez Beecham five years earlier at Horton Grange, Lance interrupted with a number of questions, but he remained silent when Philip began to link the murder of Arthur with his sister's fiancé, shaking his head in apparent disbelief.

'Arthur, as I told you, knew all about it, too,' Philip continued. 'You know what a scholar he was, and I'm beginning to think that he'd initiated some quiet investigation of his own, and that Beecham had got wind of the fact.'

A light of understanding seemed to spring up in Lance's eyes. Evidently, he had decided to believe what his uncle had told him.

'Well, well,' he said, 'what a wicked world we live in! And do you really think it was Jeremy Beecham who poisoned Father?'

'It must have been. He hates the whole Waldegrave family, you see, because he can never become your equal. His hatred of Arthur, who openly despised him, spread in that man's evil mind to embrace the whole family. If he were to marry Margaret, I wonder how long she'd survive?'

Sir Lance Waldegrave's face assumed a sudden unwonted sternness.

'That man must never cross my threshold again,' he said. 'Come, Uncle Philip. You and I have a great deal more to talk about.'

Together the two men walked slowly towards the house, deep in conversation.

'I have only a few words to say to you, Margaret,' said Aunt Letitia, 'and they are these. Today, we have buried your father and brother and that is enough sorrow, one would have thought, for a single family to endure. Added to that is the uncertainty about the survival of the Waldegraves. It all depends on whether or not Lance will marry, and so far he's shown no inclination to do so.

'And now – I watched you this morning out of the corner of my eye when your Uncle Philip went mad and made that wild, wicked accusation against Jeremy. Your face remained as frozen as a piece of cod on a fishmonger's slab, while your poor fiancé looked as though a bolt of lightning from Heaven had struck him to the heart.'

'But Aunt—'

'Oh, I know that you were petrified with horror and that, I suppose is some excuse for your passive behaviour. But what would your father have thought? What kind of love is it that you're showing for the man you have accepted to be your husband, and whom you will marry in September? Will you take the word of that fellow Grimes, a disaffected drunkard and back-yard bully, against your heart's instinct? I tell you, Philip's gone mad. He hasn't a jot of evidence for his foolish accusations. And the police have done nothing in the matter, have they? If you've any sense, you'll go to Horton Grange tomorrow, and make your peace with Jeremy. Do so, do you hear? If you don't, you'll rue this terrible day for the rest of your life.'

The murderer – for such he was, no matter how he tried to ration-alize his fearful deed – poured himself a further measure of neat whisky. The burning spirits served to deaden in some measure his memory of the scene in the churchyard that morning. He recalled the faces of Lance and Margaret, frozen, no doubt, with shock, and wondered whether they had held in addition a large measure of hostility and primitive enmity.

After all, they had come there to that bleak spot to consign their murdered father and brother to the earth. Their emotions would be raw and untamed, and their hearts would harden when they heard that terrible denunciation. Well, so be it.

How quiet the house was! No timber creaked, no mouse stirred behind the wainscot. He forgot his untouched whisky as his mind took flight from the present and winged its way back in time to the night of Arthur Waldegrave's death. Arthur ... Suspicious, frustrated, petulant – and an impediment to the future happiness of others.

How hot it had been that night! He had come into the folly

quietly through the small back entrance that gave on to a long bed of thick bushes, and Arthur had looked up from his writing-table in surprise. 'Why, what brings you here so mysteriously?' he had asked, and there had been a certain measure of good humour in his voice, though it was clear that he was vexed at being distracted from his scholarly work.

Arthur had agreed that they should each sample a glass of wine from the bottle placed ready on the table. He had taken bottle and glass – there was only the one glass – to the mantelpiece above the little fireplace, and busied himself pouring out the wine, a hand- kerchief held surreptitiously over his mouth and nose, while Arthur went back to peering at one of his old books by the dim light of the oil lamp.

It had been easy to pour some of the white powder from the blue bottle into Arthur's glass of wine. He had talked about the hot night, and the coming threat of a storm, so that his words would cover the sound of his stirring the cyanide until it was dissolved. He had brought an egg spoon with him for the purpose.

He had placed the glass beside his victim on the table, and Arthur had unwillingly dragged his eyes away from his book in order to pick up the glass. He put it to his lips and drank.

Arthur had made a little inarticulate sound, had fallen forward, and then jerked back, dead, into the secure embrace of his wheeled chair. That was all there had been to it.

There had been nothing to rearrange, nothing special to do, apart from dashing the lamp to the ground. As the flames leapt up, he had returned hastily to the dark back room of the folly, opened one of the large drums of paraffin stored there, and hurled its contents back into the blazing room, where Arthur, now engulfed in flame, sat dead in his chair.

There had been horrors to come, but the work was accom- plished. Later, much later, he had crept into the moonlit St Lawrence's room at Horton Grange, and had hidden the blue bottle with its deadly contents once more beneath the floorboards.

*

That night, while preparing to retire, Margaret looked out of the window of her bedroom, and saw a dark figure standing half hidden beside one of the trees bordering the front lawn. For a moment she thought that it was her fiancé, Jeremy Beecham, but then the man struck a match in order to light a cigar, and she saw that it was Sergeant Bottomley.

Was he keeping guard over her? What a ridiculous idea! And yet, Mr Bottomley and she shared secrets together, things that were not known either to her family or to Jeremy. They knew about the bottle of deadly poison concealed beneath the floorboards in her fiancé's house. They had sat together in the garden bower of the Lavender Lady's secluded mansion, and he had told her of the suspicions that had gathered around Jeremy – suspicions that he had committed murder in order to gain possession of Horton Grange, and the hideous possibility that he had contrived the death of poor Arthur. So perhaps he knew of dangers approaching her, and had indeed determined to watch over her.

He had been present at that day's double funeral, standing with Inspector Jackson among the servants. What had he made of Uncle Philip's terrible outburst?

After dinner that night, Aunt Letty had renewed her insistence that Margaret should call upon Jeremy as soon as possible and make it clear to him that she did not connive at all the unsubstantiated rumours linking him with murder. Aunt Letty was right. She was becoming mesmerized by suspicion, and sent off-balance by the story told to her by that appalling man Grimes. Was Jeremy to be permitted no word in his own defence?

She would go alone first thing in the morning to Horton Grange, seek out her fiancé, and beg his forgiveness. Friday, she knew, was the day when Mrs Miller, Jeremy's housekeeper, went to the market at Abbot's Langley. Both she and Jeremy would be spared any embarrassment by effecting a reconciliation before a witness.

Margaret spent a restless night, in which brief periods of sleep were visited by dreams of her father and of Arthur. They seemed to be speaking urgently to her, emphasizing their words with frantic gestures, but their message was spoken too low for her to hear what they were saying. Their words were uttered in another world.

She rose at first light, ate a couple of biscuits, and drank some water from the carafe at her bedside. By seven o'clock she had dressed and, slipping a warm coat over her morning dress, she quietly left the house by a side door.

It was a very quiet morning, sunny, but retaining some of the night chill. The sunken road from Langley Court to Horton Grange was deserted, and she was glad that no one encountered her on her clandestine visit to her fiancé.

She arrived at Horton Grange to find the front door standing open, and wondered whether Jeremy had half-expected her to make this morning pilgrimage of reconciliation. She crossed the dew-soaked lawn and stepped over the threshold into the hallway. She could hear Jeremy moving about in the great chamber and with only the slightest hesitation, she pushed open the ancient nail-studded door. Jeremy was standing near the long window that looked out on to the grounds. He turned when she entered the room, but there was no smile in his greeting.

'So, you've found the courage to come here, have you?' he asked, his voice harsh from the sudden release of pent-up resentment. 'After what that madman Garamond shouted out at the funeral yesterday, I thought you'd play safe, and look around for another fiancé.'

Margaret had never seen Jeremy like this before. He began to roam round the great chamber like a caged tiger, and for the first time since she had known him he was without a jacket. She saw how his long shirt sleeves were secured above the elbow by woven wire armbands. He was clutching a glass of whisky, and had made no effort to put it down when she appeared. She felt a sudden surge of fear, but immediately determined not to yield to it. The time had come for straight talk. She would confront him with the story that Grimes had told her, and judge his guilt or innocence by his reaction.

'Jeremy,' she said, 'I am going to tell you what lay behind Uncle Philip's outburst. It's time that you knew the truth – or maybe you know already?'

'What truth? What are you talking about?'

'Let me tell you. It's a story that our furnace man Grimes told my uncle and me. He in his turn heard it from an eye-witness, a serving-man called Owen Stubbs. It concerns the death of your late uncle, Jabez Beecham.'

Jeremy abruptly stopped his restless roaming of the great chamber, and stood quite still beside one of the writing-frames over which a blueprint had been draped. He turned to look at her briefly with fathomless dark eyes, and then turned his back upon her. Haltingly at first, and then with growing confidence, she gave him the substance of the serving-man's witness to the murder at Horton Grange, five years previously.

When she had finished her account, she felt an overwhelming wave of relief. She had spoken the unspeakable, thus destroying the demon of mistrust that had begun to separate her from her fiancé. Jeremy still remained silent, and Margaret suddenly determined to finish the business by telling him of her uncle's conviction that Jeremy had also encompassed the death of her brother Arthur. When he denied the whole iniquitous story – which, of course, he would – she would accept that denial as the truth. The time had come to side unequivocally with the man whom she intended to marry.

She stopped speaking and she felt that the very air of the great chamber was being held in check until Jeremy Beecham spoke. She watched him as he very carefully set down his glass, and turned to face her. Her hand flew to her mouth to stifle the scream that rose from somewhere in the hidden regions of her heart.

Jeremy's face was suffused with a dark, ugly blush that rose up into the roots of his hair. His eyes were wild with something beyond anger, and there were flecks of foam about his mouth. He laughed, and the sound was a mirthless cackle. Very slowly, he moved across the room towards her and instinctively she backed away. Too late, she realized that she had given him the chance to reach the door, which he pulled shut with a crash.

'Yes,' he said, 'how clever of you to find out! I poisoned my uncle all those years ago so that I could inherit his money, which is the kind of thing you'd expect from a man with no pedigree. Only aristocrats like yourself would be scrupulous over such matters. People of our sort think nothing of murder.'

Margaret thought of the tin box with its deadly contents hidden beneath the floorboards in St Lawrence's room and felt her fear almost quenched by despair. They had all been right – poor Uncle Philip, the rough but loyal Grimes, and her crippled brother, Arthur. If Providence had not intervened, she would have married a killer.

'And Arthur,' Jeremy continued. 'Well, he was ripe for extinction, wasn't he? He had opposed our marriage, and he despised me because I was an able-bodied common man with pretensions, not a useless aristocratic cripple. So I poisoned him as well, and set fire to the folly as I left. As for your father—'

'No! Jeremy, no!' Margaret screamed in horror, and rushed past the demented man to reach the door. In a moment he had seized her by the arm and more or less dragged her out of the room into the passage. His breath smelt of spirits and his gait was unsteady. She realized that he must have been drinking by himself since the dark hours. He stormed along the corridor, pulling her after him, until he came to the gaping hole in the panelling where the opening of the De Greville vault yawned. She tried to scream, but this time found that her fear had all but paralysed her vocal cords.

Still clutching her arm, Jeremy staggered down the perilous steps and pushed her into the cold chamber where the lead-cased

corpses lay in their eternal sleep. His breath came in violent, ster-
torous gasps, as though he was in physical pain. She put out a
hand to steady herself and stood trembling against the far wall.

'And now,' said Jeremy Beecham, 'you can see what a convenient place this is to bring the whole blighted family of Waldegrave
to a suitable end. No one would ever find you down here,
entombed with your fellow aristocrats. When I have closed this
door—'

Suddenly, Margaret found her voice and with it her powers of
self-preservation. With a heart-rending scream of fear, she pushed
her fiancé aside and fled up the steps into the passage. On and on
she ran through the old deserted house, and in a few moments she
heard her tormentor stumbling after her. 'Margaret!' he cried,
'Margaret!' But she had reached a door in the old rear portion of
the grange that led out on to the back garden. For one sickening
moment she thought it might be locked, but no. Hitching up her
skirts, she began to run across the lawn towards a coppice of
larches skirting the small estate. Venturing a backward glance, she
saw that Jeremy had emerged from the house and had started to
pursue her. He would soon reach her, and then ...

Summoning up hidden reserves of strength, Margaret ran
desperately until she gained the shelter of the trees. The going
was rougher here, and she knew that if she once stumbled
Jeremy would be upon her. She could still hear his frantic cries:
'Margaret! Margaret!' but within less than a minute she saw that
she had reached a road, upon which a closed carriage was
standing. With a sob of relief she saw that Sergeant Bottomley
was sitting up on the box, a whip in his hand. In a moment the
carriage door was flung open and a young man in workman's
clothes held out a hand towards her, at the same time crying,
'Come on, miss! You're safe now.' She seized his hand and, in a
moment, he had swung her into the carriage and pulled the door
shut. As Bottomley urged on the horse and the carriage moved
swiftly away from the coppice, she saw Jeremy Beecham, the

man whom she had once hoped to marry, emerge, too late, from the trees.

Jeremy Beecham, his heart beating as though it would burst, hastily assembled a few necessities and flung them into a valise. He had only minutes to flee the house and make his way unseen to London, where he would lose himself among the teeming millions. It was all over. What a mad, rash fool he had been! No, more than a rash fool – a madman. Well, perhaps he *was* mad. He looked out of his bedroom window, and saw Inspector Jackson and two uniformed constables approaching the house. What should he do? Maybe there were other policemen stationed around the house.... He would have to take his chance and make a dash for it.

Seizing the valise from his bed, he clattered down the wide wooden staircase, and ran along a dim corridor leading to a small door at the side of the house. He opened the door cautiously, and stepped out on to the grass. So far, all was well. Fool! Why had he allowed his blind anger and deep resentment to loosen his tongue?

From somewhere near at hand there came the sharp blast of a whistle and the sound of running feet. It was time to go.

Edward Pennington, Solicitor and Commissioner for Oaths, put down the letter that he had been reading and looked at his visitor. He had heard of Detective Inspector Jackson from his old friend and fellow lawyer, Leo Farmer, who had spoken very highly of his abilities. Jackson had arrived from Warwick a quarter of an hour ago and had come to seek him out here, in his office at Copton Vale, clutching a letter of introduction.

'In this letter,' Pennington said, 'Sir Lance Waldegrave instructs me to tell you all you wish to know about the wills of the late Sir Nicholas Waldegrave and his son Arthur. I take it that your enquiries are pertinent to the alleged murders of my clients?'

Pennington spoke with a deliberately cultivated dry, paper-thin voice, which matched his austere countenance. He was a man in his early sixties who contrived to look older.

'They are, sir,' Jackson replied. 'And there is nothing "alleged" about those murders. However, it would be inadvisable for me to talk of proofs at this stage.'

'Very well, Jackson,' said the lawyer. 'I take your point and I am more than willing to tell you what you want to know. I went up to Langley Court on Wednesday and read the contents of the two wills to the assembled family. Well, I say "family", but there was only Sir Lance Waldegrave and his aunt, Miss Letitia Waldegrave, present. Mr Philip Garamond – an uncle by adoption – was there, and so was Dr Savage, an old friend of the family. Miss Margaret Waldegrave was absent. No one volunteered to tell me why and, of course, I didn't ask.'

I could tell you why, my friend, thought Jackson, *but I'm not going to*. Aloud he said, 'And then you read the wills?'

'I did, and as you're obviously impatient to hear their contents, let me tell you straight away. The first will I read was that of Sir Nicholas Waldegrave. The bulk of his property, monies, lands and incomes, he left absolutely to his son and heir Arthur Waldegrave. The house and the estate were, of course, entailed to the heir and would have passed to him without specific bequest.

'After certain bequests to the servants, including four hundred pounds and a small life annuity to his butler, Lincoln, he made a settlement of ten thousand pounds to his daughter Margaret absolutely on her marriage. He left the sum of five thousand pounds to his son Lance. To his sister Letitia Waldegrave he left seven thousand in cash, and an annuity of five hundred pounds.'

'You say that Mr Philip Garamond was there—'

'Yes, he was, and he was a beneficiary, too. Sir Nicholas left him two thousand pounds in token of his esteem and, as he put it, "in thanks for a loyal and fruitful friendship spanning more than thirty years". Philip, I may say, was both surprised and very moved by this bequest. Sir Nicholas left his old physician Dr Savage the sum of two hundred pounds.

'And now we come to Mr Arthur Waldegrave's will. As he predeceased his father, none of the provisions made with respect to him in his father's will have any legal effect. Mr Arthur declared assets of fourteen thousand pounds in cash and securities lodged with Coutts' Bank. He bequeathed four thousand to his sister, Margaret, two thousand to his brother Lance, and five hundred to his uncle, Philip Garamond. He left two hundred pounds to his servant Williams, with the hope that he might be subsequently trained, and employed as a valet in the family. The remainder of his estate he bequeathed to his aunt, Miss Letitia Waldegrave entirely. That will is effective in law, and its provisions become valid immediately.'

'So what is the present legal standing of the family members, sir? You'll understand that I'm probing for motive—'

'Oh, quite. Let me tell you their legal standing. By English law, the title of baronet passed to Lance Waldegrave immediately on his father's decease. All the rest of Sir Nicholas's estate, after the various bequests have been paid out, passes now by default to Lance, as he is the sole remaining heir male of the Waldegrave family. The house and estate, by entail, also pass into possession of Sir Lance Waldegrave as of right, without specific bequest.'

'Well, thank you, Mr Pennington,' said Jackson, preparing to take his leave. 'You've been most helpful, most accommodating, if that's the right word.'

'What will you do now?'

'I shall go up to London, sir, because some of the answers to my questions lie there. Meanwhile, my sergeant has tasks of his own to perform here, in Warwickshire. It shouldn't be very long, Mr Pennington, before the whole truth of this sinister business is brought out into the light of day.'

12

Jonathan Skinner's Story

Before Jackson could leave the office, Pennington called him back.

'Don't go yet, Inspector,' he said, and his voice had lost its dry lawyer's tone. 'Sit down again. There's something else concerning the Waldegrave family that I want to talk to you about.'

Jackson did as he was bid and watched the lawyer as he sifted quickly through a sheaf of papers on his desk. This man was naturally reticent, he thought, and his training would have made him even more so. It would pay to listen carefully to anything that he chose to reveal.

'There is something called "Margaret's Dowry", Jackson, a little legal relic from the past, which is regarded as a kind of joke by the Waldegraves. But you and I have talked money today and we have also talked murder. Well, "Margaret's Dowry" is a matter of money, so I think you should know about it.

'In 1874, when Margaret was a little girl of four, a distant relative of her mother's left her the title to a parcel of land in Leicestershire. It came with a proviso, which was this: if Margaret married before her twenty-fifth birthday, the land would become hers absolutely on attaining that birthday, which occurs on this coming 18 October. She is twenty-four now, as you probably know.'

'And what happens to the property if she *isn't* married by the age of twenty-five?'

'It would have passed to her brother Arthur, but if Arthur was dead by 18 October, 1894, then the bequest would pass to Mr Philip Garamond, who was also a relative of the testator.'

Jackson was silent for a moment. Pennington's words had begun to open up a new vista of possibilities. He asked the lawyer how much 'Margaret's Dowry' would be worth.

'A few hundred pounds at the most, I should have thought,' Pennington replied. 'I know that Sir Nicholas and Mr Garamond went up to Leicestershire to spy out the land, as it were – this was ten or twelve years ago, as I recall. Well, it turned out to be a large tract of scrubland, largely derelict, running up in a kind of ribbon beyond Nuneaton. There was a mass of tangled, overgrown allotments and ruined sheds, so Sir Nicholas told me. I know we're talking about money, Jackson, but there's not much there.'

'Can you give me the name of the relative who made this bequest, sir? It sounds a quirky, eccentric kind of thing to do – to leave land to a young woman provided that she marries by a certain date.'

'It *is* odd, Jackson,' Pennington replied. 'I've no idea who it was who made that bequest, but presumably it was one of the Greggs. The late Lady Waldegrave was one of the Greggs of High Grove, near Nuneaton. However, the matter never came into my hands and the family thought it too trivial to be bothered about. When the bequest was made, Sir Nicholas was still a serving soldier in India and a little firm of lawyers in the Midlands telegraphed the details to him out in Murshidabad.'

'Do you have the address of this firm of solicitors? I'm very interested indeed in this business of "Margaret's Dowry", sir. I think there may be more to it than meets the eye.'

While Jackson was speaking, Pennington had risen from his desk and was rummaging through the contents of a deep drawer in a bureau.

'Ah! Here it is,' he said. 'I know nothing about these people or their clients, or, indeed, whether they're still in practice. But let me write down their name and address. "Henry Gough and Partner, 5 Watergate, Dorridge, Warks". I must confess, I've never heard of the place.'

'Dorridge?' said Jackson. 'Oh, yes, sir, I know it. It's a little place not far from Knowle. I think I'll pay this Mr Henry Gough a visit. But it will have to wait until I've finished my business in London. Once again, sir, thank you for all your help.'

Saul Jackson, hurrying along the crowded thoroughfare of Finsbury Pavement, stole a glance at his companion. Joe Stannard had mellowed since his days as a constable in the Warwick Force. He'd put on weight, but it was all muscle by the looks of things. His florid face told of general good health, as did his relentlessly cheerful manner. Elevation to the rank of detective sergeant three years earlier had allowed him to flaunt his liking for loud check suits, long fawn overcoats and brown bowler hats. That morning he was sporting a half-opened rosebud in his buttonhole.

'Barney Cottle, Saul,' said Detective Sergeant Joseph Stannard of 'G' Division, 'is a regular villain, but he attracts a large clientele. That's because he can lay his hands on enticingly large sums of money at practically no notice, and there are quite a few titled people who are prepared to put up with his little unpleasantnesses to have their needs supplied.'

'Little unpleasantnesses?'

'He calls them his associates. Sammy Wilberforce is a black man, a former boxer who turned to enforcement work. He's a dangerous fellow to cross, and so is the other associate, Sean Molloy. Sean is a fist man, but Sammy favours knives and razors. If a client reneges on his debt, he finds himself in serious trouble. Barney also employs freelance thugs if Sammy and Sean are fully occupied.'

The two men had walked up Moorgate from London Wall, and could glimpse the green oasis of Finsbury Square ahead of them. Jackson had been content to tag along behind his old friend, who had had several pieces of business to transact that morning before taking Jackson to see Barney Cottle. They had started from the divisional headquarters in King's Cross Road, made a foray into Clerkenwell, and thence by cab to a magistrate's office in a dark little street near Holborn Viaduct. There was something relentlessly hard and unyielding, thought Jackson, about London's pavements.

'We turn off here,' said Sergeant Stannard. 'This is Angel Lane.' Jackson found himself entering a narrow winding alley, flanked on both sides by broken-down houses and forlorn shops. The cobbles were slippery with the remains of rotting fruit and vegetables. Although it was a sunny morning, the whole area was enveloped in chimney smoke blown down from a forest of wide, squat stacks rising from the roofs.

At the far end of the lane rose a substantial building of liver-coloured brick. The ground floor was occupied by an undertaker's parlour with a coach-house adjacent. Between the coach-house and the undertaker's premises a substantial wooden door displayed a brass plaque, containing the legend:

Barney Cottle, Commission Agent and Loan Consultant.
Please enter and walk up the stairs.

Yes, thought Jackson, as they mounted the wooden stairs, no doubt those two men lounging insolently on the landing will be Sammy Wilberforce and Sean Molloy. So the idea was to intimidate potential clients with a threat of possible violence before ever they'd entered into negotiations with this Barney Cottle. How would Lance Waldegrave have reacted to those beauties?

'Well, well,' cried Sergeant Stannard, as they arrived on the landing, 'if it isn't Sean Molloy! How are you, Sean? You're looking well. Somebody told me you'd broken your wrist, but I see you only bruised your fingers. And is that Sammy? How are you, Sam? Is Mr Cottle in this morning?'

Both the men had moved themselves away from the wall and looked apprehensively at Stannard. It was evident that they knew him, but it was equally clear that he knew *them*, what they did, and how long they'd languish in gaol if he chose to reveal more than was necessary about their activities.

'Mr Cottle's in his office, Mr Stannard,' said Sean Molloy. 'I'll just tell him you're here—'

'No need to do that,' said Stannard, 'your boss'll be very glad to see us.' He opened the door without knocking, and motioned to Jackson to precede him into the moneylender's den.

Behind a substantial desk cluttered with books and battered money-boxes Jackson saw a genial, balding man wearing round, gold-framed spectacles. He looked extremely respectable and wore a sober, well-cut suit. He treated both men to an affable smile and motioned to a couple of cane-backed chairs drawn up in front of his desk.

'Why, Sergeant Stannard!' he cried. 'How nice to see you! Sit down, won't you? And this gentleman – does he require a loan? I know you'd always recommend me to a potential client.'

'Ha, ha! You will have your little joke, Barney,' said the sergeant, 'but this isn't a morning for jokes. This is Detective Inspector Jackson, of the Warwickshire Constabulary—'

'Ah!'

'Yes, *ah*! He's here making enquiries about a couple of murders out Warwick way and he'd be very happy if you could help him. He knows you've been active in that quarter, Barney – you and the boys out there on the landing. But there, I know you'll want to help him as much as you can. He's all yours, Inspector.'

'Mr Cottle,' said Jackson, 'I'd like you to tell me all about your dealings with the gentleman who is now Sir Lance Waldegrave, of Langley Court, in Warwickshire.'

'Sir Lance Waldegrave,' said Barney, joining his fingertips together judiciously, 'yes, indeed. A most valued client. Gentlemen of his class add tone to my business, you know. Sir Lance has been a client of mine for over two years. We have always worked to each other's advantage—'

'How much does he owe you, Barney?' asked Sergeant Stannard abruptly.

'Well, of course, Sergeant,' Barney replied, 'a client's details are strictly confidential—'

'*How much?*'

'Twelve hundred pounds.'

'A tidy sum,' said Jackson, smiling kindly at the moneylender. 'And has he started to pay any of it back?'

'Oh, yes, Inspector. True, he was a little tardy recently, and I had to send him a sharp reminder, but now that he has come into his inheritance, his situation has changed entirely. He may pay me in any way he wishes, now, without limit of time.'

'I suppose your "sharp reminder" came in the form of those two ruffians on the stairs?' asked Stannard.

'Well, I *did* send them down to Warwickshire, Sergeant,' said Barney, licking his lips nervously, 'and they managed to meet him in a country lane and remonstrate with him. It was a curious coincidence, that …'

'What was a curious coincidence, Mr Cottle?' asked Jackson, before the irrepressible Sergeant Stannard could venture a remark.

Barney Cottle looked undecided. He cradled his chin in his hand for a while and relapsed into thought. Then he evidently made up his mind to speak.

'It's a bit of a roundabout story, gentlemen,' he said, 'but if you'll bear with me for a little while, you'll see where it's leading. Some time in early May this year – I can't recall the exact date – a man came in here to negotiate a modest loan for five hundred pounds. He seemed an eminently respectable person and when I asked him what he wanted the money for – one does that, you know – he told me that he wished to purchase a collection of papers which were coming up for auction at Sotheby's in May. This man gave his name as Major Kirtle Pomeroy, with an address in Cornwall.

'It all seemed above-board, but then he asked me to provide him with an agent to do the bidding in his name. I wondered then whether this Major Pomeroy was as open in his dealings as he appeared. Alarm bells began to ring very faintly, if you know what I mean.'

'We do,' said Sergeant Stannard. 'It takes a rogue to know a rogue. Go on.'

'Ha! Ha! Very witty, Sergeant. But let me continue my story. I was happy to oblige this Major Pomeroy and sent little Nipper Morton to make the bidding. You know Nipper, don't you, Mr Stannard? Cheeky, chirpy little cove with a ginger beard.'

'Yes, I know him. I wish you'd come to the point, Barney, we haven't got all day.'

'Well, when the major had gone, I took the precaution of looking him up in the Army List. He was there, all right, but he had died in 1890 and was buried in Putney Vale Cemetery. So when the so-called major called here to collect his prize, I told him that I didn't like dealing with ghosts and I gave him an honest warning that he'd better pay up on the due date, or face the consequences.'

'Very wise of you, Barney. These papers—'

'They were a collection of learned essays and letters, together with a geological survey of the whole of England, written in 1880, but never published. When little Nipper Morton brought the papers here from Sotheby's, I had a careful look at them. Why not? This Major Pomeroy was a dark horse, and I didn't want to get mixed up in anything illegal. The Calton Papers, that's what they're called. All handwritten stuff. If you care to call on Sotheby's in Wellington Street, Strand, they'll be able to tell you more.'

'And what about this coincidence?' asked Sergeant Stannard. 'Or did you just say that to hold our interest?'

'You'll understand, gentlemen,' said the moneylender, 'that I didn't trust this Major Kirtle Pomeroy as far as I could throw him, and when he left here with the Calton Papers in their nice shiny wooden box, I sent Sean Molloy after him to see what he did. He caught a train to Warwick and changed there to a stopping-train to Abbot's Langley, Sean following him all the time. Well, Sean asked a few harmless questions in one of the local hostelries, and found out that this Major Kirtle Pomeroy was actually a man called Philip Garamond, who lived in a fine white house at the very gates of Langley Court, the residence of Sir Lance Waldegrave, Baronet.'

'Your shady friend Barney Cottle,' said Jackson, when he and Stannard had left the moneylender's premises, 'deserves a medal for public service. I think he's given me the vital clue to the whole business of Arthur Waldegrave's murder. I'll take his advice, Joe, and pay a visit to Sotheby's. I haven't quite got it all together yet, but I'm very near a solution. It was the name Kirtle Pomeroy that did it.'

'What do you mean by that?'

'Well, when I was alone for a while in Sir Nicholas Waldegrave's sitting-room, just after he had been found dead, I picked up an old framed photograph which showed Nicholas as a young man, posing with a friend in the uniform of the Bengal Lancers. There was an inscription which read: *Nicholas with Kirtle Pomeroy at Camp, June 1862.* That's how Garamond came to use that name as an alias. Like me, he'd picked up that photograph on some occasion in the past, looked at it, and subconsciously recorded the unusual name. Then he'd forgotten all about it.'

'So you think that this Philip Garamond murdered Arthur Waldegrave?'

'I don't quite know *what* to think at the moment, Joe. Maybe Mr Garamond was too bashful to admit that he wanted those papers and that he'd taken out a loan in order to get them. And in any case, why on earth should he want to murder his nephew? He doesn't benefit from his death. In any case, I don't see how he could have done it. And you should have seen the state he was in when he met Herbert Bottomley and me in the lane on the day after the murder. He was beside himself with grief. But he's a mystery man, is our Mr Garamond, and I intend to give him my full attention once I get back from London.'

'Talking of mystery men,' said Sergeant Stannard, 'I've been able to run your absconding valet to earth. Jonathan Skinner, gentleman's gentleman, is living at 12 Grosvenor Place, on the other side of Green Park. My constable reported that he's in service there, and goes out openly most days on shopping excursions in the West End. Whatever else he may be, he doesn't seem to be a fugitive, Saul. Maybe it's time you had a word with him face to face.'

As Jackson crossed Green Park and turned into Grosvenor Place, a hansom cab clattered past him and pulled up at the kerb some yards away. The cab doors flew open, and a tall, soberly dressed, round-faced man got out on to the pavement. He paid the cabbie and walked towards the area steps of a very opulent four-storey house.

It was Sir Nicholas Waldegrave's absconding valet, Skinner. On catching sight of Jackson, the valet made no attempt to evade him, but instead walked firmly up to him and raised his bowler hat.

'Inspector Jackson, isn't it?' he said. 'You'd better come this way, sir.'

Jackson followed him down a set of area steps. Skinner opened a glazed door with a latch-key and preceded the inspector into a cheerful basement kitchen. A fire was burning in the grate, and there were a number of different-sized flat-irons on the hob. A host of highly starched collars hung on a clothes-rack and the air smelt of freshly ironed linen. Skinner motioned to a chair by the fire and Inspector Jackson sat down.

'May I ask, sir,' said Skinner, 'whether you were on your way to see me, or whether you saw me just now by accident?'

'Oh, no, it wasn't an accident, Mr Skinner,' Jackson replied. 'As soon as ever I wanted to see you, I alerted those who knew how to find you. The police can do things like that, you see. Find people, I mean.'

Skinner smiled rather nervously, and sat down gingerly opposite the detective, with his hands folded demurely in his lap.

'This house, Mr Jackson,' he said, 'belongs to my master, Mr Julius C. Stanton of New York. Mr Stanton is a very wealthy man – very wealthy indeed. He has interests in railways – "railroads" he calls them – and timber, mining and all kinds of land in the United States. Mr Stanton comes to Europe for six months each year, and I always accompany him. I have been his personal valet for eight years.'

Skinner still found it difficult to look Jackson in the face and still spoke in the low, rather unctuous tones that he had employed at Langley Court. But whatever story he was telling, the inspector was suddenly convinced that what he was saying was true.

'We came over to England early in March and stayed for a few days at a hotel in Leeds, where Mr Stanton had some business to transact. It was there that he met another gentleman, a Mr Gregg, who told him about Sir Nicholas Waldegrave, an invalid who needed a good valet until September, when the new one he had engaged would be free. Mr Stanton asked me whether I would be prepared to step in at short notice in order to oblige this Mr Gregg. Whatever I earned there I could keep, he said, over and above my normal wages.'

'So, naturally, you agreed.'

'I did, sir. You see, Mr Stanton never tells his servants to do things. He always *asks*, and, of course, you never refuse. And that was how I came to be with Sir Nicholas at Langley Court when all the trouble started.'

'Well, now,' said Jackson, 'thank you very much, Mr Skinner, for telling me all this. But what made you bolt for it, if I may put it that way? If you'd done nothing wrong, you'd nothing to fear.'

Skinner glanced briefly at Jackson and then away again. His face assumed a look of sullen rancour.

'They never liked me – the other servants, I mean. I didn't fit in to their cosy little rustic kingdom. I could have told them ever so many interesting things about our travels all over the world. But no. They didn't speak to me, so I didn't speak to them, except for young Williams, one of the footmen, who wanted to train as a valet. He was a nice young fellow. Sir Nicholas appreciated me, that I *do* know. He gave me a pair of silver cuff-links at Easter. But the others ...'

'But what exactly was it that made you run away?' Jackson prompted. Skinner seemed not to hear him.

'Mr Lincoln was the worst. If the butler doesn't take to you you're finished in service. All he liked was to sit supping tea with that numskull Cundlett with his poems and his platitudes. Mr Lincoln found me looking at some of the books in Mr Arthur's study one day and spoke to me as though I was a stable-boy.'

His voice rose to a petulant whine.

'Mr Stanton gives his servants the freedom of the house! He doesn't think we're out to steal his things just because we're standing in his rooms!'

Suddenly he gave a rather shame-faced laugh as he became aware of the inspector waiting patiently for him to finish his story.

'So, Inspector, I was always ill at ease, as you'll understand. But there was something sinister about that house. There were shadows there, Mr Jackson, a sense of evil.... I suppose you think I'm being foolish?'

'No, Mr Skinner, as a matter of fact I don't. I know just what you mean. I felt it, too. Shadows ...'

'Yes, sir. Well, on the day Sir Nicholas died, I had come in from the vestibule into his sitting-room, and was standing at the far end of the room near the bay window. There were things I had to put out on a table for Sir Nicholas there. I couldn't see anything from where I was, but I could hear a lot, if you understand me.

'Well, to cut a long story short, Mr Lance and the young nurse – I forget her name – came into the sitting-room from Sir Nicholas's bedroom. When Mr Lance saw me there he said to the nurse, "Come out into the vestibule", and they went out through the sitting-room door. I hope this is all clear to you, sir?'

'It is, Mr Skinner. Please continue.'

'Wondering what was amiss, I hurried into Sir Nicholas's bedroom to investigate, glanced at the bed, and saw immediately that he was dead. Oh dear, what a shock it was! He'd been very kind, and was a proper gentleman of the old school. The first thing that came to my mind was, what if there's been foul play here, like with Mr Arthur? *I* would be the one who would be accused, the stranger within the gates....

'And so I "bolted", as you put it. I panicked, you see. I did my duty and broke the news and then I threw some things into my bag and fled. I came straight here, to Grosvenor Place, and told my story to Mr Stanton. He was furious. He told me to stay here until he returned from Amsterdam – that's where he is now – and that when he returned he would "blow everyone up", as he put it. But now you've found me, Mr Jackson, that won't be necessary.'

Skinner rose and opened a drawer in a tall dresser.

'Naturally, you'll want to see my references—'

The inspector held up his hand and shook his head.

'Not at all, Mr Skinner, that won't be necessary. I believe everything you've told me so far. But you've not yet told me the whole story, have you? I venture to suggest that you saw something else while you were standing at that table in the sitting-room. I'm right, aren't I?'

The valet shifted uneasily in his chair, and a curious hunted look came into his eyes. When he spoke, he was quite unable to conceal his nervous anxiety.

'Are you stating that as a fact, Mr Jackson, or is it only surmise?'

'It's only surmise, Mr Skinner, but if I'm right, then I want you to tell me what it was that you saw. However serious it is, it will be a fast secret between you and me. I suspect that what you haven't yet told me is the true reason why you abandoned all your possessions and fled the house. Will you tell me?'

'I will, Mr Jackson,' said Skinner, and there was relief in his voice. 'I'm as anxious as you are to see this matter brought to a conclusion and the wicked murder of Sir Nicholas avenged. When I fled from Langley Court, I was fleeing for my life.

'As I told you, I was standing by the little table near the bay window and although I said that I couldn't see anything from there, that was not true. I could, in fact, see through the open door leading into Sir Nicholas's bedroom. I am a silent man by training, Mr Jackson, and I stand still when I am performing a task, so that sometimes people are not aware that I am, in fact, in a room at all. That was certainly the case on that terrible 18 June.'

'So what happened, Mr Skinner?'

'I turned my gaze through that open door into the bedroom, Mr Jackson, and I saw ...'

'Yes, what did you see?' prompted Jackson urgently.

'Have you a notebook, Mr Jackson? If so, I think you should take down in writing what I'm about to tell you. You see, I looked through that open door and I saw Sir Nicholas Waldegrave being murdered.'

13

—•—

Margaret's Dowry

For what he hoped would be a brief sojourn in London, Jackson had asked to be accommodated in the section house attached to the headquarters of 'G' Division in King's Cross Road. Section houses provided living quarters for unmarried police officers and possessed all the Spartan austerity of army barracks. Sergeant Stannard had arranged for him to occupy one of the empty rooms, a sort of monastic cell, which contained a bed, a fold-down table and an upright chair. Still, it would only be for a couple of nights and then he would return to the comparative luxuries of the provincial Warwickshire Force.

Following Barney Cottle's advice, Jackson had called upon one of the directors of Sotheby's in Wellington Street and had learnt that the Calton Papers had been put up for sale by Mrs Catherine Dashkoff, the married daughter of the late Sir George Calton. He was told that the Dashkoffs lived at Highgate, and the ever-helpful Sergeant Stannard took him to Finsbury Square and made sure that he boarded one of the dark green 'Favorite' omnibuses that would take him, for a fare of threepence, to the Archway Tavern.

A short walk from the busy Highgate terminus brought Jackson to the quiet, tree-lined avenue in which Mr and Mrs Dashkoff resided. Their two-storey villa of mellow red brick stood at the far end of a long, overgrown garden. The front door was wide open and he could hear the exuberant tones of an Italian tenor rendering a passionate aria, his voice captured, presumably, on one of the cylinders of a phonograph.

Jackson pulled the bell-handle and in a few moments a woman in a long, flowered smock appeared. Her hair was confined in a kind of turban fashioned from a towel, and she was holding a sweeping-broom.

'Yes? Who shall I say it is?' she asked, and at the same moment a woman's voice from somewhere inside the house cried, 'Who is it, Mrs Tandy?' The Italian tenor was abruptly annihilated in mid-note as somebody turned off the phonograph.

'Will you tell Mrs Dashkoff that Detective Inspector Jackson has called to see her? It's to do with the Calton Papers.'

Mrs Tandy left the inspector where he was and went into a room on the far side of the hall, closing the door behind her. Jackson glanced around him. It was a spacious hall, with a fine oak staircase winding up to the first floor. The coconut matting was littered with wood shavings, evidently thrown out from a number of packing-cases cluttering the space near the front door. A stuffed bear snarled at Jackson in frustrated silence from a gloomy alcove. The air was pervaded by a strong smell of oil paint.

A moment later Mrs Tandy reappeared, her pattens clacking on the tiles. She ushered Jackson into a pleasant sunny room, announced him and returned to the hall. The room had evidently been the library of the house. Most of the tiers of open shelves had been denuded of their books and another woman in a flowered smock, who was perched precariously on top of a step-ladder, paused, feather duster in hand, to look down at the visitor. A cloud of recently disturbed dust hovered in the air.

'A police inspector? Dear me, how fascinating!' said the lady on the ladder. She had a pale, narrow, intelligent face, framed in a riot of Pre-Raphaelite auburn hair, a style which Jackson considered too young for her. 'As you may have guessed, I'm Catherine Dashkoff, and the man in the window bay is my husband, Mr Dashkoff.'

'Pleased to meet you, sir and madam,' said Jackson. 'The reason I've called today—'

'We're what you might call one of the "new couples",' Mrs Dashkoff continued. She remained perched on top of the ladder, duster in hand. 'Nineties folk, unfettered by the stifling proprieties of an age that is passing away. Aren't we, Serge?'

Serge Dashkoff, also smocked and sporting an untamed black beard, stood at an easel, dabbing viciously at a canvas. It was from Serge, presumably, that the pervading odour of oil paint and turpentine emanated. He uttered an indeterminate noise and continued painting.

'I think I am entitled to describe myself as a poetess,' Mrs Dashkoff said. 'I've had a number of poems published in the better periodicals, and am thus encouraged to work on my magnum opus, which is an epic poem about Boadicea, written in rhyming couplets. It's coming on quite well, isn't it, Serge?'

'My reason for calling on you today—'

'Inspector, why don't you sit down? You're starting to look rather untidy, you know. That's right.' Mrs Dashkoff surveyed the half-empty shelves from the heights of her step-ladder. 'This was my father's library,' she said. 'As you can see, it's still in the process of being denuded of all its books. They've already carried off the geological specimens to the Royal Geographical Society – haven't they, Serge?'

'Hum,' Serge replied. He was now grasping a paintbrush between his teeth, while he attacked his canvas with a spatula.

'He was eighty-two,' Mrs Dashkoff continued, 'which was a good age. They said he had stone-dust in his lungs, on account of all that chipping away at rocks that he did. So what is it that you want to know, Inspector?'

'I should very much like to know, ma'am, about the various documents that made up the collection known as the Calton Papers. What exactly were they? It's in connection with a case that I am pursuing in Warwickshire.'

'Ah! I wondered whether you were from the provinces, Inspector,' said Mrs Dashkoff, beginning a careful descent from the step-ladder. 'My husband needs a new studio with a proper north light – don't you, Serge? Well, I got the idea of bundling together some of Father's private papers, laying them between tissue paper in a nice box, and having them auctioned at Sotheby's. I was hoping for two hundred pounds, but in the event we got five. Splendid! So now we'll have a new studio built here in the grounds for my husband.'

'And these papers—'

Mr Serge Dashkoff threw his brush down on to the palette and strode from the easel into the room, wiping his hands on a paint-stained cloth.

'You'd better let me tell you about the Calton Papers, Mr Jackson,' he said, in a loud baritone voice. 'Catherine, sit down and be quiet. My late father-in-law was a very clever man, who knew all kinds of important people. The collection that my wife made included a goodly number of letters which Sir George received from various notables over the last fifty years which are very interesting. But the really valuable items are Sir George's unpublished account of Charles Darwin's journey to the South Seas in the *Beagle*, and a geological survey of the whole of England, which he completed in 1880. It was supposed to be published, but never was. And that, Jackson, is the Calton Papers.'

'Thank you very much, sir,' said Jackson. 'I find that my professional interest is beginning to centre on this geological survey. Could you tell me a little more about it?'

'Sir George Calton was very proud of that survey,' Dashkoff replied. 'He had trekked all over England in order to compile it, and had made many discoveries that would have been of great use to mining engineers and the like. He was a geologist, you see, so his interests were in mineral deposits of all kinds – iron ores, coal, copper seams – all that kind of thing. He had a nose for things like that. More than one interested party came to visit him in order to consult his great geological survey.'

Mrs Dashkoff, who had listened to her husband with absorbed interest, ventured a few words.

'Some of his cronies from the New Clarendon Club would come here to visit and they'd be closeted here in the library for hours, drinking port and poring over Father's great manuscript. He wrote everything by hand, you know: he wouldn't use a type-writer. What was the name of that pleasant, humorous man who used to call? He was last here about eighteen months ago. I remember that he made lots of notes on a pad that he'd brought with him for the purpose. He also brought Father a very fine bottle of claret. Maybe that's why I remember him so well. Father seemed flattered by his attentions, didn't he, Serge?'

'That was a man called Philip Garamond,' Serge replied. 'He was a botanist, I believe, but he had an amateur's enthusiasm for geology. Well, I hope we've helped you, Inspector. I really must get back to my painting, now. If you want to examine the papers yourself, you'll need to find the man who bought them – a fellow called Major Kirtle Pomeroy. He purchased them through an intermediary so I'm told. Mrs Dashkoff and I have never actually seen him.'

Oh, yes you have, thought Jackson. But when you saw him, he was using his real name of Philip Garamond who thought the geological survey so vital to some hidden purpose of his own, that he was prepared to go into debt to a dangerous loan-shark in order to get it for himself.

Did he need to ask himself why Garamond wanted the Calton Papers so desperately? No, Garamond's purposes were becoming clearer as day succeeded day. It was imperative now that he and Sergeant Bottomley should begin the inevitable frustration of Garamond's plans. But first, there were two more people in Warwickshire to interview. He would give them his full attention as soon as arrived back from London.

*

Dr John Murray, the much-respected physician of the little agri-cultural town of Sheriff's Langley, came in from his dispensary and sat down behind his desk. It had been a busy morning as he had kept open house for the poorer folk of the parish. In a minute or two, at 11.30, a Detective Inspector Jackson from Warwick would be calling to see him – ah! This sounded like him, now.

The door of the surgery opened and a comfortable, settled kind of man came into the room. He must be in his late forties, thought Dr Murray, but he's a bit heavy for his height, and that incipient double chin suggests that he eats rather more than is good for him. That brown, three-piece suit, with its array of gold watch-chain and seals, and the high-crowned blocker he's wearing make him look more like a corn factor than a police officer.

'Detective Inspector Jackson? Sit down, won't you? I'm Dr Murray. What can I do for you?'

'Well, Doctor,' said Jackson, settling himself on a chair near the desk, 'I'm investigating the murders that have taken place recently at Langley Court. I expect you've heard about them?'

'I have. Dreadful! But I'm afraid I know nothing about the matter, Inspector.'

'No, sir. But you *do* know something about the murder of Mr Jabez Beecham in 1889, as you were still physician here at Sheriff's Langley and I imagine Mr Jabez Beecham was one of your patients.'

Jackson knew from experience that doctors could get very huffy when lay-folk started asking questions that might breach profes-sional confidentiality. He saw at once that he'd have no trouble of that kind with this man in his late sixties, whose face bore many creases around the eyes and mouth born of good humour.

'Yes, indeed, Inspector,' said Murray, reclining in his chair, 'old Jabez was one of my patients. He was in very good health physi-cally for his age, so I wasn't often summoned to Horton Grange.

It was mainly a bit of chest trouble, the occasional bout of fever – things like that. And then, of course, he was murdered – or so they said.'

Jackson sat up in his chair.

'What do you mean by that, sir? "Or so they said"?'

Dr Murray laughed and treated Jackson to a rather rueful smile.

'Well, of course, you'll have been told all about the murder, won't you? Have you talked to old Pendle, who was the constable here in 1889? Of course you have. As soon as I heard of the murder, I hurried over to Horton Grange, but the police surgeon was already there – a pompous ass if ever there was one, who dismissed me as a mere country quack. He'd established that Jabez had died of cyanide poisoning and various bits of evidence at the scene pointed to murder. So it *was* murder. But I've always had my doubts.'

'But if it wasn't murder, sir, what was it?'

'Suicide, of course. I'd been waiting for poor Jabez to do away with himself for more than a year. He was suffering from acute depression, Inspector – he used to call it "that old devil". "That old devil will get me, one of these days", he'd say, meaning, of course, that his depression would lead him to suicide.'

Jackson suddenly recalled PC Pendle's account of a visit to Horton Grange when Jabez Beecham had used that very expression. 'If I'm not careful,' he'd said, 'the old devil will do for me one of these days.' Depression.... And suicide.

'But the glass containing the poison was found in another room.'

'So it was. And there was another glass there, too. So if I'm right, and poor old Jabez poisoned himself, then someone else present in the house decided to make it look like murder.'

'And why should he do that, sir?'

Dr Murray laughed and wagged an admonitory finger at Jackson.

'Come, come, Inspector,' he said, 'I'm no detective, just a poor, humble sawbones. If somebody made that suicide look like murder, it's *your* task to find out who that person was and why he did it!'

'Well, yes, sir,' said Jackson, smiling, 'but as a matter of fact, I already know who it was, and why he did it. All you've done is very kindly provided me with confirmation of what I strongly suspected to be the truth.'

When Jackson arrived at 5 Watergate, in the little Warwickshire village of Dorridge, he saw the dull brass plate, almost entirely hidden by ivy, beside the front door. 'Henry Gough and Partner, Solicitors', he read. This was the little country legal practice that had handled the details of what had come to be called Margaret's Dowry, twenty years earlier. An elderly maid admitted him to the little red-brick cottage, and ushered him into the presence of an old gentleman, who was sitting in a high wing chair near the fire. Jackson watched him as he peered at his warrant card. This man was over eighty, to judge from his frail appearance. Would he be able to recall the events of twenty years ago?

'Detective Inspector Jackson,' said the old man, in a high, quavering voice, 'sit down, won't you? My name's Simpson, and I'm the Partner whose name used to appear on our stationery. Henry Gough is long dead and I'm long retired. I expect you want to ask me about Margaret's Dowry?'

'Why, sir,' Jackson exclaimed, 'how on earth did you know that?'

The old solicitor treated him to a sly, amused smile, but refused to give a direct answer to the question.

'We lawyers have our mysterious ways, Inspector. Margaret's Dowry.... I expect you know the details? We drew up the codicil to a will – this was in 1874 – when Miss Margaret Waldegrave was an infant aged four. She was to be left the title to a parcel of land in Leicestershire, provided that she married before her twenty-fifth birthday. If she failed to do so, the land would pass to her brother Arthur, but if the said Arthur died before 18 October in this current year, 1894, then it would all pass to Philip Garamond, Esquire.'

'And can you tell me who made the bequest, and why?' asked Jackson. 'It may be relevant to my investigation.'

The old man laughed, and gazed absently at the flames leaping in the fire. He was recalling something from his younger days. Jackson was content to wait.

'The testator was an eccentric unmarried lady, Miss Hortensia Padgett, who lived not far from here at Knowle. She was well-to-do by most people's standards, but hardly an heiress, in the practical meaning of that word. She was a woman who went around doing good, being kind to the poor, that kind of thing. Very tiresome. She was well over sixty when she came to see Henry Gough and me; she was wearing a very girlish sprig muslin dress and one of those big round peasant hats.'

The old man lapsed into silence, an amused smile playing around his lips.

'Why did she leave that parcel of land to Miss Margaret Waldegrave?'

'What? Well, you see, when she was young, she was jilted – is that the right word? – let down by a fellow who said he was going to marry her. He changed his mind, you see. Lucky escape there, I should have thought – for him, I mean. She was one of those Padgetts who are related to the Greggs of Nuneaton, and therefore to the Waldegraves of Warwickshire. When Miss Margaret was born, Hortensia Padgett conceived the idea of leaving her a piece of land, provided that Margaret married before her twenty-fifth birthday. I think the idea was to encourage Margaret to "get her man", if you'll pardon the vulgar expression, before it was too late. We both thought it was howlingly absurd, you know, and rather vulgar, but we did it. We charged her four guineas as I recall, and she paid up without demur.'

'And what happened next, Mr Simpson?' asked Jackson.

'Happened? Well, Miss Padgett died in 1879, her will was proved, and we wrote to Sir Nicholas Waldegrave informing him that his daughter Margaret had inherited that bit of land. He wrote back, we filed his letter, and that was the end of the matter.'

The old lawyer chuckled, and looked at Jackson with a gleam of humour in his old eyes.

'I'll tell you how I guessed what you'd come about, Mr Jackson,' he said. 'I had another man here only last week asking the same questions. I gave him the same answers, and he went away evidently satisfied.'

Jackson hazarded a guess.

'Was the man who called last week Mr Philip Garamond?'

'Garamond? Well, it's a good guess, Inspector, but no, it wasn't Garamond. It was a man called Brassington, principal of James Brassington & Co., Steam and Gas Engineers, of Birmingham. He was trying to find out who actually owned Margaret's Dowry at this present moment. I told him that I didn't know, which is true, because of course I *don't* know, having no longer any contact with the Waldegrave family, who were never our clients in any case. Perhaps you should go up to Birmingham and have a word with this man. Big, red-faced kind of fellow: James Brassington.'

'Outside the confines of the British Empire,' said Mr James Brassington, 'the world's in a mess. A mess!'

'I'm sure you're right,' Inspector Jackson replied. Brassington, stocky, red-faced and inclined to belligerence, was the kind of man it was best to agree with.

Jackson and Brassington were closeted in the mahogany inner office of James Brassington & Co., Steam and Gas Engineers, in a thriving, smoky, manufacturing district of Birmingham. Mr Brassington radiated energy and restlessness, and looked ill at ease sitting at his desk, as though he would like to have been out among the hands in one of the yards flanking the works buildings.

'Yes,' the engineer continued, 'it's a mess. Look at Germany. Lots of sabre-rattling there, if I'm not mistaken. Bad for business. And France – well, what's brewing there, I'd like to know? But you didn't come here today to talk trade, so what exactly can I do for you, Inspector Jackson? I've some men coming from the Sheffield Steam Traction Company at half past ten, so I can give you half an hour.'

'What I'd like to know, Mr Brassington,' said Jackson, 'is why you were enquiring about a piece of lawyer's-work called "Margaret's Dowry". You called on a Mr Simpson, solicitor, at Dorridge last week. Of course, you're not obliged to tell me—'

'Why shouldn't I?' the engineer interrupted. 'It's not a secret. Yes, I saw old Simpson, and he was able to tell me more or less what I wanted to know.'

'And what *did* you want to know, sir?'

'Let me answer you by telling you what this business is all about. There's a consortium of businessmen based in London and Birmingham who are looking at all unclaimed and undeveloped bits of land on the edges of the Midlands coalfields. This consortium asked me for help in tracking down the legal owners of some of these bits of land – in many cases, you see, records have been lost. They asked me, because they know that I've many contacts in local government and the law, and that I can often oblige other businesses with my expertise. Of course, I get a commission for my trouble, which is only right and proper.'

'Absolutely,' said Jackson. 'And this bit of land called Margaret's Dowry is one of these special bits of land?'

'It is. They've been doing test-bores there, on the edge of the coalfield, and they've determined that there are massive new seams of prime coal under that land. One of the consortium members – never mind who – paid a discreet visit to the Land Registry and found out that the whole area had been willed to this young lady called Margaret Waldegrave, and then to her brother Arthur. One way or another, Mr Jackson, a certain as yet undetermined member of that family is about to become rich!'

'And could you give me an idea of how rich, Mr Brassington?' asked Jackson.

'We're speaking of potential fortunes here, Mr Jackson,' the engineer replied. 'Hundreds of thousands of pounds. Once the ownership of this "Margaret's Dowry" is legally established – and my own lawyers will see to that aspect of the business – the consortium will offer thirty thousand pounds cash down for the land. If that isn't a fortune, then I don't know what is!'

'So there, at last, Sergeant,' said Inspector Jackson, 'we have a credible motive for the murder of Mr Arthur Waldegrave, a murder plotted very carefully, probably conceived five years ago, and then refined over the course of the last year. The murderer was his doting uncle, Mr Philip Garamond, whose motive for murdering him was thirty thousand pounds.

'Margaret's Dowry was treated as a joke in the family, but Garamond knew its great potential. He also knew all the details of the family wills. Why shouldn't he? He was always regarded as a member of the family. The dowry would come to Margaret if she was married before her twenty-fifth birthday on 16 October this year. If she was still unmarried by then, it would revert to Arthur. If Arthur was dead, and Margaret still unmarried in October, then the dowry went to Philip Garamond.'

'So what it boils down to, sir,' said Bottomley, 'is this. First, prevent Margaret from marrying by depicting her fiancé as a killer, then get rid of Arthur by murdering him and portraying him as her fiancé's victim. Why should Garamond want all that money?'

'Who knows, Sergeant? Perhaps he has a secret plan to found a botanical institute with himself as director. Perhaps he wants to travel the world, visiting all the great gardens and plant collections in the different countries. Or perhaps he just lusted after money, so that he could at least begin to approach the wealth of the Waldegraves. Whatever his motive, he murdered Arthur Waldegrave to procure that fortune. I'm quite sure of it.'

'Why did he want to buy that collection of old documents? He put himself in debt to a moneylender to achieve that little ambition.'

'He was by way of being a friend of the late Sir George Calton, Sergeant, and visited him occasionally at his house in Highgate. It was there that he saw the manuscript survey of England's mineral deposits, and I'll hazard a guess that it showed the presence of vast high quality coal deposits under Margaret's strip of land. When Calton died, Garamond was anxious to buy the whole collection of papers so that the geological survey would never see the light of day.

'He was playing for time, you see. Everything had to be in order before the 16 October – Margaret prevented from marrying before her birthday, Arthur dead, and no knowledge of the true value of the dowry leaking out before Garamond had positioned himself as the legitimate heir.'

'When we first met Mr Garamond, sir,' said Bottomley, 'he was beside himself with grief. He was demented, to put it mildly.'

'He was demented, Sergeant, because he'd been overcome with a kind of self-regarding remorse that unsettled his wits. He couldn't forget poor Arthur's sudden appearance, rolling out in his flaming chair, dead, on to the little landing-stage, seemingly emerging from the flames to accuse him. I expect he still sees that horrible image in his dreams. But he wasn't too frantic, Sergeant, to begin his incrimination of Jeremy Beecham while he was still talking to us about his sorrow and grief.'

'We'll have to make a move very soon, sir,' said Bottomley. 'But there's quite a bit remaining for us to do first.'

'Yes, you're right. So let's divide our labours. It's time for me to make a discreet search of Garamond's house and all those glasshouses nestling in the trees of the grove. You know what I'll be looking for. As for you, I want you to finish off your little enterprise in Ancaster. Did you write to Canon Parrish?'

'I did, sir, and he wrote back to say that there's no need for a special licence, as both parties are orphans at law, and over the age of sixteen. He'll perform the ceremony himself in the town church of St Edmund at the Gate, at any time without notice.'

'I liked that man,' said Jackson. 'He was the voice of sanity among a lot of very self-deluded people. I'll always remember the help he gave us in solving the murder of Dean Girdlestone."

Jackson took his watch from his waistcoat pocket, and flipped open the lid. 'It's just after six,' he said, glancing at the office clock on the wall. 'That clock's two minutes fast. Time for us to go home. But early tomorrow, which is Saturday and the last day of June, we'll start to put things in train. Another few days should see the end of this sad business.'

* *The Ancaster Demons*

181

14

The End of Mr Grimes

Herbert Bottomley sat at the kitchen table and watched Miss Cecily Hargreaves shelling peas into an enamel colander. Various savoury smells wafted across the spacious room from an array of copper pans simmering on the range. Behind the smell of boiling mutton and Savoy cabbage he could just detect the perfume of lavender making its persuasive entrance through the open windows.

Cecily Hargreaves, the Lavender Lady, was sitting bolt upright in a tall, carved chair. As always, she wore black, and her gold pince-nez gleamed on the bridge of her nose. She's haughty and commanding in appearance, thought Bottomley, but this lady has a heart of boundless sympathy and concern for the fate of unfortunate girls who have fallen from grace. It was that sympathy, allied to practical kindness, he supposed, that gave her the ability to radiate calm and peace wherever she was, but especially there, in her light and spacious house. It was refreshing just to sit quiet for a while, and join in the companionable silence.

Beside Miss Hargreaves, sitting on a low stool, was Mary Connor, hemming some kitchen towels. She plied her needle with a steady hand and looked as though she had lived in the house for years. Her black hair was drawn back into a demure bun, and she was wearing a pale-blue dress over which she had tied a white linen apron. She looked very different from the girl with a face as white as chalk, who had wept and trembled at the contemplation of her total ruin. That had been in the Railway Arms at Copton Vale on the fifth, over three weeks ago.

Bottomley glanced out of the window into the quiet yard bordering the lavender garden. Young Steven Beamish, fruit porter, was carefully washing the side panels of Cecily's town carriage. He'd said that he was going to marry Mary Connor and look after her baby, too; well, he looked like the kind of lad who meant what he said....

'Mary,' said Miss Cecily Hargreaves, 'would you go upstairs for a moment and see how our guest is? Stay with her for a while, if you think it will help.'

'Yes, Miss Hargreaves.'

The girl rose from her stool, gave the lady of the house a brilliant smile, and left the room. Miss Hargreaves put the colander of shelled peas down on the table, and wiped her hands on a cloth.

'She's only in her first month, Herbert,' she said without preamble, 'so the birth will not take place until next March. But I shall keep her here with me all that time and teach her housecraft. She loves the country, you know. She's so happy here that the thought of going back to Copton Vale depresses her.'

'How is she coping with your guest? It was a good idea of yours to call Miss Waldegrave that, ma'am.'

'It's a sensible precaution, Herbert. A lot of people come and go here. If no one hears a name spoken, no one can retail gossip. As for Mary, well, she was very timid at first, as is understandable, but she's very much more at ease now. In some way they're like sisters. Adversity makes strange bedfellows, as someone once said.'

Miss Hargreaves glanced out of the window for a moment and then continued to talk to Bottomley.

'That young man Beamish loves it here, too; he comes whenever he can get time off from his work in the market. He's making himself alarmingly useful around the house and garden. What a fine boy he is! They'll make an attractive couple. I've persuaded them to marry in the autumn before Mary's condition begins to show more than is wise. Mr Parry, our rector, will perform the ceremony very nicely, and without fuss.'

Herbert Bottomley cleared his throat, and gave vent to a very cryptic remark.

'House parlour-maid, and coachman. All we lack is a butler.'

Cecily Hargreaves drew in her breath sharply and sat up in her chair.

'Herbert,' she said in a half whisper, 'you've seen the end of it all, haven't you? I wondered, you know…. So it's to be like that? Oh dear, God help them all!'

The door opened and Mary Connor came back into the kitchen.

'Our guest seems much better this morning, ma'am,' she said. 'I've settled her into a chair, and tidied her hair a little. I think she'll want to see Mr Bottomley now.'

When Sergeant Bottomley had left the kitchen, Mary Connor resumed her work. After a moment she looked up at Cecily Hargreaves, and said, 'Mr Bottomley was my good angel. He came just in time, you know. I was going to throw myself into the River Best.'

'Don't talk nonsense, child,' said Miss Hargreaves, robustly. 'You'd have done nothing of the sort – and if you had, someone would have rescued you straight away, you silly girl.' Mary smiled, and resumed her work of hemming towels. After a moment Miss Hargreaves said, 'But you're right about Herbert Bottomley. He *is* like a guardian angel. I could tell you many tales of people he's rescued from danger and despair.'

Sergeant Bottomley mounted the stairs, knocked at a door at the end of the passage and entered a bedroom at the rear of the house, overlooking the lavender garden. Margaret Waldegrave, pale and drawn, started up from the chair in which she was sitting near the open window.

'Oh! Mr Bottomley! I thought you'd never come. What is happening? It's over a week since you rescued me from that – that nightmare at Horton Grange. Miss Hargreaves is very kind, but she tells me nothing. What am I to do? I've lost the man I hoped to marry – have you found him yet? My brother Lance, I find, got this poor girl Mary into trouble and refused to help her. Only a few weeks ago I was the lady of the manor and Mary was a lost soul. Now we're like sisters – both betrayed by the men we loved. Oh, what's to become of me? Does Aunt Letty know where I am? What—'

Herbert Bottomley drew up a chair beside Margaret's and sat down. He placed a big hand over hers and regarded her gravely with his rather fine grey eyes. She suddenly stemmed her flow of words, and looked at him expectantly.

'Miss Margaret,' said Bottomley, 'you and I have been allies ever since you found that tin box with the cyanide bottle inside it, so I think that you'll trust me to do what's right in this terrible business of murder. I'm going to talk to you very frankly, miss, and if you think I'm being too familiar, I'd better tell you that I have eight daughters, all living. Two are married, two are in service, and the other four are still at home with the wife and me. Maybe it's having that little tribe of girls that makes me talk to you in this way.'

Margaret relaxed in her chair, some of the restless anxiety fading from her eyes. Bottomley gently removed his hand from over hers, then began to talk in a quiet, grave voice. His soft Warwickshire accent held its own soothing quality.

'I'm afraid, my dear,' he said, 'that there's more sorrow for you in the offing. I'd be failing in my duty to you if I didn't warn you of that fact.'

'What do you mean?' Margaret whispered.

'I mean that, very soon, you will find yourself almost entirely on your own, with your own way to make in the world. Your time at Langley Court has come to an end. I can't tell you more than that at present, but what I've said to you is true. This quiet, healing house of Miss Cecily Hargreaves is like a staging-post from which you'll move on to a new life elsewhere.'

'I wondered myself, after Father died, whether my time at home was over,' said Margaret in a low voice. 'A staging-post? Yes, I can see that that could well be true. But where am I to go? What am I to do?'

'My advice to you, Miss Margaret,' said Bottomley, with the ghost of a twinkle in his eye, 'would be to get married just as soon as you possibly can. That would go a long way to solving your problems.'

'Are you mad?' cried Margaret hotly. '*Marry*? The only man I want to marry is Jeremy Beecham—'

'Then marry him!'

'But he's a murderer! I can't believe that I'm hearing you aright. Am I dreaming? He murdered his uncle, Jabez Beecham—'

'He did not, miss. Jabez Beecham committed suicide. You and Jeremy have been caught up in a devilish plot hatched by a man who is either wicked, mad, or both. There's a lot that you don't know, and this, I'm afraid, is not the time for me to enlighten you.'

Margaret shook her head in disbelief.

'But Jeremy confessed to me, Mr Bottomley; he confessed to those murders and, but for your intervention, he would have murdered me, too!'

'Listen, Margaret,' said Bottomley, earnestly. 'Jeremy Beecham did *not* confess to you. And at no time were you really in danger from him. If I wanted, I could tell you what that so-called confession of his meant – yes, I know what he said, because he told me all about it, later! But it wouldn't be right for me to act as his interpreter. If you want to know what that confession meant, then you must ask him yourself.'

'Are you saying that Jeremy was innocent all along?' Margaret cried. 'That he didn't poison his uncle, or murder poor Arthur? Oh, what have you done with him? You're right, dear Mr

Bottomley, I must see him as soon as possible. They were all wrong about him – poor, dear Uncle Philip and that hateful man Grimes in the gas-house – and *me*! Oh, Mr Bottomley, where is he?'

'He's in Ancaster, miss, and I want you to go there with me this very day. Miss Hargreaves knows all about it and she'll speed you on your way. And on Monday of next week, miss, you must marry Mr Jeremy Beecham in the church of St Edward at the Gate, in Ancaster. I will give you away – begging pardon for being so presumptuous – and your maid of honour will be your aunt, Miss Letitia Waldegrave.'

'I'm bewildered, Mr Bottomley. Are you being serious? Yes, I suppose you must be—'

'I'm in deadly earnest, Miss Margaret. There's a vital reason for your getting married so soon, but now is not the time to discuss it. You will be lodged in the house of Canon Parrish, a gentleman very well known to Inspector Jackson and me, a married man with daughters of his own. You will find your aunt, Miss Letitia Waldegrave, there, too. Will you trust me, miss, and do as I suggest?'

'I will,' said Margaret, with sudden decisiveness. 'If what you say is true, Mr Bottomley, then you have given me new hope for the future. Let us go now, at once, to Ancaster.'

While Sergeant Bottomley was talking to Margaret in the Lavender Lady's house, Inspector Jackson was entering the grove of oaks which formed part of Philip Garamond's demesne. He came in from the little hamlet at the summit of the hill and made his way slowly down the winding path which would take him to the handsome white dwelling known as the cottage.

Philip Garamond, he knew, had left for London earlier that morning on business of his own. It was cool under the shade of the oaks and the grove was pervaded with the aromatic perfumes of wild flowers and exuberant giant ferns. Presently, a long line of glasshouses came into view to his right; it was to these that he made his way, a set of pick-locks in his hand.

He would search the cottage last, because he considered Garamond to be too shrewd a man to leave the box containing the Calton Papers where it could be so easily found; no, he would be more likely to conceal it somewhere in this long line of well-tended and well-preserved glasshouses, his pride and joy.

There were five in all. When Jackson entered the first of them, using his pick-locks, he was assailed by a blast of hot air, which bore the heavy, heady perfumes of a riot of exotic blooms. He found nothing of significance there, nor in the next three glasshouses, all of which, he saw, were connected together by heating-pipes, running in brick conduits built among the riot of ferns in the grove.

The final glasshouse, the one nearest to the cottage, contained another fine collection of rare plants, all of which evidently thrived on the heat of the sun radiating from the glass roof, but here, too, the heating-pipes were going at full blast. Jackson wondered whether he would faint from heat stroke before he'd even begun his investigation.

The far end of this glasshouse consisted of a brick wall with a green-painted door let into it. Jackson opened it and found himself in a little chamber containing a large cast-iron industrial stove, which hissed and hummed to itself as it delivered boiling water from a hidden tank into an upright cylinder standing in a frame beside it. Lagged pipes led away from the cylinder and disappeared through the adjacent walls.

There were two large cupboards built against one wall to ceiling height. They contained a vast array of tins and bottles, tools, watering cans and all the other paraphernalia needed to operate a battery of glasshouses, and it was on the top shelf of one of these two cupboards that Jackson found the mahogany box containing the Calton Papers. It had been wrapped roughly in sacking and thrust behind a collection of oil cans. Stepping carefully down from the ladder which he had commandeered, the inspector placed the box carefully on a table and then unlocked it with one of his keys.

The contents were exactly as they had been described to him by Mr Dashkoff. The geological survey proved to be a thick volume of 150 manuscript pages, sewn into a sturdy cardboard backing. Jackson flicked through the pages until he came to a chapter entitled 'The Midlands Coalfields'. Here, someone – presumably Garamond – had made copious notes in pencil and there were exclamation marks liberally dotted over the text. Then, turning over a page, Jackson saw a circle scrawled over part of a carefully drawn map. Beside the circle, written this time in ink, were the words: 'This is all Margaret's, now. £30,000!'

All Margaret's, *now*.... Those words must have been written after the death of Arthur Waldegrave, which had occurred well after Philip Garamond had acquired the Calton Papers and hidden them here, in his greenhouse. Why had he put himself in debt to acquire the papers? Because no one else was to be allowed to know of the potential value of Margaret's Dowry. If someone else had outbid him at the auction, then that someone might well have published the survey.

Why had he not destroyed it? Because he was a man who would, no doubt, recoil in horror at the prospect of destroying part of a unique collection. Destroying human life was, of course, another matter entirely.

Oblivious now to the overpowering heat and the cloying perfumes of the colourful exotics filling the greenhouse, Saul Jackson continued to think of the ramifications of his find. Philip Garamond, perhaps as long ago as five years, had hatched a plot to possess himself of Margaret's Dowry. That plot had involved making Jabez Beecham's suicide look like murder. He had kept the solution of that 'murder' as a fast secret until the time came for him to incriminate Jeremy Beecham, in order to ensure that Margaret Waldegrave never married him.

What about the poisons-book in the chemist's shop at Ancaster? Well, although Sergeant Bottomley had seen the signature 'J. Beecham' signed in that book, he had not been convinced that it was Jeremy's signature. It could easily have been that of Jabez and almost certainly was. Moreover, the original witness to the purchase of cyanide had died and the shop was in other hands.

Dead men, they say, tell no tales, but that wasn't quite true in this case. Grimes, the stoker, claimed that he'd been told the truth about old Jabez's 'murder' by a former servant; but that servant, too, was dead and could not be called as a witness. Had Garamond himself primed that man Grimes with the whole false story, knowing that he would co-operate with him for money? The veracity of it rested entirely on the testimony of Garamond and Grimes. Of course, it was Garamond who had hidden the tin box with its deadly contents under the floorboard in St Lawrence's room at Horton Grange, after he had contrived the death of Arthur.

A strong breeze had blown up out in the grove, sending a wave of moaning protests through the tall oaks. Some of the windows began to rattle and, from somewhere nearby, a door began an incessant slamming.

Dead men's tales, clues scribbled on scraps of paper, things hidden where he, Jackson, could find them.... Did these people think that the police were stupid? It was time for that man Grimes to be taken out of circulation.

Confound that banging door! Jackson looked around him and saw that there was another door behind the stove, evidently leading out into a yard of sorts. It was open and flinging itself aimlessly to and fro against the outer wall. He carefully replaced the Calton Papers in their box, locked it, re-wrapped it in the piece of sacking, then mounting the ladder once again put it back on the shelf behind the oil cans. Then he went out of the door behind the stove.

It gave access to a little paved yard where an open shed held a vast quantity of coal. A number of shovels and rakes lay on the flags. Jackson walked round to the back of the shed, his feet crunching on the coal dust. In the long grass beyond it lay the dead body of the stoker, Grimes. A brief examination showed the inspector that he had been first stunned by a blow to the back of the head, then his throat had been cut with a kitchen knife, which lay, bloodstained, beside the corpse.

'What kind of curse has fallen upon us here, Jackson? First poor Arthur, cruelly poisoned and his body left to burn, then Father, poisoned, too.... At first, I suspected that skulking fellow, Skinner, the valet, but that was only because I didn't want to think that this killer was someone near to us in blood. And now, the wretched Grimes. In God's name, why should anybody want to kill a humble yard-servant? Have you made no progress in detecting the perpetrator of these foul crimes?'

Saul Jackson looked at Sir Lance Waldegrave and saw in the baronet's haunted, bloodshot eyes the realization that his ancient family was doomed. What answer could he give to his frantic questions? It was not yet time for him to reveal all that he knew.

It was several hours after his discovery of Grimes's body. Superintendent Mays had been informed by telegraph and two young, uniformed constables had been dispatched to Langley Court to help Jackson in his enquiries. They had arrived by railway, but a police van from Copton Vale was on its way to take away yet another body from the stricken house.

'The house is deserted, Jackson,' Sir Lance Waldegrave said. 'My sister has fled from that man Jeremy Beecham – have you not apprehended him yet? Surely he's a prime suspect? I've no idea where Margaret's gone. My aunt has left the house to stay with friends. The whole place is as quiet as the tomb.'

Jackson and Lance Waldegrave were standing near the archway under the clock turret. To their left they could both see the burnt-out ruin of the folly. Lance was dressed in riding kit; some moments earlier a groom had led away his steaming horse. In the long yard behind the house the two constables were conducting a search of the gas-house.

'I'm not the man I was,' Lance was saying. 'It's all I can do to mount my horse and go riding across country. But it takes my mind off all this tragic business. And Grimes's throat was cut, you say? What kind of man would do a thing like that?'

'I'll tell you, sir,' Jackson replied. 'It was done by a man overcome with hatred, a man who had found himself in the power of a crude, ill-conditioned rogue who hadn't the sense to know when his luck was running out. Grimes was blackmailing someone, and his victim knew that he would never escape his clutches. So he waylaid Grimes in the grove, as he arrived to tend to the glasshouse stoves, and felled him with a single blow. But then, you see, his mad rage at being at the mercy of that dull man made him cut his throat. I've seen that kind of thing before, Sir Lance, where the revenge of a victim of blackmail boils over into atrocity.'

Lance watched as Jackson's gaze was directed beyond the folly, along the pathway leading to the cottage.

'Good God! Surely you don't suspect Garamond?' Lance whispered. 'You horrify me, Jackson! For heaven's sake, hurry, will you, and bring all this horrible business to an end. I'm beginning to wonder how much more of it I can stand.'

Sir Lance Waldegrave turned on his heel and walked slowly away along the yard.

A moment later one of the constables emerged from the gas-house.

'Sir!' he called to Jackson. 'We've found something rather odd in here. Will you come and have a look at it?'

It was dark inside the gas-house. The furnace was dead and a pile of ashes had been raked out on to the hearth. The retort was cold and silent. Jackson knew that there would be a gas-holder somewhere behind the building, and that later in the day, if death had not taken him, Grimes would have fired up the gas plant once more in order to keep the supply of gas to the house flowing.

Two fresh-faced young constables saluted him when he entered and he raised his high-crowned blocker in reply.

'I'm PC Smith, sir,' said one of the young men, 'and this is PC Hughes.'

Smith pointed silently to a dark bundle of clothes tied roughly with string which was lying on a small table.

'It was crammed into the space between the furnace and the back wall, sir,' said PC Smith. 'It's a suit of clothes, but the material's too good to have been worn by that furnace-man.'

'Well done, lads,' said Jackson. 'That's the kind of observation that can help to solve a complex case.' As the two pleased young men watched, Jackson untied the string. The parcel consisted of the three parts of a high quality tailored suit – jacket, waistcoat and trousers. The left side of the jacket was wet and, when Jackson examined the inner pocket in the silk lining, he winced as a sliver of broken glass pierced one of his fingers. The whole jacket smelt of some substance that he could not recognize. He tied the parcel up again, and turned to the constables.

'Your work here is done,' he said. 'I know what this suit means and I know who it was that murdered the man Grimes. Well done, both of you. You can go back to Copton Vale, now. Wrap that suit up, and take it back with you to Peel House. Tell Mr Mays that it needs to be examined immediately by an analytical chemist.'

As he stepped out into the sunlit yard, he thought to himself: This whole case will be closed this coming Tuesday, and its ending will usher in a grim time for the Waldegraves. God help them all.

In the crowded little study of Canon Parrish's house in Dean's Row, Margaret Waldegrave and Jeremy Beecham were making a valiant effort to become reacquainted. Margaret saw the lingering anger and resentment still lurking in her fiancé's face and he saw her expression of shame and bewilderment. They would have little time to iron out their misunderstandings, as they were to be

married on the Monday morning, and this was Saturday afternoon.

'I've been here over a week,' said Jeremy Beecham, 'ever since
Sergeant Bottomley and his men seized me in the grounds of
Horton Grange, and spirited me away here, to Ancaster. And it
was Bottomley who told me that no suspicion of any kind
attached to me, and that I was a free man. Then he began to tell
me things.... When he had finished, he proposed a course of
action which included my marrying you this coming Monday.'

'And you agreed?' asked Margaret, faintly.

'Well, yes, of course I agreed, even though you'd treated me so
abominably. So on Monday, we'll get on with it. Your aunt will be
your maid of honour, or whatever it's called, and Bottomley will
give you away. The best man will be Nicholas Arkwright, the
cathedral dean.'

Jeremy suddenly permitted himself a rather cynical laugh.

'Until last week, I'd never heard of any of these Ancaster
people, and now they're busy arranging all the intimacies of my
life.'

'Why did you confess to all those murders? Why did you
frighten me nearly to death, and threaten to entomb me in that
vile crypt in the foundations of your house?'

Jeremy had the grace to blush, but when he replied to her questions his voice still held its tone of sullen anger.

'You remember the day of the funeral, I expect?' he said. 'I
came to pay my respects, and was driven away like a cur by that
raving madman Garamond. And I was *innocent*, do you understand? I had committed no crime of any kind. I was a rising star
in the world of landscape design, with a growing list of clients; I
ended up the very next day as a frightened fugitive.

'And where did *you* stand in all this, Margaret? At the funeral
you stood like a statue, unmoved, while I endured the most humil-
iating moment of my life. My anger was kindled then, and was
still burning the next day when you came in to the great chamber

to confront me with what you called "the truth". Can you wonder that I went mad with rage when you started to treat me like a recalcitrant infant in need of correction? You stood there, solemnly recounting some lying tale dreamt up by one of your yard-servants – you, my fiancée! – and then challenged me to deny that I had murdered my uncle, your brother, and your father! *And I was innocent!*

'At that moment I was suddenly possessed by a devil of perversity. I thought, if she believes all that of me, then I'll *let* her believe it! Why should I crawl and cringe to you aristocrats any longer? I'd endured your brother Arthur's intolerable insolence for your sake, and had been happy to subsidize your brother Lance whenever he was in dire need of five pounds. Well, no longer, my proud miss, I thought. And so I "confessed" and enjoyed seeing your horror; and the more you shrank from me, the more I determined to make you pay for your faithlessness—'

'And so you dragged me down to that frightful tomb, and threatened to bury me alive! Oh, poor Jeremy, I must have driven you desperate for you to behave like that!'

'You had, but as soon as you screamed and broke away from me in fear, I woke up, horrified, from my wicked trance and ran after you to apologize and to make amends. But the more I called your name, the faster you ran. In the end Sergeant Bottomley rescued you and I was left to rue my pride and folly. Maybe I really *was* mad, then.'

'Poor, dear Jeremy!' Margaret cried. 'I should have known better! I am to blame for all this misery that you've suffered. Can you forgive me?'

'Can you forgive *me*?' said Jeremy, moving towards her with open arms.

At that moment Canon Parrish opened the door of the study.

'Oh! Sorry,' he murmured in some confusion, and closed the door softly behind him.

15

·•·

A Man Consumed by Envy

Philip Garamond paused on the landing, and glanced into the dim old silvered mirror that had hung on the wall at the top of the stairs since the eighteenth century. For a brief moment he saw his own reflection, that of a gentleman in his mid-fifties, with thinning grey hair, a genial face and shrewd eyes looking out gravely from behind round gold-framed spectacles. And then, in a moment of vivid recall, he saw beyond the present and its petty constraints to the brilliant future that lay ahead of him on the island of Madeira.

Madeira! The jewel of the Atlantic, it was called. He had visited it once, long ago in 1857, as a carefree youth of eighteen. That was long before he had come to live at the cottage, and none of Nicholas Waldegrave's children had yet come into the world. He had accompanied a wealthy young man of his acquaintance as a travelling-companion, and had found himself enthralled by the beautiful mountainous island lying some 400 miles west of the Moroccan coast. The climate was mild and pleasant, with the temperature seldom dropping below sixty-five degrees. He had dreamt fondly of living on Madeira one day.

His friend and he had stayed on the estate of a gentleman called Joao da Silva, in the fertile northern part of the island, and it was here that he had been introduced to the absorbing study of botany which was to become a lifelong passion. Da Silva had created his own botanic garden which lay on a hillside, sloping gently down to a little sheltered cove. There had been a number of conservatories, but most of the plants had been able to thrive in the open, where one could stroll among them before returning to the long, single-storey villa set in the midst of the garden. Experts came from all over Europe to view the plants, and also to attend lectures and learned discussions at the little school of botany that da Silva had established on his estate.

And now, after half a lifetime's wait, he would return to Madeira, having secured the da Silva Botanic Gardens for himself.

His young friend of 1857 was long dead; but he, Philip Garamond, had kept up a correspondence with the da Silva family ever since that visit. The father had died, and the son, another Joao, had succeeded him. Like Philip, he had sought academic recognition for his botanical work and at much the same time that Philip had been elected to the Linnean Society, Joao da Silva had been made an Officer of the Portuguese Academy of Sciences.

It had been in 1893 that Joao had written to say that he was retiring through poor health and that he would be returning to Portugal. The estate, gardens, and school of botany would be put up for sale, but he would make Philip an offer for friendship's sake and would not move in the matter of a sale until he had heard from him. He had mentioned a figure in escudos, which in English money amounted to £7,000.

A noise from somewhere in the grove recalled Philip Garamond to the present and he continued his progress downstairs to the drawing-room. He had lived in this tired old house for too long. It was a pleasant enough place, of course, but it fitted him now like a faded and tattered old overcoat. It was time to go. The fellows at the New Caledonian Club liked to rib him about his fond dreams of Madeira, but they'd laugh on the other side of their faces when they found out that he was going there after all! Seven thousand pounds would secure his own particular paradise, and there would be a veritable small fortune left from the balance of the £30,000 which would come to him from Margaret's Dowry.

Margaret.... She would be all right, her brother Lance would see to that. She would learn to forget Jeremy Beecham, a man tainted with the suspicion of having committed murder, and would marry into one or other of the gentle families in their part of the shire. The wretched Jeremy had fled, presumably in fear of his life, but he had not got far. Providentially, the police had been lying in wait for him at Horton Grange. Margaret would never marry him now, that was the important thing.

Philip's dramatic outburst at the funeral had succeeded beyond his expectations. Beecham had behaved like a madman, apparently confessing to crimes he could not have committed. Margaret had been frightened out of her wits and Lance, as head of the family, had, in effect, forbidden the marriage.

After the funeral he, Philip Garamond, had sat in this very room recalling how he had made away with Arthur. He had liked the boy well enough while he was strong and fit, but he had grown to despise the fretful invalid who was going to inherit the whole Waldegrave estate, title, land and fortune. Da Silva's offer had been more than enough to determine him to send Arthur quickly to eternity.

Years earlier, at Jabez Beecham's request, he had gone to Ancaster and purchased a quantity of cyanide, signing the poisons book 'J. Beecham', the J standing for Jabez. If ever that signature were seen by the police now, in 1894, they would inevitably think that it stood for 'Jeremy'. It was that cyanide that he'd used to poison Arthur.

He'd always been 'Uncle Philip' to the children, ever since he had come to live at the cottage, soon after Nicholas and Mary Jane had married. But he was an uncle in name only: he came from the scarcely acknowledged Garamond clan, a large, poverty-stricken family who were distant relatives of Nicholas's wife.

His father, an amiable wastrel, had died when he was still a young boy. His mother had seen Philip's potential to do well in the world and had prevailed upon one of her wealthy relatives, Maurice Gregg, of Nuneaton, to sponsor him. It was with Gregg's son, Rupert, that he had embarked on his visit to Madeira in 1857.

It had all worked very well, and he had carved out a very creditable position for himself in the scientific world of London and beyond. But it had all been achieved through the charity of others and through the self-denying devotion of his consumptive mother who had died when he was twenty. However equally he was treated, he was conscious of being a dependent at another man's table, claiming a spurious equality with the Waldegrave family – spurious, because it was founded on charity and condescension.

And so he had dreamed and plotted for years to make himself free of the Waldegraves' patronage. If only he could secure Margaret's Dowry for himself, he would be independent at last. If Margaret remained unmarried until her birthday was past, and if Arthur were to be removed from the scene, then £30,000 would become his by legal right.

The Calton Papers posed a threat to his ambition, so it had been essential for him to secure them in order to remove Calton's geological survey from curious eyes. His ruse of employing a third party to bid for the papers in a false name had succeeded admirably and, after a short stay in London, he had conveyed them secretly to the cottage. The box of papers was safe enough where he'd concealed it and, perhaps, one day, he would bring himself to burn its contents to ashes in the greenhouse stove. He'd had to borrow the money to buy the papers, but now that Nicholas had left him a legacy of £2,000, he'd have no difficulty in paying Barney Cottle when the debt fell due on 30 July.

He'd begin a new life on Madeira, an independent, moneyed life, dependent on no one, but he'd return to England for a month or two in the summer. He'd buy the lease of a Town house where he could hold court for a season among his many learned friends.

There was a very handsome property on offer in Bruton Street, Mayfair....

What a pleasant morning it was! What day was it? The third of July. Only three months to go before Margaret's birthday. The Dowry was now his in all but deed.

Who was this walking along the lane from the main road? Inspector Jackson and Sergeant Bottomley. Perhaps they were coming to the cottage? They'd be very welcome. The inspector was a rustic plodder and the sergeant some kind of bibulous oaf. Perhaps they'd come to stare dumbly at the spot where the wretched Grimes had been done to death.

Grimes had proved to be a willing accomplice, a man who would do anything for money. He'd carefully tutored the fellow in the fictitious tale of a serving-man who had witnessed old Jabez Beecham's 'murder', and he had proved an apt pupil. The police had swallowed the story hook, line and sinker, and so, apparently, had Margaret; but the truth had been rather different....

He had come to know Jabez Beecham, his near neighbour down the sunken road at Horton Grange, because the man had revealed a genuine interest in botany, and had shown him some specimens of native Australian plants that he had carefully nurtured among the shabby ruin of his dilapidated home.

It had been a pleasure to get free occasionally of the family at Langley Court, and talk with this simple, brusque old man with the troubled eyes. Something terrible had happened to him in Australia, but he would never talk about it. Whatever it was, it had left him in the grips of a pathological depression from which he was quite unable to free himself.

And then, one cold winter's day in the February of '89, with the whole area blanketed in snow, the two of them were sitting over glasses of whisky in the great chamber, and Jabez had made the suggestion which, five years later, would lead to Philip taking possession of his botanical paradise on Madeira, the jewel of the Atlantic.

'I've reached the end of my tether, Garamond,' old Jabez had said. 'That old devil, depression, has dogged me for years. I intend to set him at defiance by ending it all. I want you to go to some town far away from here, and buy some cyanide. You can say it's for getting rid of vermin.'

'Cyanide?' he'd said, feigning an unwillingness to become involved. 'That is a very dreadful request, Beecham. I don't think it's fair of you to ask me to do such a thing.'

The old man had laughed and wagged an admonitory finger at him.

'Don't be so faint-hearted,' he'd said. 'You can sign my name to the poisons-book and add my address. And, when you've brought the poison here to me at Horton Grange, I'll give you one hundred gold sovereigns.'

That had clinched the matter. He had found an apothecary's shop in the old cathedral town of Ancaster, had bought a bottle of cyanide, writing Jabez's signature in the book, but instead of giving the address as Horton Grange, he had written that of old Jabez's nephew, who, at that time, was living in one of a row of cottages in the nearby village. It had seemed a judicious act at the time; later, he was to see it as an enormous stroke of luck.

Jabez Beecham had given him the hundred sovereigns in a stout leather bag, and thereupon had bade him farewell. Next day, curious to find out whether the old man had made good his threat to do away with himself, he had trudged through the snow to call upon him at the Grange, found the house deserted and Jabez lying dead on the floor of the great chamber.

All at once he had realized the extreme danger in which he had placed himself. Aiding or abetting the act of suicide was a crime punishable by imprisonment. How easy it had been, simply by removing the fatal glass from one room to the other, and drinking a measure of old Jabez's whisky from a second glass, to turn suicide to murder! He had left the Grange unseen and the next day news of the 'murder' was on every tongue.

He had found the bottle of cyanide standing on the table in the great chamber and had removed it, concealing it in one of his glasshouses. Years later, when he had conceived the idea of discrediting Jeremy in the most effective way possible – by making him seem to be a murderer – he had retrieved that bottle from its hiding-place, so that it could become part of his deadly design. Unseen by anyone, he had concealed it under a loose floorboard in one of the rooms at Horton Grange, and had manufactured a written clue, entrusted to Grimes, that would ensure its discovery.

The good Jackson was executing a fine double rap on the front door. It was time to see what news he and his lump of a sergeant had to tell him.

Inspector Jackson and Sergeant Bottomley stood at the garden gate of the cottage, Mr Philip Garamond's graceful white house nestling among the oaks of Langley Grove. At the turn in the dusty lane, and contriving not to be seen from the house, stood an olive-green police van, a constable on the box, and a grey shire horse between the shafts.

'There was enough evidence against him for Mr Mays to obtain a warrant,' Jackson was saying, 'and Garamond will most certainly stand trial for the murder of Arthur Waldegrave. But he's a clever man, Sergeant, a learned man, as they say, and I don't want him to leave here reserving his defence, and plotting ways of extricating himself from the gallows.'

'So what will you do, sir?'

'I'll go straight into the attack, so that he gets rattled, if that's the right word. I'm hoping that he'll betray himself as he tries to fend off my accusations. I'll start by telling him of Jeremy and Margaret's marriage, which will immediately deprive him of Margaret's Dowry, and bring whatever plans he may have had crashing down in ruins. After that, I'll tell him what he did, as though you and I had been witnesses of his villainy, then I'll use the death of Grimes to bring him to his knees.'

'Grimes? Surely you don't think—?'

'No, I don't, Sergeant, but it's Grimes's murder that I'll use to deliver the *coup de grâce*.'

They opened the gate in the wooden paling, walked up the short garden path and Jackson knocked at the door. In a few moments it was opened to them by Philip Garamond himself. He seemed in very good spirits and greeted them affably.

'Inspector Jackson!' he cried. 'And Sergeant Bottomley, isn't it? Come in. What news do you bring?'

He ushered them into the elegant, high-ceilinged drawing-room in which they had first spoken to him on 12 June. He was wearing the same rusty old frock coat, and Jackson hazarded a guess that he was about to leave the house to tend his beloved plants, sweltering in their specially heated accommodation up in the grove. Garamond motioned to them to sit down and chose for himself a high-backed oak chair near the fireplace.

'The first piece of news I've brought for you today,' said Jackson, 'is that your niece Margaret Waldegrave, and her fiancé, Jeremy Beecham, were married yesterday at Ancaster parish church.'

They both saw how Garamond tried to master his shocked reaction to these words, and fail. His face turned suddenly as white as chalk and he sprang up involuntarily from his chair.

'What?' he cried. 'You're mad! What are you saying? Beecham is a felon, an arraigned murderer—'

'He is nothing of the sort, as you know only too well,' said Jackson. His voice was stern and forbidding. 'I tell you that they are well and truly married. She is beyond your envy and he is beyond your hatred. You planned and plotted for years to bring that particular inheritance known as Margaret's Dowry into your grasp—'

'What do you mean? Margaret's Dowry is a mere few hundred pounds—'

'It won't do, sir!' Jackson cried, striking the arm of his chair with a clenched fist. 'Do you think the police are stupid? That so-called dowry is worth thirty thousand pounds, as you most certainly know, a sum of money well worth murdering for! I know all about your dealings with Barney Cottle, and your acquisition of the Calton Papers using the false name of Major Kirtle Pomeroy. Did you imagine that you'd invented that name? During my investigation, I found an old photograph in Sir Nicholas's sitting-room, which showed him posing decades ago with an army friend called Major Kirtle Pomeroy. That's where you got the name from. It showed me that whoever used that name as an alias would have to be an intimate of the Waldegrave family, or a servant in its employ. It was an easy enough matter to trace that name back to *you*.

'I have seen and read those papers. I discovered them where you had hidden them in the first of that range of greenhouses in the grove. I have read the notes that you made in the margins – notes that convict you of plotting to acquire your niece's legacy.'

It was appalling to see how the mask of the gentleman was replaced by that of a cornered felon, partly defiant, partly cringing in the presence of the man who was exposing his villainy. His voice still retained its cultured tones, but it was now much higher, as though his lungs were in the paralytic grip of total fear.

'Very well, I confess to having plotted to acquire the Calton Papers. But what has that to do with the law? What gives you the right to hector me as though I were a common criminal? Your superintendent will hear of this—'

'But someone stood between you and that thirty thousand,' Jackson continued, ignoring Garamond's interruption, 'your nephew, Arthur Waldegrave, and so you encompassed his death by giving him a glass of wine into which you had put a quantity of cyanide. You left him dead in his wheeled chair, and set fire to the folly, hoping to conceal your crime. When that did not happen, you saw an opportunity to shift the blame for Arthur's death onto Mr Jeremy Beecham. You were seen hiding

a bottle of cyanide beneath the floorboards of a room in Horton
Grange—'

'Seen? Who could have seen me? There was no one in the
house.'

'So you admit that you were there. That admission alone damns
you. Do I need to go on, Mr Garamond? I tell you it is as if I had
been present as a witness to all your felonies, particularly your
vicious murder of your fellow conspirator, the stoker Grimes.
Your murder of that man alone, here on your own premises, will
be enough to send you to the gallows.'

'It's a lie!' Garamond shrieked. 'I never harmed him! Grimes
was quite content with the money I gave him to tell the story that
I'd concocted – the story about Jabez Beecham's so-called murder.
I never killed him, I tell you! I abhor violence, I—'

'You have condemned yourself out of your own mouth by
these admissions,' said Jackson. 'Very well, the death of Grimes
can lie on the file for the moment. Meanwhile, I show you this
warrant, and say: You are Philip Garamond, and I arrest you on
the charge that, at Abbot's Langley, in the county of Warwick,
on the day and date specified herein, you did administer to
Arthur Waldegrave a noxious thing, so that he died; and that
you did murder him.'

Jackson and Bottomley stood in the dusty lane and watched the
two uniformed constables who had accompanied them half carry
Philip Garamond into the police van. The driver, who had got
down from the box, slammed the stout iron doors shut, and
secured them with a tie-bar.

'He's the type of man who'll confess all,' said Jackson, watching
the van as it turned awkwardly in the lane, and rumbled back the
way it had come. 'What we don't know for fact he'll supply in the
end. Not that it'll do him any good. He's not mad, just beside
himself with anger and fear.'

'Well, sir,' said Bottomley, 'I suppose we'd better get up to the house.' He suddenly uttered a sigh, his normally cheerful countenance assuming an expression of deep despondency.

'You can feel the desolation in the air this morning, sir,' he said. 'The air's thick with ghosts and goblins.'

'It is, Sergeant,' said Jackson. 'But come: Sir Lance Waldegrave must be told the truth about his brother Arthur's death.'

'Sir Lance is working in the estate office this morning, sir,' said old Lincoln when Jackson and Bottomley called at Langley Court. 'If you will follow me up this little flight of steps, I will take you there.' He had conducted them from the hall into a side passage which led to a part of the house that neither of them had seen before. It seemed to consist of a number of store rooms and pantries, leading off from narrow passages paved with York stone flags. Their feet echoed on the steps as they mounted to the estate office.

Jackson glanced covertly at the old butler and noticed the grim set of his jaw, as though he was steeling himself to accept what was rapidly becoming an intolerable situation. He placed a hand gently on the old butler's arm.

'How are you, Mr Lincoln?' he asked. 'How are things with the family?'

Lincoln's eyes filled with tears and he shook his head sorrowfully.

'It's kind of you to ask, Mr Jackson,' he said. 'I'm tolerably well and, as you may know, Sir Nicholas left me a lump sum and an annuity, so I can retire at any time I choose, but I can't bear the thought of leaving poor Master here to cope with new servants. He's ... he's not as robust as he was; he seems to have aged over this last week. You see, Mr Jackson, the spirit's gone out of the house with Sir Nicholas dead and Mr Arthur, too; and with both Miss Waldegrave and Miss Margaret away at the moment, the place seems forsaken. But here we are at the estate office, sir.'

Lincoln opened a stout oak door and ushered the two detectives into a spacious, dark-panelled room with windows looking out on to the gardens to the west of the mansion. It was furnished as an office, with tall wooden cabinets of drawers, and long tables upon which had been placed wire baskets containing papers and folders of all kinds.

'Mr Jackson and Mr Bottomley to see you, Sir Lance,' said Lincoln, before leaving the room and closing the door quietly behind him.

Sir Lance Waldegrave sat at a table placed before one of the windows. He had evidently been writing letters, because he was still holding a pen as he looked up at them. Both men started in shocked surprise at his appearance. He was, they knew, only 25, but he now looked much older. His face was drawn as though in pain and there were dark shadows around his eyes. He glanced at them and they both had the uncanny feeling that he was not really seeing them, but looking beyond them into another world. He seemed unnaturally calm and this lack of restiveness belied his age. Bottomley thought to himself: This man's body is holding up under the strain, but his soul is dying.

Sir Lance put down his pen, and sat back in his chair.

'Gentlemen,' he said, 'I can see from your expressions that you are the bearers of evil tidings. Well, I am quite disposed to hear what you have to say. But first of all, I have something to ask of you, Mr Bottomley. That girl—'

'She will be all right, sir,' said Bottomley. 'There are those who have already begun to protect her and who have promised to take care of the child.'

'Good, good. And now, sit down and tell me your news.'

It took Jackson nearly half an hour to give Lance a full account of his uncle's murderous treachery. When he had finished, the young baronet seemed to lapse into a reverie. It was some minutes before he stirred, as though from sleep.

'I would never have believed such a thing of my uncle Philip,' he said at last. 'So it was he who murdered my brother and then plotted to cheat my sister of her inheritance. I'm very glad that she has come into a private fortune. Even more glad that Jeremy Beecham has been exonerated. I always liked him and he was very decent to me in the days when money was short, but my uncle poisoned my mind against him. And they are married, you say? Well, I should like to have provided them with a public wedding worthy of the Waldegrave family, but there: necessity apparently decreed otherwise.'

Lance gave vent to a deep sigh and his shoulders sagged under the burden of some unexpressed sorrow.

'Do you know, gentlemen,' he said, 'that I am tired – weary unto death? I feel in my heart that I have achieved the number of my days, yet I am still only in my twenties. You see me here today, working on the estate books until I can appoint a new factor, and yet a mere three months ago I would not have dreamed of setting foot in this place. I expect you know that I was obliged to leave the army. I had thought to build an honourable career in the regiment, despite my addiction to gambling, but it was not to be.

'I have had an unenviable reputation, gentlemen, and no doubt I deserve it. But people assume that I was cashiered from the army for dishonourable conduct – or they think that I was told to resign my commission or face the consequences. Well, none of that was true. The truth is, that I was judged physically unfit to serve. The regiment was due for a long tour of service in India, but the medical officer said that I would not survive the climate out there. The colonel's advice was that I should resign through ill health, so that is what I did. But then, as you know only too well, the devil finds work for idle hands to do…. In this last week, I have suddenly grown up into a man and hoped that I was leaving the gambler and scapegrace behind me. But it was too late, gentlemen, too late….'

The baronet lapsed into silence, it seemed minutes before he spoke again. Jackson had the conviction that Lance Waldegrave had withdrawn almost completely from the ugly realities of the present.

'So it was Uncle who murdered my poor brother,' said Lance, at length. 'What about Father, and the furnace man, Grimes?'

'Well, sir,' said Jackson, quietly, 'we all know the answer to that question, don't we? Because it was *you*, Sir Lance, who poisoned your father Sir Nicholas Waldegrave and who cut the wretched Grimes's throat.'

16

The End of the Waldegraves

Sir Lance seemed not to react to these damning words. He merely regarded the two men with a curious absence of commitment. They both heard him repeat in a low voice, 'Tired, tired.'

'There was a witness to the murder of your father,' Jackson continued. 'The valet, Skinner, was actually standing in Sir Nicholas's sitting-room and saw you take a vessel of ruby glass from an inside pocket of your coat. It had been fitted with some kind of lid, which you removed, and administered some of the contents of the glass to your father as he lay in bed. Skinner saw you replace the lid, and secrete the glass once more in your inside pocket.'

'Skinner.... Yes, I saw him standing there when I came out of Father's room and wondered then whether he had seen what I did. It was the lid from a drum of zinc ointment, which fitted tightly over the top of the glass, which I'd purloined from Father's room. I thought it was rather a neat idea.'

'Nurse Stone saw you, too,' Jackson continued, 'but only in a mirror in the dressing-room. Once you moved away from the bed, the original ruby glass containing harmless water, which stood on the bedside table, came back into her view. It was a clever device, Sir Lance, but you forgot how furtive Skinner was. He had a habit of standing stock still on occasion, part of his belief that a good servant should never be seen when he's not wanted.'

Lance had closed his eyes for a few seconds. Then he opened them, and said, 'I don't think Father would have minded very much. I'd collected quite a lot of digitalis from his bottles, you know, and mixed it very successfully in a quantity of sal volatile. It certainly did the trick. Poor Father! He died almost immediately. He shouldn't have been so confoundedly mean at a time when I was damnably in debt.

'You can have no idea, Jackson, or you, Sergeant Bottomley, how constant debt rots the soul. You try to pull what rags of self-respect remain about you, but you always fail. You become naked to the contempt of your inferiors – you can have no idea what it's like. I did what I did through desperation and resentment. Father shouldn't have been so merciless in the matter of advancing money. Still, with respect to what I did, I don't think he'd have minded very much.'

'Sir,' said Jackson in a low voice, 'you have just confessed to the murder of your father.'

'Well, what would be the point of doing otherwise? I'm so tired, you know, that all I want to do is sleep. I've been like this ever since I killed Grimes. Something seemed to burst in my breast and my youth fled from me. You seem to know such a lot, Inspector. Do you know why I sent that fellow out of this world?'

'I believe I do, sir. After you'd concealed that fatal medicine glass in your inside pocket, you rushed away into the yard, bent, I've no doubt, on disposing of it immediately in the middens beside the gas-house. But then, a passing groom collided with you, smashing the glass to pieces, and soaking your coat with the remaining contents. I witnessed that collision, sir, and remember your desperate anger with the man. I wondered then whether you, too, suffered from heart disease.'

'Barlow's a good fellow,' said Lance, 'but he's always been a clumsy clodhopper. Yes, you're quite right. I went up to my rooms and changed into a different suit. Some time later, I thrust the old suit, with its broken glass tumbler still in the pocket, into one of the middens.'

'I know what happened next, Sir Lance,' said Jackson. 'Grimes fished the suit out of the midden, examined it, and saw an easy way to blackmail you. Like many stupid men, he had an innate cunning which was able to make him see that you had murdered your father and the means that you'd used to accomplish that murder. Parricide, they call it.

'We retrieved that suit from where Grimes had hidden it in the gas-house, and the police analyst found that the left-hand side of the jacket was soaked in a mixture of digitalis and sal volatile. The inside pocket contained the broken and crushed fragments of the Venetian glass – one of a pair, as Sir Nicholas once told me – and the lid from the ointment jar.'

'Grimes became insolent, Jackson,' Sir Lance continued in the same weary voice, 'swaggering, and over-familiar in a way that was quite insufferable. I said we would talk later, but when the opportunity offered itself, I stalked him up to the grove when he went to tend Uncle Philip's glasshouse boiler, then I struck him down like a mad beast.' A very faint colour returned to the baronet's face as he recalled the incident, but it was soon gone. 'I had brought a knife with me, you know, and it seemed a pity not to use it. So I cut his throat for good measure.'

Sir Lance Waldegrave began to tidy up the papers on his table. He seemed to Jackson to have become totally detached from the world.

'Well, Inspector,' he said at last, 'I expect you'll want me to come with you now?'

'I have a warrant here for your arrest—'

'Oh, yes, I'm sure you have. We can take it as read. Will you want me to wear handcuffs? I'm not *au fait* with all the details, you understand.'

Jackson looked at the shattered young man, wondering what had aged him so in so little space of time. Was it remorse? He seemed to show no compunction of any kind for his fearful crimes. Was he, in fact, insane? The answer to that question, he knew instinctively, was a resounding 'no'.

'It would be a good idea, sir, for you to tell your people to prepare your covered carriage, and to bring it round to the front of the house. There will be no need for handcuffs. My sergeant and I will accompany you to the police station at Sheriff's Langley, where arrangements will be made for your formal arrest and detention.'

Some time later, the carriage turned out from the estate and so on to the public road to the little agricultural town of Sheriff's Langley. Sir Lance Waldegrave was very pale and his eyes were still looking into some other world that was not the present. Jackson sat beside him, facing the impassive Sergeant Bottomley and one of the constables who had come up from the police station. Nobody spoke as the closed carriage, with the Waldegrave crest on the door panels, made its slow progress towards Sheriff's Langley. In his mind's eye Jackson saw Langley Court again, the lake, and the ruined folly at its edge, the clock turret rising above its archway that led into the long working yard. He saw the great and gracious ivy-covered mansion, and thought of old Lincoln and his staff doing their best to maintain some kind of order in the face of an indomitable chaos.

That house and its demesne would now become the home of a lonely maiden lady, Miss Letitia Waldegrave, who would withdraw from society to nurture her memories. It was an irony of fate that he and Bottomley had played their own inevitable part in securing the demise of the Waldegraves of Abbot's Langley.

Eventually the carriage came to a halt in a small flagged yard in front of the police station, a long building contrived from two Cotswold stone cottages, that stood in a lane on the outskirts of the town. Leaving their prisoner in charge of the constable, Jackson and Bottomley entered the dim whitewashed office at the front of the building where an elderly uniformed sergeant was waiting for them.

'Inspector Jackson, sir,' he said, 'I'm Sergeant Hopcroft. Mr

Mays sent me here for the day from Sycamore Hill. There are only two constables here in Sheriff's Langley.'

'Pleased to meet you, Sergeant,' said Jackson. 'This is Detective Sergeant Bottomley. Now, I have Sir Lance Waldegrave outside in a closed carriage. I intend to bring him in here now, read the warrant, and formally arrest him. What arrangements have you made to get him from here to the Copton Vale Bridewell?'

'Well, sir,' said Sergeant Hopcroft, 'when the formalities are over in here, I think you should all get back into that closed carriage and go immediately to Langley Platform. There's a little special train waiting there, with one carriage, and steam already up, which will convey you straight to Copton Vale Central. You'll be met there by a posse from Peel House.' He added, with a little frown of vexation, 'This is a titled gentleman we're dealing with, sir, that's why we need to be as discreet as possible.'

'I take your point, Sergeant,' said Jackson drily, 'but this particular titled gentleman murdered his own father, and cut another man's throat, so there must be a limit to the discretion involved in this case. But I take your point. You've done well, Sergeant Hopcroft. Well, let's get the formalities over and done with.'

Jackson and Bottomley were to remember long afterwards what happened next. They walked across the little flagged yard to where the carriage stood, the sun glinting off its brass lamps and accoutrements. The constable had left the carriage, and was standing beside the horse, which had become restless. Jackson opened the carriage door.

Sir Lance Waldegrave still sat upright in the corner of the seat, his eyes apparently surveying some other, different, world, but when Jackson addressed him and put out a hand to assist him from the carriage, he saw that his prisoner was dead.

'Poison? No, nothing of the sort. He died of a ruptured aorta.'

It was the day following the seizure of Sir Lance Waldegrave. Jackson and Bottomley were listening to Dr James Venner, who had called on them at Barrack Street Police Office. He had conducted a post-mortem on the body of the baronet on the previous evening.

'I asked Dr Murray, the local man at Sheriff's Langley, to assist me,' Dr Venner continued, flicking a particle of dust from the sleeve of his dove-grey morning coat. 'A very sensible and inventive fellow. He told me that you and he had talked together about an old suicide that had been tricked up to look like murder. Waldegrave's post-mortem was a sad affair. He was only a young man, and I should have thought that he was in good health. But we found that his heart was badly damaged and I suspect that he had suffered more than one minor heart attack over the last year.'

'He told us that he had been virtually invalided out of the army,' said Jackson, 'but he didn't go into details. I think he was ashamed at not being one hundred per cent fit.'

'Very likely. Heart disease can run in families, you know; evidently it did in this case. So there it is. He died of a ruptured aorta, and had that not taken him when it did, he would have very soon succumbed to a heart attack. I gather that no one suspected that he was in such a bad way. He must have died just after that constable got out of the carriage to attend to the horse. Well, he's escaped the gallows, but that, I venture to suggest, is nobody's fault. Why did you think he'd poisoned himself?'

'I thought it was a possibility, sir,' Jackson replied, 'but in my heart of hearts I felt that it was most unlikely. I think he would have borne his fate with a great deal of fortitude. The other one, now – Philip Garamond – I could imagine *him* trying to slip away from us by secreting poison about his person. But I can assure you, Doctor, that he won't get the chance. We'll watch him like a hawk until he steps up on to the scaffold.'

'I gather that, of the two killers, you preferred Lance Waldegrave?'

'I preferred neither of them, sir! Lance gently eased his terminally afflicted parent out of this world, and later, in what I'm convinced was a fit of temporary madness, cut the throat of the man Grimes. But Garamond poisoned a young crippled man, sitting helpless in a wheeled chair, then contrived to burn his body to ashes in a kind of heathen funeral pyre. Both men were beyond the pale, but Garamond distinguished himself by being a cringing, heartless and cold-blooded sneak. The world will be a better place once he's been sent out of it.'

One year to the day following the death of Sir Lance Waldegrave, on Wednesday 3 July, 1895, Inspector Jackson retraced his journey along the winding path through the trees that would take him to the gates of Langley Court. This time, though, he was not afoot, but riding in a smart little pony cart with Sergeant Bottomley up on the driver's seat. The two policemen had been visiting the police station at Sheriff's Langley on official business, and Sergeant Hopcroft, now installed there permanently, had suggested they hire a conveyance from the local livery stable and pay a visit to Mr Jeremy Beecham at Horton Grange.

'He was in here on Monday, sir,' Hopcroft had told him, 'and we got chatting about the tragic end of the Waldegraves. He said how much he'd like to see you and Sergeant Bottomley again if ever you were in the district.'

They had set out along the main road in order to approach the Grange from the sunken road lying behind Langley Court. There was no logical reason for doing this, but both men were impelled by a strong spirit of curiosity. What was Langley Court like, now?

'Sergeant Hopcroft said that the estate had passed to a family called Nicholson, from Westmorland,' said Jackson. 'Apparently, they were the nearest kin to old Sir Nicholas, and the entailed house and estate passed to them by default. But the title, of course, died with Sir Lance Waldegrave.'

After a while they clattered on to the stone-paved drive that would take them directly into the grounds of Langley Court. Bottomley reined in the pony, and the two men surveyed the scene.

The extensive lake glittered in the morning sun, but there was no sign of the folly which must have been completely demolished. Two young boys were paddling a skiff across the lake, while on the grass beyond, an impromptu game of cricket seemed to be in progress. The air rang with the careless cries of a whole tribe of boys, two excited little girls, and the barking of attendant dogs.

'We're not needed here, any more, Sergeant,' said Jackson.

'Or wanted, sir, for that matter,' Bottomley replied. 'You and I belong to the tragic past of Langley Court. Those lads and lasses have brought the old place alive again.'

Sergeant Bottomley gently urged the pony away from the main path and down into the sunken road that would take them to Horton Grange. It looked very much as though the Nicholsons of Westmorland had effectively driven away the lingering ghosts of the defunct Waldegrave family.

The changes to Horton Grange were immediately apparent to them as Bottomley halted the trap at the end of the sunken road. The front lawns had been expertly mowed and a gardener was busying himself about the flower beds. The house itself had been freshly painted, and its black and white façade glowed in the bright morning sun. Jackson pulled the bell at the side of the front door.

They were surprised when the door was opened to them by Lincoln. Although still stooped with advancing years the shadows had lifted from his brow and he greeted the visitors with a genuine smile of welcome.

'You'll have come to see the master, gentlemen,' he said. 'He'll be very pleased that you're here. I often hear him talking about you both and the wonders that you performed at Langley Court.'

'Well, now, Mr Lincoln,' said Jackson, as the butler took their coats and hats, 'this is a surprise – to see you here at Horton Grange, I mean.'

'Well, Mr Jackson, I followed Miss Margaret, you see – Mrs

Beecham, as she is now. Mr Beecham very kindly asked me to come, and of course it's a smaller house to supervise.'

'As I recall, Mr Lincoln,' said Jackson, 'there was only a house-keeper here and a little daily help from the town.'

'Oh, yes, that was so; but now we've brought together a very nice little household. Mrs Miller is still here, of course, and Williams – you remember Williams, sir? He's come here as Mr Beecham's valet, but he also doubles as footman when he's needed. We're not as grand as we used to be when we were at Langley Court, but between us we've brought this dear old house alive again. And then there's Mary Beamish and her husband, but you know all about them, especially you, Mr Bottomley.'

Lincoln seemed to have forgotten that they had come to see his master. He stood in the old Tudor hallway and talked about the momentous changes of the last year.

'Mr and Mrs Piers Nicholson and their family have settled in very comfortably up at the house, sir. They have nine children, six sons and three daughters, so it's very lively now at Langley Court! Of course they brought most of their own staff with them from Westmorland, so I've lost my friend Joe Cundlett, I'm afraid. He's gone as head coachman to Mr Ambrose Danecourt of Belphegor House at Henley. He'll like it there, I'm sure, him being a south-erner, but I miss him. He used to recite all kinds of beautiful poems to us.' He looked very serious for a moment. 'Sir Lance Waldegrave has been buried in the old churchyard at Temple Heath, sir. Mr Nicholson wouldn't let him be put in the family plot at Abbot's Langley church, and indeed it wouldn't have been right. But dear me, I'm keeping you waiting! Let me take you to Mr Beecham.'

They followed the old butler along the hall passage, noting that there was no trace of the gaping hole in the wall that had led down to the hidden vault. The panelling had been replaced and the spot covered by an enormous Tudor dresser bearing a display of ancient pewter.

They were shown into a long, many-windowed chamber at the rear of house, overlooking the well-tended lawns across which, just over a year ago, Margaret Waldegrave had fled from Jeremy Beecham in fear of her life. The room was newly furnished in modern styles, its elegant furniture standing on vibrantly coloured Turkey carpets. Over the mantelpiece at the far end of the chamber hung a portrait of the late Sir Nicholas Waldegrave, baronet, of Langley Court.

Mr and Mrs Beecham rose from their chairs to greet them. Jeremy, wearing a pair of flannel trousers and an alpaca jacket, looked as though he had taken a second lease of life. Jackson noted that his fingers were stained with ink, and that the top pocket of his jacket was laden with an array of pencils. Margaret, the chatelaine of Horton Grange, was wearing an artlessly simple white frock, acquired at great expense from Liberty's.

'How kind of you to call upon us!' cried Margaret. 'You were the two wonderful men who wrought miracles to bring my husband and me together again. Do sit down, both of you. How are you, Mr Bottomley? Do you still see Miss Cecily Hargreaves? She's by way of being a regular visitor here, now. We're gradually acquiring our own circle of acquaintances, both here, and in the little Town house we've bought. It's in Bruton Street, Mayfair; Jeremy receives some of his more exalted clients there.'

Jackson thought: Margaret Beecham is an heiress in her own right. She's using some of her money very judiciously to further her husband's career. Aloud he said, 'I remember Horton Grange as it was last year, ma'am. There have been great changes since then. The house seems to have sprung up into new life.'

'That's my wife's doing,' said Jeremy Beecham. 'We both intend to put our roots down here, which is why Margaret is kept so busy transforming the Grange from a rather gloomy house to a gracious home.'

Margaret Beecham smiled fondly at her husband and rose from her chair.

'I hope you'll excuse me, Mr Jackson,' she said, 'but I have to see Mrs Miller about various domestic matters. Maybe I will see you again before you go.' As she moved towards the door, she seemed to remember something that she wanted to say.

'And may I please borrow Sergeant Bottomley for a while? There's someone in the house who's very anxious to see him!' Without making any reply, the sergeant lumbered out of his chair and followed Margaret from the room.

'Jackson,' said Jeremy Beecham when they were left alone, 'I've wanted to thank you personally all year for what you and Mr Bottomley did for us both. By bringing us more or less unscathed out of that nightmare of murder and suspicion, you enabled both of us to start afresh. We are Mr and Mrs Beecham of Horton Grange and, although we make frequent visits to the Nicholsons at Langley Court, we do not consider ourselves as gentry. We're professional folk, Jackson, and it's in that capacity that we'll face the future.'

'And your business is thriving, sir?'

'It is. I finally secured extensive commissions from the Prince of Wales to construct new conservatories at Sandringham, and that royal connection has given me at last the necessary *cachet* to open the purses of some of the aristocracy. Yes, I am positively thriving.'

'What has become of Miss Letitia Waldegrave, sir?' asked Jackson.

'Aunt Letty? Why, she's here, with us, Mr Jackson, but she's visiting friends in London this week. She wanted to go and live in Cheltenham, but neither of us would hear of it. She was virtually a mother to Margaret for most of her life, so here she stays, with us.'

Jeremy was quiet for a moment; his face became grave and almost embarrassed. Finally, he uttered a single word.

'Garamond?'

'I witnessed the hanging of Garamond in Birmingham Gaol last August, sir. His lawyers tried to plead insanity, but he was as sane as you or I. He was sane, sir, wicked and wilful. He would have been content to see you hanged for the crime that he had committed. The earth is a better place without him.'

'I would never have suspected him of murder for a single moment,' said Jeremy. 'And neither would Margaret. She had known him all her life.'

'I'm not surprised to hear that,' Jackson replied. 'He was a smooth, polished scoundrel. But you know, he was careless in covering his tracks because he was arrogant enough to think that the police are stupid. He took a false name when he went about acquiring the Calton Papers, but it was the name of an old friend of Sir Nicholas Waldegrave's youth, inscribed on the back of a photograph which I myself saw in his sitting-room. That little slip told me that "Major Kirtle Pomeroy" was someone intimate with the family. After that little discovery, Philip Garamond's fate was sealed.'

'I used to lie awake at night,' said Jeremy, 'wondering whether poor Uncle Jabez's ghost was walking in this house seeking vengeance for his murder. But now that I know he wasn't murdered at all, I can sleep easy – and so, I hope, can he. And Lance?'

'Lance might well have got away with his most wicked crime because he was not the kind of man to complicate things. He hatched a simple plot, with none of the convolutions that Garamond loved. But Providence decreed that the murder of his father should be witnessed by the valet, Jonathan Skinner. Had Sir Lance Waldegrave come to trial, Skinner's testimony would have hanged him.'

Jackson stirred restlessly in his chair. He looked almost comically vexed with himself.

'I made a grave mistake in the matter of Lance Waldegrave, Mr Beecham,' he said. 'I should have trusted Nurse Stone's instinctive conviction that Lance Waldegrave had been up to no good when she saw him giving his father what seemed to be a drink of water. Because of that mistake, I allowed my initial examination of Sir

Nicholas's bedroom to be too superficial. As there was only water in the glass on the bedside table, I foolishly assumed that Lance could not have administered anything sinister to his father. Lance had set a trap into which I fell all too easily.'

Jackson permitted himself a rueful, self-critical laugh before he proceeded.

'Do you realize, Mr Beecham, that Lance Waldegrave murdered his father while Nurse Stone was actually watching him from the dressing-room, and while I was still in the house? It was sheer bad luck for Lance that poor Skinner actually saw what he did, and was able to tell me once he was safe in London.'

'You can't expect to get everything right first time, Inspector—'

'I should have been more alert, sir! I continued to be dense even when I saw how wildly Lance reacted to being bumped into by a servant in the yard. "Damn you!" he cried, and clutched his side, as though he were suffering a sudden heart attack. But, of course, it was not his heart but his pocket that he was clutching, and his anguish was caused by the breaking of that little tumbler – the poison tumbler – into smithereens.'

Jackson looked at the young man sitting opposite him in the old Tudor window bay. When he and Bottomley had gone, Jeremy Beecham and his wife could bury the past for good and all, and get on with what appeared to be a bright future.

'He told me, you know,' Jackson continued, 'Sir Lance, I mean. He told me that he'd taken small quantities of Sir Nicholas's digitalis over a period of time until he had enough for his purpose. I remember that Dr Radford was surprised at how much tincture of digitalis had been used up, and it was extremely dense of me not to have realized what that might have implied.'

'And then,' said Jeremy, 'Lance used sleight of hand to perform what must be one of the most sinister conjuring tricks of all time.'

'He did, sir, and that "trick" encompassed the death of his father. Well, there's the bare bones of the tale of the Waldegrave murders. It has been a great pleasure to see you today, Mr

Beecham, but if you'll excuse me, I'll go now and find out what's happened to my sergeant!'

Herbert Bottomley stood in the stone-flagged kitchen of Horton Grange. It was hot, because the coal-range was busy heating an array of pots and pans, but the windows were open on to the rear lawns of the old Tudor house, and a pleasant breeze was finding its way into the room.

'It's lovely here, Mr Bottomley,' said Mary Beamish, formerly Mary Connor. 'The house is being refurbished, and seems to be springing to life after years of neglect.'

Mary wore the black dress, white apron and cap of a house-maid. Bottomley could scarcely recognize in this smiling, confident young woman the desperate, trembling girl in the Railway Arms who had been contemplating drowning herself in the River Best.

'I can't believe that I'm actually living in the country and that I'm now a married woman. The master gave Steven and me the empty cottage near the sunken road, and we're nicely settled there, now. Steven's the coachman, and the ostler, and one or two other things, too! As Master gets richer, he'll employ more servants, but it's really nice at the moment with just a handful of us running the Grange.'

Mary suddenly placed a hand on Bottomley's sleeve and kissed him on the cheek.

'I never knew that there were people in the world like you and Miss Hargreaves,' she said in a low voice. 'In the evening, after we've served dinner, we sit here around the big table – Steven and me, dear old Mr Lincoln, Williams the valet, and Mrs Miller, and Mr Lincoln tells us tales of his years in service up at Langley Court. Well, one of these days, Steven and I will tell them *our* story, and the part you played in it.' She added, rather shyly, 'Would you like to see my baby?'

Bottomley followed her out of the kitchen and into the housekeeper's sitting-room nearby. Lying asleep in a little cot was a tiny baby, almost hidden by various frilly sheets and blankets. The sergeant bent down and peered intently at the little face.

'She's very nice,' he said. 'Very like you, my dear.'

'It's a boy,' said Mary, laughing.

'Why, so it is,' said Bottomley. 'What have you called him?'

Mary paused in embarrassment for a moment before replying.

'Herbert,' she said. 'After all, he owes his life to you. If you hadn't come along when you did—'

'Ah! There you are, Sergeant,' said Inspector Jackson, coming into the room. 'I thought I'd lost you for good. Excuse me, Mrs Beamish, but I must take him away with me now. There's a lot of work waiting for him and me to do back in Warwick.'

Mary accompanied the two detectives to the kitchen door and, as they walked away round the corner of the house towards the sunken road, she shaded her eyes with her hand, and watched them, giving thanks silently but profoundly for the part that they had played in securing for all who lived at Horton Grange the hopeful future that lay ahead.